Praise for the Rare Book Mystery Series

"A page-turner...gripping and engaging... or, as dealers rate rare books, definitely VF—Very Fine!"

—Carolyn Hart, *New York Times* bestselling author of the Death on Demand mysteries

"Anyone who enjoyed John Dunning's Bookman series will enjoy The Dirty Book Murder."

—*Reading Reality*

"...an entertaining and action-packed adventure reminiscent of Indiana Jones, delicately seasoned with the allure of rare old books."

—*Library Journal*

DIRTY BOOK
MURDER

Rare Book Mystery
Book 1

THOMAS SHAWVER

**ROUGH
EDGES
PRESS**

Dirty Book Murder
Paperback Edition
Copyright © 2023 (As Revised) Thomas Shawver

Rough Edges Press
An Imprint of Wolfpack Publishing
9850 S. Maryland Parkway, Suite A-5 #323
Las Vegas, Nevada 89183

roughedgespress.com

Paperback ISBN 978-1-68549-272-4
eBook ISBN 978-1-68549-271-7

DIRTY BOOK
MURDER

Chapter 1

Sunday, June 20

The young women disappeared, one after the other, a week apart. One had been an all-state basketball player, another placed in the high jump at the Kansas Relays, and the third was a National Merit Scholarship finalist. The pictures of them that appeared on television revealed well-scrubbed Midwestern coeds blessed with the silk-haired, snub-nosed beauty of unsoiled youth, their eyes alight with hope and steady resolve.

Six months later, the initial media frenzy had run its course without any significant leads, the grief-stricken parents were left to handle their agonies alone, and the bewildered investigating team was reduced by half due to ongoing budget concerns. I went back to reading the classifieds first.

Most weekend mornings, I sit on my back porch, sipping Irish coffee and checking the newspaper for upcoming estate sales. This is followed by a glance at the sports headlines and if I have time, the Metro section. The sequence has more to do with the nature of my job as owner of Riverrun Books than a lack of curiosity regarding the news, although the disappearance of those local college girls at the beginning of the year had altered my weekend reading habits for a while.

Normally, I'll pay two or three dollars for common novels and non-fiction, then price them for my shop or on the Internet for ten. Rare and important works are a different story, of course. That's when being a bookman can get interesting.

Consider, for example, two advertisements that caught my eye one such morning in June. While each piqued my interest for different reasons, both contributed to the strange business that is this story.

The first was an item in the auction column.

I ordinarily avoid such sales. Not only are they time consuming, they tend to be depressing affairs where bankrupts desperately seek to unload tractors and restaurant tables for a tenth of their value to Bubbas in bib overalls partial to spitting tobacco juice on other people's shoes.

Nonetheless, in the midst of the listing for restaurant equipment, I spotted a bit of gold among the dross. Possibly fool's gold, but one never knows.

"...*barstools,*" *it proclaimed. "Tables, electric can opener (industrial), lots of erotic books (includes Shakee Hen), towel dispensers...*"

Whoa. I might have passed the "erotic books" with a smirk if there had been no parenthetical addendum, picturing nothing more than a mildewed collection of girlie magazines and yellowed paperbacks with selected pages stuck together by some unspeakable substance.

But the parentheses held the promise of something else. Did the words Shakee Hen in the advertisement actually refer to a sample of Shoku-hon, also known as Shunga, the erotic art of Japan?

These woodblock prints, when produced by feudal Japan's greatest graphic artists like Utamaro and Hokusai, conveyed the sexual practices and conventions of a lively, uninhibited society in the most intimate detail. I recalled enough art history to know that when these prints first reached Europe in the waning days of the nineteenth century, they influenced the post-Impressionist movement and western art was never the same.

The auction was scheduled to begin the following Saturday afternoon at a warehouse on Eighth and Main in the River Market area. It meant missing a Royals baseball game, but that hasn't meant much to me since George Brett hung up his glove in 1993.

I turned to the second classified advertisement, reading it with amusement dimmed by concern that Anne, my twenty-year-old daughter, might have seen a similar notice posted on the bulletin board at the University of Colorado's drama department.

WANTED: Local actors as extras for the filming of "The Life of Jesse James." Send black-and-white glossy photo and brief background info to Gayle, Box 32, Kansas City Star.

It was an invitation guaranteed to keep dozens of starry-eyed western Missourians up all night working on their "brief background" letters. I must admit that for an unguarded moment I, too, felt the siren call.

After all, the entertainment channel was buzzing with rumors that the movie was to be directed by the great Robert Langston. No motion picture actor had gone as far or fallen as low as "Long Bob" in his thirty-year career. Who wouldn't want to be part of his heroic comeback? Who, indeed?

Anne, an aspiring director and theater major who admired Langston's early work before drugs, booze, and three disastrous marriages destroyed his career, would be first in line to associate with this Hollywood legend, no matter how faded his star. I was all for her getting practical experience, but she, who in her first two years at school had shown a far greater affinity for parties and skiing than Moliere and Arthur Miller, could ill afford to cut any more classes. A month earlier, she had informed me I'd be getting a bill for a summer of make-up classes she intended to take.

Somewhat comforted by this reminder of her renewed dedication to getting a degree in Colorado, I felt reasonably assured she wasn't aware of the casting call. So I relaxed, poured a cup of coffee and imagined what my own response to "Box 32" would say:

"*Michael Malachy Bevan, age 44: former lawyer, rugger, Marine. Currently a book merchant. Full head of hair, handsome in a jug-eared, farm boy sort of way. Like you, Mr. Langston, I have suffered. Widowed. Disbarred. Freaked out. Padded cell or modern equivalent. Unforgiving former clients with ties to the mob. Similarly unforgiving daughter. Character lines around eyes.*"

As I folded the newspaper, the telephone rang. It was Anne calling from Boulder. Collect, of course.

"I'm coming home for a few months to work on the Jesse James movie as a gaffer or something."

"What about school?"

"I'm taking a sabbatical from my studies."

"Honey," I said. "Only tenured professors and disgraced CEOs are allowed to do that."

"Really, Father! This is a one-time chance to be involved in a major motion picture and I'm not going to let it pass."

I had learned long ago not to argue with Anne once she had made up her mind. "How'd you get the job?"

She didn't respond, so I asked again.

"I know someone in the picture," she finally answered.

"Really?" I said with a chuckle. "Let me guess. Is it Long Bob Langston?"

Fifteen seconds of silence followed.

I laughed again, but it was an uneasy "Please God, don't let this be happening" kind of laugh.

"Why, yes," she said, somewhat surprised. "I've been seeing Bob the past few months. You didn't read about this in the tabs, did you?"

Something started doing cartwheels in my gut, but my native wit came to the fore.

"Afraid not. Can't believe I let my subscription to the *National Enquirer* expire."

Silence again answered my sarcasm, but this time for a mere ten seconds.

"If you must know, we met last September in Telluride. I was volunteering at the Nugget during the film festival when he came up to my table and said he was an old friend of yours."

"What!"

"My reaction as well. It took a minute or two listening to him talk about 'ramblin' with Roddy in Edinburgh' that I realized he'd mistaken me for Rod Stewart's daughter. Kimberly was at the Fest and we *do* rather look alike. My British accent must have also reinforced his first impression. Anyway, he was very apologetic when he realized his mistake and invited me for dinner at the New Sheridan. We've been together ever since."

"Annie, the guy is thirty years older than you."

"I grew up, Father. You just didn't notice."

"Right," I said, resisting the urge to hurl the telephone through the front window. "I'll have your room ready at the house."

"Fine."

"We need to catch up on a few things. Now, about school—"

"Try to be nice to Bob," she interrupted. "It's very important for him that things go well on this movie."

"Nice, huh? 'Nice' like I'm happy about this or 'nice' like I really don't care? No can-do either way."

"I'm only asking you to be civil. Please. We'll be in next week."

"All right," I said, but not before clearing my throat four or five times. "I'll try to channel my inner Oprah."

After slamming the telephone down, I wondered why humans are the only creatures who bother to have anything to do with their half-grown offspring.

Chapter 2

Saturday, June 26

Steam rising from the tar-papered warehouse roof matched my mood as I pulled between twin pickup trucks in the graveled parking lot. I hadn't spoken to Anne since her telephone call the previous Sunday and if she and her aged Lothario had arrived in town, they hadn't bothered to let me know.

Inside the overly lit auction hall at the River Market, a battalion of bargain hunters inspected the flea market junk that passes for antiques in the Midwest: round oak tables, rocking chairs with cane-webbed seats, colored glass globes, milk cans topped by seat cushions, iron plows, wagon wheels, graphite telephones and hundreds of "rare" depression glass bowls.

The auctioneer wore a wide-brimmed Stetson hat tilted precariously on the back of his head. Pink suspenders held up a pair of lime-green pants. Over the left breast pocket of his denim shirt, a plastic name tag announced "Colonel Herl Bender." An empty holster hung on his waistband.

A hundred or more hopeful entrepreneurs, woefully short of meaningful lines of credit, shifted impatiently in the stifling atmosphere for the lots of barstools, cash registers, and commercial dishwashers to come up.

Finally, the colonel, after solemnly instructing the audience to keep their bidding cards close at hand, waddled over to where a dozen barroom signs hung and proceeded to talk them up as if they were the Elgin Marbles.

"This fine example of the Mr. Peanut character is made of one hundred percent molded plastic…"

God, it was hot—sticky hot, the kind that causes a neck rash even after using a clean razor—and the odor of two hundred sweaty armpits was enough to make a middle school janitor blanch.

It didn't take long before a sallow-faced woman skittered from the room, clutching a lace hanky to her mouth. The auctioneer, oblivious to her sudden departure and the heaving sounds she made in the hallway, prattled on about the virtues of the original Naugahyde barstools that had taken center stage.

"Now what am I bid…"

I had decided to give him ten more minutes when I spotted my fiercest competitor in the antiquarian trade standing by a table loaded with books, most of which were covered by a pale-yellow bedsheet.

Blessed with the charm of an Afghan warlord and the subtlety of a cement mixer, Gareth Hughes had once wrenched a copy of *To Kill a Mockingbird* from the hands of an elderly woman at a library sale. When it turned out to be a worthless book club edition, he tossed it back on the table without apologies.

He tried a similar tactic with me when I was new to the business. Only I wasn't old, little or a lady. It came down to bare knuckles in somebody's living room with an audience of horrified suburban bargain shoppers. Fortunately, "Jumbo" Ralph Sadecki was in charge of that particular estate sale and he parted us before the police had to be called.

I saw Hughes a few weeks later at a book fair in St. Louis. By mid-afternoon, each of us had acquired our quota of Americana and sat down at a table to share talk and a pitcher of beer.

Having grown up in Cardiff, he spoke with a Welsh accent, but there were traces of other languages that muted the musical lilt of his native tongue. He said he admired me for standing up to him. I countered by acknowledging his expertise and his ability to survive without having an open shop. If his ethics weren't up to Plato's standards, they were no worse than most of the lawyers encountered in my prior career.

A solitary man, grossly fat and opinionated, he could be as touchy as a polar bear with an ass full of razor blades. Once, near the end of a long drinking session, he admitted to never having known the companionship of a woman. The only surprise to me in that revelation was that he appeared to deeply regret the situation.

Curmudgeons are not uncommon in the antiquarian trade. When asked, most will admit to preferring books to people. And why not? What personality could be more charming than a 1910 edition of *Pervigilium Veneris* bound by the Doves Press; or more amusing (and rarer) than Beau Brummel's *Unpublishable*

Memoirs, a little volume that was published, the title notwithstanding, in 1790?

In Gareth's case, however, the noble thoughts contained in the classics and the beauty of illustrations in old manuscripts meant nothing to him other than how they enhanced the material value of the object.

Despite his limitations, he had a fine knowledge of collectibles and enough line of credit to buy what he wanted in the midrange. He wasn't in the rarefied league of great bookmen on the East and West Coasts —people like Ken Lopez, Peter Stern, and Ed Glaser —but he held his own in the Midwest.

The only other person I recognized in that squalid River Market warehouse was Richard Atwood, a former book scout who now sold exclusively on eBay. He was a squat, one-armed lout with stringy hair that cascaded to his shoulders as if he were a lost member of Black Sabbath.

Among other misdemeanors, he cadged beers off unsuspecting locals at dive bars by claiming he'd lost his wing to an IED in Falluja (the enemy in fact being a guardrail on I-29 and a fifth of McCormick vodka). I'd kicked him out of my shop a year earlier for selling books to Prospero's Bookstore that had mysteriously vanished unpaid from mine.

Staying clear of Atwood, I snuck up to Hughes and gave him a friendly nudge. It startled him more than I intended.

"Jaysus, you bloody shite," he said with a hard glance. "What brings your sorry ass down here? Auctions and flea markets are my territory."

I pointed to the partially covered books.

"It's nothing but old Bibles, magazines, and World

Book encyclopedias," he said. "Go back to your store where people bring books to you."

"What about the erotica?"

His feigned look of innocence confirmed that whatever the sheet concealed was enough reason to stick around in the airless, hundred-degree heat.

"Ah, hell," he conceded, nodding in Atwood's direction. "Just don't let that parasite see that we're interested in them."

"It's too late," I said. "Anyway, he's only good for paperbacks and reprints."

"Ya think so? With you and me hovering over this pile like a hen on her chicks, he'll do his best to be a player when he gets a peek at what's under the sheet."

Edging past Gareth, I pulled the cloth up for a closer inspection. What I found astonished me. When I looked back at him and silently whistled my appreciation, he answered with a peevish frown instead of the knowing wink of a fellow book lover.

As predicted, Atwood gravitated toward me as soon as I picked up the first leather-bound book. Carefully opening it, mindful not to let sweat drop on its beautifully illustrated cover, I saw that it was in French. That gave me an advantage since I could read and speak a fair amount of the language.

L'Ecole des Biches, the title read. *Ou moeurs des petites dames de ce temps (School for Courtesans, or habits of the little ladies of today)*, # 53 of a limited edition of 64 copies.

A dozen short vignettes graced its pages, at least two of which centered on lesbianism. It was in perfect condition with a supple leather binding that gave slightly when handled. The linen-threaded pages displayed a strong yet feathery texture that had maintained its cream color for over a century. Although there were no illustrations, the feel of the book conveyed its own sense of tactile sensuality.

Laying *L'Ecole* down gently, I turned my attention to an oversized book of etchings and ink drawings by Andre Masson that reeked of violent sex. Etching #72 displayed a couple kissing, tears flowing from the woman's closed eyes as a dagger sliced into her shoulder. A more colorful and delightful book of watercolors followed. It was by the female Danish artist Gerda Wegener, whose charming illustrations were filled with costumed characters diving under petticoats and into trousers, merrily seeking the not-quite-hidden forbidden fruit.

Each book I handled topped its predecessor in beauty or perversion, the common denominator being exceptional condition and, despite their subject matter, surprising literary merit. It was enough to make me forget about the Shunga until Gareth pointed to a large Japanese scroll.

I untied the silk bow and carefully unrolled the rice linen paper as the auctioneer started the bidding for a dozen barstools. The watercolor revealed a beautifully robed geisha engaged in intercourse with a handsome young warrior. His bow and quiver of arrows leaned against a table as they made love. Although he was obviously about to explode, she maintained a chilling aloofness.

Unrolling the horizontal scroll further, I saw couples engaged in a variety of artfully arranged debaucheries, the men looking comical with their lustful grimaces while the women maintained a look of slightly bored obedience. This subjugation of the female lover, I gathered, was the essence of the Shoku-hon prints in reinforcing the precept of the master-servant principle.

Intended to excite patrons of bordellos in 17th, 18th and 19th century Japan, the prints portrayed better than words how courtesans and geishas were trained to satisfy men without regard to their own pleasure. They were also used as how-to books for blushing brides of the middle classes.

I knew enough from reading Edmond de Goncourt's *Le Peinture des Maisons Verte* (along with English lit, art history was one of the few classes I never cut as an undergrad) that after Utamaro died in the early 1830s, the erotic ukiyo-e prints lapsed, with the exceptions of Kunisada and Hokusai, into a coarser style portraying little more than crude posturing. But to my untrained eye, the work before me seemed more like fine art than the decadent efforts of the later period and represented an important find.

With Atwood hovering nearby, I hid my enthusiasm by shrugging my shoulders and turning away from the table. I needn't have bothered. This bottom feeder of the book trade may not have had a thousand disposable dollars to his name, but he wasn't an idiot and he answered my posturing with a knowing smile.

Still, I figured that only Gareth Hughes stood in the way of my winning those treasures, and while he was worth far more than the likes of Atwood, he didn't have the resources to outbid me on most of them.

Being a practical man, the Welshman whispered to me a proposal that made a great deal of sense.

"They're worth tens of thousands, but we can get them for a pittance. Why don't we come to some arrangement so as not to out-price each other?"

"You mean collude? Why, Mr. Hughes, I'm

shocked."

"You're as much a pirate as I," he said with what passed for a grin. "And if Christie's and Sotheby's can do a bit of topping, I figure we can, too. I want the Colette."

"The Colette?"

He nodded. "You missed it entirely. Promise you won't gouge me on that one?"

"Sure. I'm mainly interested in the Japanese scrolls. But show me the one you're so keen on."

We walked back to the table, followed by Atwood, but ignored by the others whose interests were focused on the aluminum napkin holders proudly raised by the auctioneer for all to admire.

Gareth pulled back the sheet and reached for a book that he had concealed beneath a 1964 issue of *Fortune Magazine*. Titled *L'Ingenue Libertine* by Colette, the cover portrayed a man kneeling before a beautiful girl who held a whip over his bare buttocks. I wasn't particularly impressed until he opened to the title page containing the following inscription in green ink:

To Sylvia Beach, my most beautiful American friend. I give this book to you in the hope you will share it with Hemingway (un homme tres jolie!) whom I believe will appreciate its delicacies. Je t'aime, Sidonie-Gabrielle Colette de Jouvenal.

Impressive enough, but the real kicker followed. In blue ink and different handwriting were the words:

And back to you, Sylvia. It was a damned fine week despite the guilt. Blame it on the book. I've been in worse places than this and I bet you have as well. All will be o.k. My best to Adrienne who is good at forgiving. Ernie.

Wow. From Colette to Beach to Hemingway.

The history of significant possessors of a book could be the most important feature of a collectible work, particularly if it had anything new to say about a major literary figure. For literature scholars, the provenance of this book was the equivalent of baseball's double play combination of Tinker to Evers to Chance.

Sylvia Beach had been the founder and owner of Shakespeare and Company in Paris when it was the literary headquarters for Ernest Hemingway, Ezra Pound, T.S. Eliot, and James Joyce. She had published Joyce's *Ulysses* when no one else would touch it.

The inscription meant that Colette, author of *Gigi* and one of the more outlandish personalities of that extravagant era, had given her book to Sylvia in the hope that she would sexually excite Ernest Hemingway. If the ink writings were genuine, it would significantly alter the historical perception of Sylvia Beach, a lesbian who had lived happily and, supposedly, faithfully with her lover Adrienne Monnier.

I wondered if Hadley Hemingway ever chanced upon that inscription or whether her husband used the affair associated with it to write *The Garden of Eden*.

"Any others like that in there?" I asked Gareth.

"Perhaps. I haven't had time for a proper inspection. You can have all the Japanese stuff. I don't have contacts in the art world."

After twenty minutes, Gareth and I had divvied up most of the books and scrolls we would share and were inspecting a few more when the auctioneer directed the crowd's attention to the table we had by then assumed was ours.

"Now we got some purty books here!" Colonel

Bender bellowed as he lumbered over to us, microphone in hand. "Some ain't as nice as the others and some don't have no pictures at all, but most of 'em is old and all of 'em is saucy."

The first thing he held up was the Colette.

"Ten dollars," I bid casually, aiding Gareth with an artificially low start.

"Ten dollars, ten dollars, ten dollar', ten dol'...do I hear fifteen?"

"Forty," Atwood shouted as he stepped away from the pile of Harlequin romances he had pretended to examine.

Gareth and I looked at each other with annoyance, but secure in the belief that the book scout didn't pose an undue threat to our finances, we looked back to the auctioneer and proceeded to raise the bid in cautious increments.

Surprisingly, Atwood got the bidding up to a thousand dollars before conceding to Gareth's ante of another hundred. That seemed to do it, but the auctioneer had to earn his commission.

"Come on, folks," the colonel pleaded. "I know it ain't got pictures and it's in a funny language, but these came from a fancy home."

I held my tongue, but it wasn't easy honoring my promise to Hughes, knowing that the fat bastard was getting an incredible piece of literary history for a tiny fraction of its worth in exchange for me getting some Japanese prints.

"Okay then," Colonel Bender exclaimed. "Going once, going twice, for one thousand one..."

"Ten thousand for the lot," said a voice behind us; a voice that most certainly did not belong to Richard Atwood.

Chapter 3

I f you've ever had a new bicycle stolen on Christmas Day, you might understand how Gareth Hughes and I felt at that moment.

"Did yew jes' say ten thousand?" the auctioneer said after recovering his voice.

A tall, wide-shouldered man dressed in a brown silk shirt and black linen trousers stepped from behind a post, tapping his fingers against the side of his pants impatiently. His long, narrow head, book-ended by two grossly cauliflower ears, was completely bald. Take away the dark sunglasses he wore in the hazy light of the auction hall, he looked like the eraser end of a #2 pencil.

"Yes, I have a check to present in that amount. You will bring the sale of these books to an end."

He spoke with a Dutch Afrikaner accent, one I'd heard often in my rugby career. As I pondered what a white South African was doing in Kansas City bidding on erotic books at Colonel Herl Bender's flea market auction, Hughes piped up, refusing to accept defeat.

"Point of order!" he shouted. "These books weren't offered as a lot. I'm prepared to offer five thousand dollars for one of the items. Just one book."

The auctioneer, clearly out of his league, looked beseechingly at the stranger who slowly shook his head.

"This one," Hughes insisted, holding up the Colette. "Just this one."

"No," the South African repeated. "All or nothing."

Colonel Bender held out his palm seeking patience, then sat down to confer with a pinch-faced woman who looked ready to throw her calculator at him. After listening to her urgent advice, he rose red-faced to announce a decision.

"My wife says they were offered as erretatica... eroica...or somethin'. Ah, hell, them's all the same, them dirty books."

Mrs. Bender could stand it no more and rose, all five feet of her, to announce in a shrill voice that the books were not described individually in the newspaper but rather as "erotic books" in general. Therefore, they could be sold as a lot.

The auctioneer shrugged his shoulders apologetically in response to Gareth's impotent snarl.

"Going once, going twice..."

"Eleven thousand five hundred," I said quietly.

I was gambling with Anne's college education. It cost that much for just one semester at CU. But my bookman's intuition had taken over, and I didn't want those beautiful Japanese scrolls and that piece of literary history to go to a bad home without a challenge.

"Twelff five," sputtered the man in the brown shirt.

"Fourteen," I countered with a nonchalant shrug, but my sphincter felt so tight I couldn't have passed a raisin.

A long silence followed in which I ignored my competitor. Nonetheless, I felt his eyes boring into the back of my head.

"Fourteen thousand dollars," squeaked the colonel. "Do I hear fourteen five?"

He didn't. "Awright then, goin' once..."

I turned for the second time to look at the man who continued to stare at me. He had taken off his dark shades, most likely to better size up his competition, and I noticed his eyelids had narrowed to slits. Beads of sweat gathered on his forehead.

I guessed that he wasn't buying the books for himself and we were now beyond his employer's authorized limit. I wondered what kind of person could put that kind of apprehension in such a hard man.

"Twenty thousand," the man hissed as the colonel raised his gavel.

Now it was my turn to sweat. I glanced at Hughes who quickly avoided my look. He would be good for ten thousand just to get the Colette, but he didn't have the money for more at the prices being bid.

I was alone, betting my entire livelihood on a pile of paper and leather, discovering how focused one becomes when success or failure rests on nothing more than gut instinct and a momentary perusal of the goods. I could sell two hundred and fifty shares of inherited stock for six thousand dollars, use a ten-thousand-dollar line of credit at Midwest Bank, and unload a later first edition Faulkner that I'd been saving for myself. But did I really want to risk that kind of money for books I hadn't researched thoroughly?

"Twenty-five thousand," I said.

The room erupted in applause.

Gareth Hughes barked a surprised laugh and the colonel performed a brief jig as if struggling to control his bladder. Even his wife emitted a constipated smile as she tallied up the commission on her calculator.

The Afrikaner leveled his porcine eyes at me as if I was the only person in the universe. His look confirmed that he would make up the difference out of his own pocket.

"Thirty-five thousand," he said.

"Forty," I countered blithely and totally beyond reason, except for my renewed belief that, up to a point, my opponent could not afford to let me win. The trick was to guess where that amount stopped.

Everyone in the room stared at me, including Gareth Hughes who stepped forward and gave me a cool, one-sided smile accompanied by a shake of the head that made it clear I was not to count on him. Whether it was the stifling heat of the room or the insane position I had placed myself in from misplaced pride and an old-fashioned devotion to rare books, I felt dizzy and nauseous.

"Forty-five."

"Damn," I muttered under my breath.

Those near enough to hear my curse smiled sympathetically, assuming I was disappointed because I could bid no higher. But my small outburst was only for the effect it would have on the Afrikaner.

Sick as I was with worry, I knew with all my quivering heart that we had not yet reached the end sum. We were close, however, and I shed my poker face just long enough for him to see I was near the end of my challenges.

I waited for Herl Bender to threaten dropping the hammer before quietly upping the count by twenty-five hundred. To have raised the ante by another increment of five grand ran the risk of scaring away the competition; the last thing I wanted.

My opponent studied me long enough for mankind to evolve into something else. Meanwhile, the colonel went through his by now well-practiced prolonging of the raised gavel, letting it quiver in the left hand he held high above his head, his patience bubble-gum stretched as he aimed his oily smile at the man, urging the final bid to top mine.

But the stranger stared silently at the auctioneer and slowly shook his head, causing my bowels to sink into my Nikes.

Outside Christmas and St. Patrick's Day, I'm not a religious man, but my eyeballs shifted upward, seeking divine deliverance from owing a fortune I did not have for items I had inspected for less than two minutes. Add to this the miserable fact that they were offered by an auctioneer with about as much credibility handling rare books as Mike Tyson.

If there was any consolation to be had, it was that the Afrikaner seemed as concerned as I at what was about to transpire, confirming that his boss was not a very understanding individual when it came to losing.

Except that he had nothing to worry about.

If I couldn't honor the bid, which was extremely likely, he would get the books for the first price he bid before I originally countered.

Namely, ten thousand dollars.

Not only would I owe a substantial amount in

damages to the auctioneer and face possible felony charges for fraud, my credibility as a book dealer would be ruined unless I could make good the $47,500.

I began to calculate the fair market value of my house (naturally, the economy was experiencing the worst recession in modern history) when I heard a quivering voice from the back of the room utter the magic words that renewed my faith in Catholicism.

"I bid fifty."

The voice didn't belong to the Afrikaner but to Richard Atwood, that thieving book scout who wasn't supposed to have a pot to piss in. On the other hand, the person at the other end of the cell phone that Richard held to his ear with his plastic prosthesis probably did. The sneaky bastard must have been reporting my bidding with the Afrikaner to his client, waiting for the right moment to jump in.

And thank Jesus, Mary, and Joseph for that.

For a few seconds you couldn't have heard a mouse fart, then the room exploded in wild applause and laughter louder than before.

The Afrikaner appeared as startled as I, only now he had his own cell phone to his ear and the look of renewed interest. He didn't hesitate to top Atwood's bid by another twenty-five hundred while I looked on in relief and wonder. Atwood reported the raise into his cell phone and raised the ante, which, in turn, was quickly countered by the person calling the shots on the Afrikaner's phone.

Sixty grand is what Richard Atwood's client and I cost the stranger's boss that day.

After Colonel Bender slapped down the gavel, the crowd remained silent for a few moments before madly rushing toward the table to see what prizes had laid before their unschooled eyes. The pandemonium provided enough diversion for Gareth Hughes to sneak the Colette into his leather satchel and skulk out a side door.

I didn't pursue him. My colleague was long past reason. It happens sometimes with bibliophiles; that "gentle madness" Nick Basbanes is always writing about.

If the stranger noticed that Gareth had fled with the Colette, he didn't show it as he shoveled the books, far too carelessly for a true book lover, into four cardboard boxes. When they were filled, the colonel motioned for three of his helpers to pick them up, leaving the fourth on the floor.

"Are you ready to go?" Colonel Bender asked the man.

"I'm ready."

"Well then, you'd best get that last one and show the boys to your car."

The set of the big fella's jaw made it clear he wasn't doing any physical labor, even though the remaining box weighed all of twenty-five pounds.

"One of the boys will come back and get it," the colonel said diplomatically.

"I want 'em taken out togetter. Now."

Bender's crimson face puffed up like a blowfish. He still held the check for sixty thousand dollars in his right hand and, for an instant, I thought hillbilly pride would prevail over common sense.

No such luck.

"I'll get this one, Colonel," I said, picking up the box. "Go ahead with the rest of your business."

"Why, thank you, son. That's mighty decent of you."

I figure it never hurts to protect another man's dignity, especially if there's no threat to my own in doing it, and, as I'd have some questions for the colonel later, I thought it wise to get on his good side.

"Show us the way, Shakespeare," I said to the Afrikaner.

He snorted contemptuously, aiming those piggy eyes at me again until satisfied he had stored my features in his memory bank. Then the other three book haulers and I followed him out of the building.

His black Lincoln Continental sat in a no-parking zone near the front door. He opened the trunk with an electric key and watched in silence as we put the books in place. Then, showing a two-inch smile that promised to drain my liver sometime soon, he got into the car and sped away, the tires spraying gravel against our kneecaps.

I barely had time to jot down the personalized license plate.

It read 2 L 8.

Chapter 4

After the auction, I headed for Riverrun Books, my shop located in the heart of Brookside.

It's a middle-class urban neighborhood where people glide away summer afternoons on porch swings, nodding friendly greetings to strollers on shaded sidewalks under the canopies of hardwood trees four and five stories high. Although well-tended, the lawns are not particularly wide or deep so that the houses lie close to the street, expressing their owners' trust in the outside world and pride in their handsome oak doors and exterior walls of native stone.

The soft, fresh air after the heat of the River Market warehouse lightened my mood. I counted my blessings, such as they were, while I drove to what many considered the best used bookstore in town.

After all, I'd narrowly escaped owing Colonel Bender's client an amount I couldn't possibly have raised in the foreseeable future, my health was excellent after years of trying to destroy it, and the used book trade, like movie theaters and liquor sales, was proving to be recession proof, picked up by ever-increasing sales on the internet. Even last week's shock of learning that my twenty-year-old daughter was having an affair with a notorious celebrity more than twice her age had retreated to the back of my consciousness, hovering like a faintly disagreeable odor.

At least she was coming home for a while.

Riverrun Books anchors the middle of a quaint shopping center built in 1924. It is bordered by a tailor shop to its south and a bakery to the north. An inside open door connects the bakery with the bookstore so that the smell of baking bread and brewing coffee permeates the place.

As I approached Fifty-Fifth Street in my Jeep Cherokee, I saw customers sitting outside my shop at green bistro tables under a broad awning drinking café lattes and reading *The New York Times*. A dog, lazing at the feet of a young couple, chewed on a leather bone while a little boy sat on crossed legs contentedly reading a picture book.

I pulled into my regular space in a church lot across the street, turned off the engine and set the automatic lock before exiting it. Three paces from the car I realized I'd left the keys in the ignition. Returning to the Jeep, hoping against hope that I hadn't really locked myself out, I reached for the door latch hesitantly, preferring empty uncertainty to the confirmation of a locked door.

I jiggled the handle.

Locked.

I jiggled the handle again.

Same result.

I cursed under my breath and looked over my shoulder to see if anyone had noticed my predicament. Only the boy with the picture book seemed concerned.

I gazed morosely at the asphalt and, finding no answers there, decided to swallow my pride and seek help in the shop. But first I had to do the manly thing and slammed my fist against the offending door.

The car alarm went off, scattering pigeons and causing Father Patrick Doogan's cup of hot chocolate, propelled by his startled knees under the café table, to spill onto the virginal laps of Sister Mary Catherine Browne and her cousin, Mary Margaret Scanlon.

While I scuttled across the street to the bookstore, apologizing to what seemed like half of St. Peter's parish, Weston Preston, towel in hand, leaped from behind his coffee cart to clean up the mess.

"You'd best turn that noise off, boss," he said unnecessarily in his southern Missouri drawl as he sponged the steaming mess off the nun's habit.

"I locked myself out," I said, equally unnecessarily.

"Well now, that would be a problem, if…"

Leaving the cousins to clean themselves with paper towels, Weston set up the table that had fallen over and began wiping off the top, lost in mid-sentence as if the whooping and clanging of the alarm had rendered him catatonic.

"'If' what, for God's sake?" I said. "Why aren't you looking for a wire coat hanger or something?"

"If," he said, looking up at me with the slightest hint of superiority. "You didn't have an extra key in a magnet box stuck under the left-front wheelbase; the one you had me put there a year ago after another one of these episodes."

"I don't remember that."

"You was drunk."

"Oh."

He went back to wiping the table while I ran across the street to bring peace and quiet once again to the neighborhood.

A round of applause and laughter led by the priest greeted my return to the shop. It being Saturday, the store was crowded. Some of the regulars sat inside at tables arranged in a semi-circle in front of the coffee cart.

Brian Canady, Scottish Dan Muldoon, and Kiki Bates had been strangers to each other until developing common bonds through the bookstore. Their tendency to stay long and spend little had aggravated me in the beginning, but I soon came to appreciate the kindnesses, large and small, that they showered upon me and my other customers.

They were soon referring to themselves as the Riverrun Irregulars and if their debates over religion, politics, and the merits of certain authors sometimes became too heated, they rarely failed to entertain. A used bookstore, like any small retail business, can get pretty lonely in the slow seasons, but I could always count on one or two of the Irregulars to brighten up the place, whether on a bone-chilling January morning or a humid August afternoon.

Opposite the cart, separated by the front door and a library table stacked with newly arrived books, was a long sales counter where Phyllida Law sat perched before a computer screen.

She wore a silk blouse and a light cashmere jacket. Her long dark hair, streaked with gray, was gathered in the back into a braided bun. A loosely tied silk Lacroix scarf barely concealed the wattles that draped her throat. Her dark linen skirt was long and tailored in such a way as to make allowance for a rather thick waist and full hips.

She was a woman who had probably always fought her weight, never quite to her satisfaction. Nonetheless, she could be attractive in the manner that a once-glowing debutante thirty years later can be when not rushed to put on makeup. The glow may have departed, the flesh loosened, but the good high cheekbones remained, as did the Lady Duff Cooper nose.

Only the mouth failed inspection. Thin lips, permanently pursed, reflected the soul of an intelligent but grasping woman sliding toward sixty who was haunted by a lifetime of high expectations followed by inevitable disappointments.

She looked up, brushed back a wisp of hair that had escaped the bun and said in a voice as hard as a park bench: "We've been busy. You're late again."

"I was at an auction."

"They're a waste of time," she said, going back to the monitor.

I noticed two boxes of books stacked on the floor behind the counter.

"Who brought these in?"

"Look at the note," she said without looking away from the screen.

"Okay," I said, resisting the urge to fire her on the spot. Just as quickly, the reasons why I shouldn't came to mind.

Prior to her bookstore being lost in a fire ten years earlier, she had been the doyen of Kansas City's antiquarian book trade. She had little patience for botanical works, but her knowledge of other rare books, particularly travel/adventure, nineteenth-century children's illustrated and collectible contemporary fiction, was vast. She needed a paycheck, meager as it was, and I felt sorry for her. It was hard for her to forgive me for that.

I looked at the three-by-five card stuck to one of the crates and, forgetting for the moment my lost opportunity at the auction, felt the anticipatory thrill that comes with the second-hand book business three or four times a year if one is lucky.

"Greetings from Charles Walsh," it said in a neat script penned with India ink. "Perhaps you can find a home for these old friends. Let me know what you want to pay."

Charles was the retired curator for incunabula— hand-printed books published prior to 1501—at the Linda Hall Library, one of the top reference libraries in the world, and a man of refined and varied tastes. When we first met, he hadn't let on what he knew about books, but after we became friends, the octogenarian felt compelled to hone my expertise.

Phyllida rose from her chair, brushing baguette crumbs from her lap, to join me as I pulled a box onto the counter for inspection. The first book was a leather-bound beauty written by James Boswell, best known for his remarkable biography of Samuel Johnson. I slowly opened it, careful not to crack the spine.

The title page declared a delicious boast: "*An Account of Corsica, the Journal of a Tour to That Island; and Memoirs of Pascal Paoli. London, 1769.*" My mind filled instantly with images of dry, mountainous land dotted with fig trees and donkeys ambling up a rocky corniche.

Being a third edition, it wasn't rare by antiquarian standards. The engraved frontispiece portrait was browned, and it had offset onto the title page as well. However, for its age, it was in good shape and a note-worthy book by an important author.

"We'll finally have a decent travel and exploration section," I said while unfolding a beautiful map affixed to page eighty.

Phyllida answered with a saccharine smile. "My old shop had *Cook's Voyages*; including the charts, of course."

When I didn't respond, she shrugged and nodded indifferently toward the boxes. "You'll like the rest of them as well."

I brought out a fine limited edition of *Merchantmen-at-Arms* by David W. Bone. Printed in London, it was one of only a hundred and sixty numbered copies and contained illustrations by his brother, Muirhead, including a signed drypoint etching.

Phyllida gathered it lovingly in her hands and sighed. Turning the pages as if they were butterfly wings, she felt the texture of the white linen sheets, mouthing a particular phrase as she read them, then traced with her fingertips the lines of the engravings.

"So beautiful," she said mostly to herself. "Yes, I think we have the beginning of something here. I never had one of these in my shop. Could never find one for the right price. Although once in Edinburgh…"

She caught herself before the nostalgia made her seem all too human. "Well, it doesn't matter. Would have lost it in that damned fire anyhow."

There were thirty more such books in the three boxes, all related to travel, adventure, or sporting activities such as hunting and fishing. I didn't expect to find any incunabula, but these beautifully bound editions covered a period from the mid-eighteenth century to the early nineteenth that was in a price zone I could afford.

If Charles accepted my offer, I'd no longer feel presumptuous advertising that Riverrun sold rare books as well as the second-hand variety.

"I'd better get my application to the Antiquarian Book Association ready, Phyllida."

"Are you sure you can afford them?"

"That's not the way to look at it," I said as if money was a mere inconvenience, and I hadn't been staring at the modern equivalent of debtors' prison a few hours earlier. "Choose a book as you would a friend and you'll never regret the cost."

"Some friends," she said, but let the rest pass, it being too nice a day even for Phyllida's highly developed cynicism.

"I hope Charles didn't try to lug these in by himself," I said.

"His wife did the heavy lifting. As always."

"How were they? I haven't seen them for a while."

"Agnes was her plump, annoyingly cheery self, and Charles obscene as ever. He recited that same disgusting limerick."

"'There was a young lady from Aberystwyth?'"

"Yes, Michael, that one," she said with the tight, knowing frown of a nun who might have strayed once or twice. "He insists on aggravating me with those naughty stories."

"Care to name others, Phyllida?"

"Please, let us not be coarse. As Cicero once said, 'Be thou familiar, but by no means vulgar.'"

Just then, Josie Majansik interrupted her jogging to tap on the window.

I hoped she would come in and stay awhile. Her looks had appealed to me the first day we met three months earlier when she popped in for coffee before going to work. I was impressed when she told me she was a reporter for the *Brush Creek Gumbo*, the alternative newspaper with a reputation for taking on the local establishment. It meant that not only was she a writer but feisty as well.

One weekend morning I found her at a table outside the shop busily jotting down answers to questions she had posed to a handsome man in his early thirties. His thinning black hair was combed straight back, and he sported a blue and white polka dot bow tie. A shirt with French cuffs and a chalk-striped custom-tailored shirt beautifully matched his earnest, glistening expression. He seemed far more interested in her than the questions being asked.

Although he wasn't a regular customer, I had no trouble recognizing him. If Edward Worth IV wasn't the richest man in town, he was in the top four—his father, uncle, and an older cousin possibly edging him out. The aptly named family owned the largest brokerage firm in the Midwest and Eddie was majority shareholder of the region's Coca-Cola distribution and bottling plant. His portfolio also included ten thousand acres of grazing land in the Flint Hills that supplied McDonald's franchises in four states with hamburger meat.

Eddie's reputation wasn't limited to his aristocratic good looks, Jermyn Street tailor, and business acumen, however. In his younger days, he was considered East Coast society's randiest bachelor.

Having sown the wildest of oats at Choate, Yale, and with friends from the New York Athletic Club, at the age of twenty-five, he returned to the family firm in Kansas City determined to prove himself worthy, not only in board rooms but through philanthropic leadership as well. A decade later, he had become a paragon of noblesse oblige and every society matron's dream of a son-in-law.

Because I didn't usually get to the shop until after ten a.m., I rarely saw Josie during the week. Lately, however, she started dropping by at noon on Saturdays to buy *The New York Times* and browse the contemporary fiction section. She favored women authors, especially A.S. Byatt and Virginia Woolf, but knew her way around Barry Unsworth and Peter Carey as well.

She seemed just shy of thirty, wore her silky dark hair cut short, laughed with sparkling green eyes, and walked in the bouncy, flirtatious manner one associates with the women of Paris. Her wide smile also endeared her to me, not the least because she wore a retainer to correct slightly crooked front teeth, suggesting she was not to the manor born.

Her high cheekbones and slightly tilted eyebrows indicated an Eastern European background, so I wasn't surprised when she told me her maternal grandparents came from Budapest. She certainly had the exotic looks of a gypsy. The blood of Attila probably coursed through her veins as well. I felt a presumptuous surge of jealousy at the thought that she and Eddie Worth might be having an affair.

I set aside the box containing Boswell's book and motioned for her to come in. But Josie just waved and then did something that stirred me more than I thought possible. It was a purely innocent sign of affection, nothing more than a quick farewell, but it seemed at the time to be a life-changing experience.

She blew me a kiss.

Pleasantly flustered, I touched my cheek in response. I'm not sure she saw the gesture before she walked away, but my hand was still at my face when I heard a commotion coming from the art section near the back entrance.

Bob Langston and my daughter had arrived.

Chapter 5

Kansas Citians tend not to stare at special people, whether they have a physical affliction, drive exotic cars, or play professional football. Just isn't polite, you know. But this was *the* Long Bob Langston of action movie fame and suddenly my bookstore erupted in a frenzy of Hollywood mania.

Any presumption that he was a decrepit roué knocking on death's door was immediately shattered when he bounded into the place and yelled, "Hello, K.C. MO! Your dreams have been answered."

A shaggy mop of dishwater blond hair topped an overly large head that sat on a chest as solid as a Nevada dam and when he flashed his famous gap-toothed grin the customers swarmed around him. Not one to seek refuge in a corner, he wrapped an arm around Anne's shoulder and cheerfully answered questions while I stood behind the counter attempting to make eye contact with her.

I couldn't help noticing how thin and tired my daughter looked in contrast to Langston's vitality.

She was stunningly beautiful, but the coltish charm I once associated with her seemed to have faded since our last encounter in Boulder. Even though she smiled at the raucous banter between the customers and Langston, I knew she wasn't as amused as she pretended to be. She looked like a strung-out super-model forced to appear at a grand opening of Kmart.

Langston, however, seemed to be sincerely enjoying the attention. Despite skin that appeared tired from surgical stretching, he exuded charisma. I doubted that he could jump from boxcar to boxcar as he had done in *Hell Train*, his first major motion picture, but his manner was that of a man who still did his own stunts.

"What's it like filming a love scene with Rhonda Ashworth?" a matronly woman asked.

"Do you really want to know?" Bob said with a conspiratorial smile that drew the crowd closer to him. His craggy face with its deep-set eyes, long crooked nose, surprisingly sensuous lips, and anvil jaw beamed with emotional involvement and good humor.

"If you think it's all right."

"She has bad breath."

"No!" the lady shrieked. "Really?"

"Really. I'd rather kiss Rin Tin Tin."

That brought plenty of laughs and calls for more Hollywood insights.

"Well, most scenes take eight hours to shoot," Langston said seriously. "But nothing is ever sustained. It's like bad sex—all over in thirty seconds, and it's an hour before you can do it again. Doesn't matter whether you're with Miss Ashworth or Miss Piggy. After a while, it's just a rather common, silly little job."

Nobody bought that, and Bob seemed pleased that we hadn't.

"I suppose there are plenty of downsides to being so famous," said Kiki Bates as she guided her wheelchair to his side.

"You mean 'infamous,' don't ya' darlin'?"

Kiki blushed, a rarity for her, and continued: "Well, you *were* the favorite of the tabloids for a while."

"A while?" he said, pretending to be insulted. "Hell, I've been king of the grocery store rags for three decades. I'm in the Mighty-Have-Fallen Hall of Fame. My Fruit of the Looms are hanging on the wall of the Smithsonian. I have my own butler at the Betty Ford Clinic."

The crowd loved it. He may have been a rascal who in the past couldn't keep his pants up and his nose undusted, but he could laugh at his faults. Then he got serious and they loved him all the more for it.

"You know," he said, sitting in a chair so he could look Kiki directly in her eyes. "There's no hiding place when a movie star makes mistakes. Even when we don't. In the distant past, actors like Grant and Hepburn were considered sacred. Now...well, you know the public perception. We don't pay our bills, we don't bathe very often. We're seen as silly grownups playing life as a child's game."

"And we seduce your daughters," I said to myself.

While we had yet to be introduced, I figured Anne had done a good job of describing me. Or perhaps I just had that puzzled, steamed look of a father concerned that his daughter doesn't know what she's getting into. At any rate, he suddenly looked at me and nodded as if he had read my thoughts. I acknowledged the greeting with a smile as genuine as a Robert Mugabe promise.

As concerned as I was for my daughter, I wondered if Langston knew what *he* was in for. Anne Bevan had yet to sink a battleship, but she had yet to turn twenty-one, and you only had to look at her to know her most destructive period was going to begin any day.

She was tall, blonde, and leggy with a slightly oval face, a straight nose upturned at the end, a wide mouth with sparkling teeth that five thousand dollars' worth of braces had set to perfection, and the bluest eyes this side of Iceland.

Her sorority sisters had nicknamed her "the Palomino." The moniker was as much for her wild behavior as her thoroughbred looks. I learned this the first month into her freshman year when the Kappa Kappa Gamma housemother called me expressing concern for Anne following unbecoming antics at an off-campus barn party.

"It wasn't that she drank cup after cup of schnapps and smoked a large marijuana cigarette," Mother Morsbach had said. "I'm afraid such overindulgence is not uncommon anymore. But then she tore off her blouse and…"

The housemother carefully searched her vocabulary for the appropriate words but failing that, simply said, "Please suggest that she act more lady-like in the future. She has become a bad influence on the other girls in her pledge class."

That was my little girl all right. She might have toned things down by her junior year, but I suspected she had just gotten better at covering up her transgressions.

After the initial excitement of the movie star's

appearance in Riverrun had run its course, my customers began to notice her. I doubt anyone realized that she was my daughter. She rarely visited the store when in town and, when she did, emphasized her upper-crust English accent as if to nullify any connection to me.

The looks came from her mother and the voice from living with her maternal grandparents in the ritzy London neighborhood of Holland Park. For nine years following Carol's death, I let them raise her. Mental demons haunted the child and I was in no state to be an effective parent. That's what I tell myself, anyway. I needed her then as much as she needed me, but there was so much hurt and confusion at the time neither of us realized it.

So I shuttled her off to England where Duncan and Marie Christie-Miller did the best they could. They taught her beautiful social manners and provided a first-rate primary education, but they never succeeded in taming her wild nature. When Anne turned fourteen, they returned her to my care.

The day I met her at the airport she experienced her first period. Things didn't get any better for us after that.

I put aside those memories and locked eyes with my daughter's seducer, who then raised his hand for silence in order to make an announcement.

"Now, ladies and gentlemen, if you'll excuse me, I'd like to meet the owner of this fine establishment."

The crowd dispersed very gradually and reluctantly as he and Anne made their way to the counter. A few of the men shook his hand, a teenage girl jumped up and kissed him on the cheek, and Kiki wheeled back to the coffee cart to order another espresso from Weston Preston.

"Hello, Father," Anne said with cut-glass diction as she gave me a Princess Diana mwah-mwah air kiss. "Dad, Robert. Robert, Dad."

Langston smiled broadly and his eyes twinkled just like in *The Last Man* when he stood on that barren hill after the battle of Culloden to shout with his dying breath, "Bastards all!"

Well, maybe 'twinkle' isn't the right word, but they seemed to catch the light from somewhere and reflect it back. He was a star, no doubt about it, and his handshake, featuring fingers thick as Wisconsin brats, was firm and dry.

"Anne tells me you played rugby," he said.

"A bit," I answered, trying not to look pleased.

"You must have been good to have started for the Eagles."

"Canada beat us forty to fifteen in 2005 and the Welsh tour was pure disaster. We weren't exactly New Zealand's All Blacks."

"Still, capped for your country is no small thing."

He knew the way to my heart.

"Did you play?" I asked.

"A little," the hero of *Red Tide Running* answered. "When I was at Northwestern in '82 I played for the Chicago Lions RFC."

"Well, up you old Zulu warrior! Did you know Mick Daily?"

"Of course." He laughed, and it was a beautiful laugh, full of manly bonhomie and Falstaffian cheer. "Mickey was our scrum half; a great guy but slow with the pass to the standoff and best remembered for singing 'Sweet Mary of Knock' after every match."

"I suspect you played second row," I said, eager to avoid the subject of rugby parties. The moronic escapades of young athletes fueled by testosterone and buckets of beer do not weather well in the retelling.

"Actually, I was a strong-side wing."

I arched an eyebrow. You don't see many running backs outside of New Zealand or the NFL who are six feet six inches and two hundred fifty pounds.

"I clocked a nine point eight hundred-yard dash before the knee blew out," he continued. "I missed playing in the national tournament, but with nothing better to do, I auditioned and got a part in the Toronto production of *Camelot*."

Anne gave him a sideways look with a frown as cold as January, unhappy to be frozen out of a conversation between two old ruggers.

"We'd better be going, Bob," she said, stifling a yawn. "You have the meeting with your producer."

"Yes, yes, I know," he said. "At three thirty."

Like a chastised boy, he nervously checked his watch.

"Are you okay?" I asked.

He frowned, checked himself, and flashing that gap-toothed grin, answered with the catchphrase from the film that had garnered him an Oscar nomination.

"No worries, mate."

Anne took his hand. For an instant she seemed the older of the two, the mother of the child, as Langston's smile faded behind a blank mask.

"He's been working awfully hard. Shooting begins tomorrow."

"I understand," I said. "When will you be coming home, Anne? I'd like to catch up on things."

"We'll try."

"I thought you were staying with me."

"Perhaps," she said.

"They wouldn't let us in," Langston muttered, waking from his semi-trance. "The bastards denied us lunch."

"What are you talking about?"

"That damn Stable Club. The manager showed us the door. Apparently, they don't care for actors."

"You aren't a member," I said feebly.

"But he was with a member," Anne explained quietly. "A very nice fellow named Martin Quist who has put quite a lot of money into the picture. They still wouldn't let him enter. It was quite humiliating."

"I won't forget it," Langston said bitterly. "The Hotel Ritz barred Laurence Olivier back in the fifties. Even today, the LA Country Club is thought to set a quota for actors. I just didn't expect it in this neck of the woods."

He sighed before going on.

"You know what Olivier did the first time he was in Paris after receiving his knighthood? He returned to the Ritz where they made a special point of welcoming him. In the bar, with a fawning manager attending him, he ordered a glass of tap water, took two sips, and left, never to return."

"Nice touch," I said.

"Yeah, but Sir Larry knew what it took me a long time to learn. People don't trust people who can fool them. Actors are just tricksters and anyone who can become another person must be lacking a proper self. Peter Sellers was a master at inhabiting personalities, but never knew his true identity. Like him, I honestly don't know any more how much of me is real."

I wondered, too.

A *Time Magazine* article featuring Langston reported that he grew up in Pueblo, Colorado, the son of a prison guard who would beat young Bobby's mother, then tell the boy he'd been conceived by another man. Years later, when the old man lay dying of emphysema, Bob whispered in his father's ear to remind him of those words, adding that he hoped they were true.

Back in the bookstore, Langston's face had become a shimmering canvas of mood and feeling.

"Sometimes," he said. "I feel that I'm on the verge of committing real violence. Acting is my way of staying out of the asylum."

"And you're in love with my daughter? Gee, that's reassuring."

Langston's laughter broke the somber mood.

"You're my kind of guy," he said, slapping me on the back. "You want to be in my movie?"

"Not if I have to sleep with you."

It just came out; a sarcastic line from a peeved father who wished to make a point. Naturally, without my intending it, the comment insulted not only the super-sensitive Mr. Hollywood, but my daughter as well.

Suddenly, Long Bob and I weren't rugby buddies anymore. We weren't even on the same team. He and Anne stomped out of the store, followed by most of my customers.

Chapter 6

I spent the next two hours in the storage room sorting and pricing recent trade-ins. It's a job that usually takes no more than thirty minutes, but I was in no mood to chat. When I finally felt calm enough to emerge, Phyllida greeted me with a sneer.

"I hope you didn't buy any junk at the auction this morning."

"Nope," I said, settling into my chair behind the counter. "All I got were ugly looks from an unpleasant man who outbid me on what may be the finest stock of books I'll ever have the chance to obtain in my lifetime."

Phyllida looked up from the computer. Her green eyes studied my face for an instant, then looked back to the screen.

"Did you know him?" she asked as she resumed tapping on the keyboard, scrolling down our inventory list.

"He wasn't from these parts, but Gareth Hughes and Richard Atwood joined in the bidding as well."

"Hughes I can understand, up to a point. But Atwood? That miserable creature who suffers from petrified adolescence? What could he have possibly afforded?"

"He was bidding for someone else; someone interested enough to offer fifty thousand dollars over the phone. Richard didn't stick around long enough for me to find out who."

Phyllida glanced back at me before standing.

"Tough day, huh?"

"Yeah, you might say that. I'd just as soon not discuss all the reasons."

"Given your present attitude," she said, gathering her purse. "I think it's in both our interests that I take the day off."

"I'm sorry, Phyll," I said, rising from my chair, "It's just…"

She placed her hand on my shoulder. "Don't get up. And stop worrying about Anne. She's infatuated with that Hollywood coot for now, but she's strong and has enough horse sense not to get carried away."

I found no comfort in her words and told her.

"All right, have it your way," she said sharply. "You men know so much about women, why don't you try screwing yourselves." She headed to the front door, waved her hand in dismissal and marched out.

So much for "let us not be vulgar."

Weston Preston's eyes closely followed Phyllida as she exited the store. He expelled steam from the espresso machine, wiped his hands on the plaid ladies' apron he always wore, and walked over to me. A T-shirt and cutoff jeans covered the rest of him, leaving exposed a hairless chest, knobby knees, and in testament to ten years in the Merchant Marine, an anchor tattoo on a skinny right biceps.

"A long nose is a lady's liking," he said, leaning over the counter and exhaling stale coffee breath into my face.

"You can take off as well, Weston."

"But I've only put in ten hours."

He wasn't being sarcastic. He averaged twelve hours a day during the week and more on Saturday and Sunday. The long hours were his choice. It wasn't just the money. The coffee customers and the shop constituted his entire social life. His goofiness delighted the children as well as their mothers who found him harmlessly amusing. I could never get a handle on him, but he was a good barista.

More importantly, Phyllida, who considered coffee in the shop an unnecessary hazard to the inventory, was surprisingly tolerant toward him. That alone seemed enough to keep him on.

"You got to take better care of yourself, Captain Mike. Don't want to be a mud-head."

"Right. Don't want to be a mud-head. Last thing in the world I'd want to be accused of."

Sometimes it was best to humor Weston when he began to spout nautical terms harkening back to another century.

"You sure you don't need me? Vic and Karen are goin' to miss their coffee fix tonight. They always land at four bells."

"Leave a pot for them to pour themselves."

"But Vic expects his latte and Karen a cappuccino."

"Go, Weston. Please."

Two hours after Weston left, I had yet to close the

shop. Vic and Karen had come and gone, deeply disappointed. Near the poetry section in a quiet corner, two customers lingered, reading lines of Keats to each other.

I pulled a fifth of Jameson from under the counter, poured half a glass and worked on some bookkeeping.

It hadn't been a bad week for the business. Our efforts to list first editions on Advance Book Exchange and Alibris were starting to pay off. We recorded twenty sales for the week from those sites on the Internet. They included two from England, one from France, and another from Japan.

To top it off, I'd taken in a fine dust-jacketed first edition of *Suttree* by Cormac McCarthy from a scout who either didn't realize the value of the book or was desperate for cash. I paid his asking price of thirty dollars and sold it through Alibris two days later for eight hundred. The rush I felt making that quick seven hundred seventy dollars felt as satisfying as any big personal injury settlement from my old days practicing law.

With things going so well in my life after years of courting disaster, I asked myself why Anne had to get involved with that Hollywood character.

It wasn't just her hooking up with Bob Langston. I couldn't get over the feeling that she was rejecting me for another father figure, someone against whom I felt unable to compete, and I felt the cold winds of disaster beginning to blow again.

Phyllida was doubly wrong about Anne. She wasn't tough and she lacked good sense. Her years in London had given her a superficial strength that comes with good schooling, but the upper-class Sloan Ranger facade hid a frightened, emotionally stunted girl.

For all her proud nature, she was capable of self-destructive acts. I knew enough about drugs to suspect that cocaine or something worse was behind the bizarre behavior reported by her housemother that went beyond normal college hijinks.

But who was I to judge?

I'd had a pretty rough childhood until my grandparents took over parental duties. If there was any advantage to having a schizophrenic mother and a father who could be bear-trap mean when drunk, it was to discover that outside their grasp, the world could actually be quite nice.

I played football on scholarship at Iowa University and followed that with law school, where I served as Notes Editor on Law Review. Four years as a judge advocate in the Marine Corps, including a tour in Iraq, added some extra confidence.

I seemed to have everything in those early years after my discharge from the Corps—a wife as intelligent as she was lovely, a darling little girl, and partnership in an up-and-coming law firm. But there was something in me that had refused to grow up.

Until a man reaches thirty, he is often a self-centered idiot, and in many ways, that rang true for me. Looking back, all my self-important posturing—the screwing around with other women, the blackouts—was all an attempt to recapture a time that never was; a mythical place where Mother set a decent table and a sober father there to tuck me in at bedtime. Despite outward appearances, I was just a bunch of molecules without a clue as to who I was.

The law firm of Winter & Bevan, LLC, had done remarkably well almost from the day we put up our shingle. We focused on trial work, Tim Winter representing clients in personal injury cases while I defended business owners that blue stocking firms wouldn't go near—payday lenders, trash haulers, and after-hours bar owners.

Most of my clients wore suits, attended mass, and enjoyed Sunday dinners with their families, but that didn't prevent them from employing others to do some very dirty business on their behalf.

In my defense, I fancied myself a stout defender of the First Amendment. If that meant a large part of my income came from keeping strip clubs open and modern-day shylocks rich, I was still able to sleep at night. It was lucrative and, with Supreme Court precedent on my side, not very difficult. It was also plentiful, there always being some civic do-gooder or politician trying to outlaw their idea of lewd and lascivious behavior.

The trouble started when I began to accept certain fringe benefits associated with the juice bar trade. At first it was free booze, then women, and inevitably, cocaine. Plenty of that.

Carol saw what was happening and threatened divorce more than once. I made a few feeble efforts to get out, but always came up with an excuse to be pulled back in. Representing vice was, after all, the money train that paid for our country club membership, ski vacations to Aspen, and other perks deemed necessary by the upwardly mobile.

Tim Winter attempted to help by referring some of his personal injury cases to me. But medical malpractice and product liability lawsuits required the kind of patience I no longer had. Word got out about my late-night activities and my law license was suspended for six months.

During the period of my suspension, I kept off drugs and focused on saving my marriage. Although barred from appearing in court, I earned my keep assisting Tim prepare his cases for trial.

At the end of the six months, I found myself ready to take my career in a new direction. Carol stuck by me with unending patience. I took time off and we visited her parents in England. On a summer evening while on a hill in the Lake District, we rededicated our lives and love for each other. But happiness isn't something you decree to yourself; it's not a thread you can pick up when you feel like it any more than you can choose your parents.

One of the healthier aspects of my life at that time involved rediscovering a rugged game I had learned in the Marines and played at an international level for a time.

Rugby kept me fit and my teammates on the Kansas City Blues, a wholesome cross-section of hard-working cops, bartenders, post-grad students, and a trio of Samoan Mormons, were in direct contrast to my clients.

Not long after my reinstatement to the bar, Carol and I traveled to a tournament in Tulsa. I hadn't meant to play on the 'A' side, but a lock forward had been injured, so I borrowed his boots and went in for him. I played well despite being the oldest man on the pitch and afterward insisted to Carol that we attend the post-tournament party. As the daughter of a former British rugby player, she knew full well what that might entail, but she reluctantly agreed.

After consuming four or five beers, I gave in to her demand that we return home that night and that she would do the driving.

The car shot off the highway somewhere past Fort Scott while I dozed in the back seat. The trooper's report concluded that Carol, who had not been drinking, must have fallen asleep at the wheel as there was no evidence of skid marks. She died of head injuries before the Life Flight helicopter landed. Unhurt except for a three-inch scar on my forehead, I was left to grieve with our then five-year-old daughter who had been left at home with a babysitter.

Friends said I did the right thing by not driving while intoxicated. Carol's parents, bless their hearts, even told me at the funeral it was God's will. I've been told a lot of things. But it comes down to this: my irresponsibility killed the love of my life, the mother of my child.

I hung in there for three months, maintaining a semblance of sobriety and struggling to show up at the firm each day before ten a.m.

Isn't that what you do, particularly when you have a five-year-old motherless child depending on you?

Well, I couldn't do it. The man whom Carol had so carefully brought back from one abyss, couldn't handle her loss. One night I went out drinking, leaving Anne home alone without a babysitter. The next morning after realizing what I had done, I bought an airline ticket for her and sent her to live with her grandparents in London.

I managed to get by at the firm for another year, but the loss of Carol, accentuated by unrelenting guilt at her death and relinquishing my parental duties, sent me spiraling downward in a haze of drugs and booze.

My law career came to an abrupt end when I was disbarred at the instigation of a hotshot assistant DA named Denton Crowell for commingling a client's funds with my own. It was unintentional neglect, but that didn't matter. I had frittered away a once-promising career long before that and was in no shape to defend myself.

In the following decade, Crowell went on to become the white knight of Missouri's moral majority, attacking sin wherever it lurked. That included my former clients' establishments, as well as birth control clinics. He was incapable of stopping the proliferation of gangs and meth labs in our county, but he made national headlines when he filed criminal charges against teenage girls who failed to disclose the names of doctors who had prescribed birth control pills for them.

Now he was his party's front-runner for the United States Senate and looking for another cause to emblazon his name among the electorate. I wondered if he had found that cause in my case.

It took the disbarment and a kick in the ass from my British father-in-law to get me thinking halfway clearly again. I swore off drugs, reduced my drinking, and six years ago, thanks to a generous loan from Tim Winter, opened Riverrun Books.

Since then, my profits from the shop have been enough to feed myself and make house payments on time. The rest of the income goes for a modest social life spent mostly in neighborhood bars, traveling to book fairs, and covering my daughter's fees at the University of Colorado.

Such parental tithing had not brought with it redemption, however. Nor had it brought respect, love, or forgiveness from Anne.

It was nearing seven thirty and I was putting the day's receipts away when I noticed her walking across the street looking as if she had just stepped off a Grecian urn.

Strands of her silken hair streamed in the light wind and the setting sun gave her skin a golden glow. A simple dress, soft and gentle in cut, hung loosely on her tall, slender figure. Despite my frustration and anger at what she was doing with her life, I couldn't help feeling proud that she was my daughter. She really did have the looks and style of a movie star. No wonder Bob Langston was making a fool of himself over her.

A boy, seven or eight years old, swept around the corner on a skateboard. She moved to avoid him, but he panicked and collided with her so that both fell hard onto the concrete. Anne picked herself up, oblivious to the cinders embedded in her forearm, and leaned over the boy who was trying unsuccessfully not to cry. She put one hand on his back to comfort him and with the other, gently wiped gravel and dirt from his skinned knees. She helped him to stand and, with arms entwined, they limped across the street to my store like two veterans of trench warfare.

I had the first-aid kit out by the time they entered. After dressing their wounds, I added a couple of cookies and soft drinks to aid the healing process. His tears dried, the boy soon jumped back on his board in search of new sidewalk victims.

"Thanks," Anne said.

"No problem. I'm proud of you."

She shrugged. "I don't think it's worth mentioning."

"Still, I'm proud of you for a lot of other things as well."

"You don't have to elaborate," she said as if

sensing a lecture. "I was coming to see you. I didn't drop in for medical treatment."

"I'm glad you're here for whatever reason."

"Well, you always say that we ought to talk. I'm here to talk."

"But not to listen?"

She looked away, then back again. "Are you jealous of him?"

"That's a strange way of putting it. I'm your father. I don't want you to be hurt."

"Don't try to protect me. It's not as if I were in some kind of danger."

"Aren't you? A guy like that, so much older than you, for all his charm and glamour, will toss you aside when he gets tired of ..."

"Of what? Bob is doing more for me than you ever did. He believes in me and doesn't treat me like a child. While you blew a lucrative career to become a used book salesman, he's fighting to get back on top. You have no right to prevent me from loving him."

"I'm entitled to share my opinion. For one thing, I'm still in financial bondage to Sallie Mae on your behalf."

She pretended not to hear.

"Have you ever thought why he might be attracted to you? Aside from your beauty and tender age, of course."

Her response was to pick up a book from the new arrival table. It was a National Geographic photography book about bees. She had never shown any interest in bees before that moment, although she could be about as unpredictable as a swarm of them.

I waited for her to put down the book and answer

me. When it seemed as if she would read the whole thing, I changed tactics.

"How about joining me for dinner? It's closing time."

The couple who had been reciting Keats to each other hovered near the counter, an audience to our test of wills.

"I'm not hungry," Anne finally said.

"That's not the point."

"What is the point then, Father?"

"What's this formal 'Father' stuff?"

"It's the most proper word I can think of, given the way I feel about you. Or would you prefer I call you something else? Something more appropriate to your status. 'Loser,' perhaps? 'Barfly'? Less charitable names come to mind as well."

The customers put down their poetry and silently left by the back door. Not knowing whether there were others lurking in the stacks, I moved closer to her.

"Try to understand my concern," I whispered. "Langston's been ridden hard and put away wet a hundred times. He's about as stable as a hand grenade with a pulled pin. It's in your best interests, if not as a matter of respect to me, that you listen."

"That's your point?" she said, smiling. It was a feigning, mocking smile; an empty smile on a cold face. So unlike the face she had presented to the boy who had run into her on his skateboard; so unlike the coy, seductive smile that she gave to a has-been movie star. I wished that she was six years old and we could start all over again.

"Come on," I said. "I'll give you a ride home."

"Don't bother. I've changed my mind about staying with you. If you want to reach me, leave a message with Laura Dowell. She's a production assistant on the movie who takes messages for Bob. Here's her number."

Then she was gone, leaving me with a silly grin on my face and a piece of shrapnel in my heart.

I finished the drink, turned out the lights, and walked over to the door to lock it when Weston Preston appeared.

"You still here, honcho?"

"No, Weston. I left hours ago and am actually getting shit-faced at Fitzpatrick's Galway Pub."

"Hey, that's funny. Wish I'd thought of it."

"What are you doing here?"

"I forgot somethin'. You go on to your Hibernian hootenanny. I'll close up."

"All right. Check the bathroom towel dispenser before you go."

I walked to my Jeep, put in a CD, and listened to Chris Isaac wail "Diddley Daddy" while I drove two miles to the Country Club Plaza for a friendly pint or two.

Chapter 7

Fitzpatrick's was one of those 'authentic' Irish theme bars that sprouted like shamrocks throughout the country in the late '90s. Despite its manufactured charm, it had the liveliest craic and the prettiest women between Denver and St. Louis on Saturday nights. People sat in comfortable snugs listening to the Pogues, Black 47, and the Clancy Brothers on the sound system while attentive barmen from Donegal and Kerry helped to lend a bit of authenticity.

So in I went, greeted by a charming hostess named Siobhan who promptly told me the wait for dinner was an hour at least.

"Well fine," I said, giving her my name and made my way through the noisy, chain-smoking crowd to the smaller of the two bars in the second room where Ronan Gill was tending drinks.

Ronan was a fine fellow, three years off the boat and working during the day for Sprint as a computer analyst. I'd met him and his pretty Belfast-born wife at a few Celtic Fringe meetings.

I ordered my first Guinness.

"How are t'ings?" he said as we waited for the stout to settle.

"Hundred percent."

"To be sure. Every day a holiday. Every paycheck a fortune."

"And every line a parade," I said, laughing.

"Ah, you're a good man, Mike. May your daughter grow up to be Pope."

Ronan was full of blarney and a few other things but he always managed to make me smile. By the time my stout was presented, he was on to drawing more for others and I turned to the job at hand.

The first sip of the Guinness is the second best, followed by the second long pull, which is the best. By the end of the jar, I was feeling much better. Black 47 was cranking out Irish reggae over the speakers, the girls were looking saucy and I'd seen several old acquaintances from the days of practicing law who didn't care that I'd been disbarred. I waved at them and ordered another pint.

I listened to a long, not-very-funny joke from a stranger at the bar and ordered a round for him and for me when it was over. An informal seisún began in a corner with a fiddler, a bodhran player, and a girl with a penny whistle. They played "The Bold Fenian Men" and followed that with "Black and Tan" to put the crowd in a fine rebel mood. Happy wars and sad love songs were the themes for the evening and so I ordered another pint to celebrate.

When the performers took a drink break, I chatted up the penny whistler. She was dark-haired, sloe-eyed, slender, and pretty with a smile that made you remember Vermeer. She said her name was Sandra Epstein, played second chair flute for the Kansas City Symphony and could I buy her a whiskey soda as she was a little short of cash. So I did and sat with her for the next series of tunes and even chimed in with my voice which, when properly oiled, isn't half bad. I was good for the "Gypsy Rover" and "Finnegan's Wake" and we all got friendly with everyone else, which is lovely and magical and not easily acquired, and then I sang "The Wind that Shakes the Barley" a cappella:

> *I sat within the valley green, I sat me with my*
> *true love.*
> *My sad heart strove the two between, the old*
> *love and the new love.*
> *The old for her, the new that made me think on*
> *Ireland dearly*
> *While soft the wind blew down the glen and*
> *shook the golden barley…*

The ladies were lining up for me by the time I'd finished, but my sights were on Ms. Epstein, whose hand had been on my thigh for the entire second verse. An unhappy day was settling into a pleasant evening and then the winds shifted again.

"Aren't you the jolly bloody Irishman, Mr. Bevan."

I looked up at the staggering figure of Gareth Hughes. The broad face was bloated, his red eyes rheumy with yellow crusts in the corners. He was the last man in the world I wanted to see that night.

"Are you enjoying your book?"

The bloated face got harder. "What book might that be?"

I set Ms. Epstein's pretty hand aside and reluctantly stood up. "The book you stole today."

Hughes raised his right fist, thought better of it, and picked up a half-filled pint of stout off a stranger's table. He chugged the contents, stared belligerently at the young man whose pint it had once been, then returned his attention to me.

"Buy me a pint," he said.

"Buy your own."

"I'm out of cash."

"You did a damn stupid thing taking that book."

"That man didn't deserve a rare gem like that."

"His sixty thousand dollars said he did."

"It wasn't his sixty thousand."

"He'll know that book is missing soon enough and he's a hard case. He'll be calling on you."

"The Dutchman wasn't buying it for himself. Ever see him before when you were lawyering?"

"No," I said.

"Well, I have. He works for a big shot. Major money."

"Are you going to tell me who?"

"You didn't buy me a pint."

"And I'm not going to. It's your problem, not mine."

The seisún started up again and Sandra Epstein began singing "The Road to Mayo." I turned my back on Hughes to rejoin the group when I felt his hand grip my right shoulder.

Blame it on the beer or the bad mood he had suddenly put me back in. Or maybe it was a natural reaction for a former Marine who gets pushed too far. Whatever the reason, I dropped my shoulder, spun around and introduced my left fist to his chin. He went down hard, pulling a table and pints of Guinness on top of him. The music stopped for a beat or two and a woman screamed. An Irish voice shouted back at her, "Ahh, hold your gob. It's just two bloody arseholes looking to dance with their fists," and then the music started up again.

Hughes got to his feet and swung at me, but he was too drunk and slow by nature to cause any damage. I took one of his wrists, spun him around into a bear hug and tried to reason with him. Before I could give my speech, however, the manager and a bouncer had me in their grip.

They weren't in a mood to listen and that's how I found myself on the curb outside of Fitzpatrick's with Gareth Hughes instead of Sandra Epstein.

Nothing for it, but to apologize. We had both knocked some sense into each other.

"Sorry," I said. "Didn't crack it, did I?"

He rubbed his jaw. "Too much padding for that."

"Do you need a lift?"

"No thanks, Mike. I live just past the creek at Plaza Point. The walk will see me right."

Hughes turned to go, then stopped and turned around.

"I just can't stand it when someone with money shoves me around when it comes to books. I don't mind losing a bid to a bookman like you. It's when the idjits who don't really care end up with the goods that bothers me."

"I understand, Gareth." And I did.

"You want to know who the foreigner works for?"

"Sure."

"Martin Quist."

"That's the second time I've heard his name today."

"Do you know him?"

"I heard he's backing a motion picture. The family owns some banks in Lawrence or Salina, don't they?"

"And Medicine Lodge, Goodland, and about fifteen other small towns. Their real fortune comes from their oil and gas leases, however. Martin's the black sheep. He lets other family members take care of business while he lives off his trusts. About a year ago I sold him a first U.S. edition of *Mein Kampf*. He sent the South African to collect it. The fellow's name is Kramm, Rolf Kramm."

"That book isn't particularly hard to come by. Is Quist a serious collector?"

"I don't know any dealers who have worked with him. I think he just likes Hitler."

"Given today's purchase, we can add classic erotica," I said. "Thanks for the tip. Now I owe you that beer."

"Save it for another time." He paused for a moment, then asked, "Did you phone me earlier this evening?"

"No, why?"

"No reason," Hughes said as he turned to walk away.

"Gareth?"

"Yes?"

"I understand why you wanted that Colette, but one way or the other, you're going to have to return it. It's not worth the risk."

His answering smile was about as smooth as a handful of tacks.

"Oh, I think it is, Mike. And, just so you know, it

wasn't the only Hemingway prize I rescued from that pile at the auction. Are you familiar with *in our time*?"

"Sure. It's considered his earliest published work. You stole that as well?"

Another smile. "The ghost of Dr. Guffey would never forgive me if I'd let it fall in the hands of a man like Quist. There's more to this than you can imagine. Maybe I'll tell you someday. Yes, for sure I will. Someday in our time."

"Dr. Guffey? Who in the hell is he?"

But Gareth had already gone, lumbering down the street toward the Wornall Bridge like a fat French goose which, as it turned out, he'd be just as lucky. It was the last time I saw him alive.

Returning to Fitzpatrick's and the loving arms of the symphony's second chair flutist wasn't an option after that fight with Gareth.

It was just as well since pretty Ms. Epstein was considerably younger than me. The last thing I needed was to give my daughter additional ammunition to use against my position that Langston was too old for her. Anne didn't respect me for a number of reasons— some valid, some not—but, so far, hypocrisy hadn't been one of them.

It was starting to rain as I walked past half a dozen hand-holding couples to my Jeep. Five minutes later, I arrived home to a hungry cat and an empty bed.

Chapter 8

Sunday, June 27

I awoke early the next morning to a beautiful day. The heat of the previous week had broken and a cool breeze blew in from the south, bringing a hint of rain. I put on my running gear and went outside filled with enough positive thoughts to make Norman Vincent Peale blush, determined to come up with a solution for Anne's misguided infatuation with Bob Langston.

After jogging for a mile and a half, nothing had come to mind (nothing legal anyway) and as I approached Brush Creek, the old funk that comes with parental helplessness settled in.

Heading west toward the low skyline of the Country Club Plaza, I descended to the concrete path that runs parallel to the man-made canyon containing the waterway. I paused to catch my breath under the Main Street Bridge, then jogged into the sunshine again.

To my left, a stone wall hunkered below a gently sloping hillside covered with flowers and prairie grass. A series of stately apartment buildings designed and built in the 1920s, when Art Deco meant something, towered above the slope. Brush Creek flowed lazily on my right, fifty feet wide and ten feet deep, bordered by another hill and the shops, restaurants, and tennis courts of the Plaza shopping district.

The tangy scent of barbecue wafted from a restaurant and the carillon bells from a campanile tower played a Haydn concerto. Flocks of pretty girls dressed like Easter trinkets in shorts and halter tops sat on marble steps leading down to the creek or lounged on grass as they watched wiry college athletes exchange volleys on the tennis courts. Gaudy banners promoting blue jeans, cologne, and Boulevard Beer festooned the juniper trees and wire fences surrounding the courts. A voice on a loudspeaker announced a match and politely called for a player from the University of Kansas to report to the head referee's chair.

On such a perfect morning, it occurred to me that given any sort of good weather at all, it's hard to beat a Midwest city in its scrubbed-up places.

The water matched the color of the bluebird sky, the slight wind creating tiny whitecaps on its otherwise clear surface. A finch on a branch cocked its head. A pair of chattering beauties, their faces bright as sunflowers and their bodies shaped like reeds, waved from the street above.

I felt flattered to warrant such attention until I realized the girls weren't looking at me at all but at something over my shoulder in the distance.

I followed their stares downstream where two pontoon boats floated next to the dock just past the

Wornall Bridge. A man dressed in white overalls stood in the center of the first boat gazing at an object directly across from him. An ambulance slowly drove across the bridge, followed by a police car.

I jogged toward the scene, curiosity picking up my pace until I joined the crowd of gawkers gathered on the hillside above a bend in the creek.

A yellow plastic police tape hung across the path. Thirty feet beyond it, emergency medical technicians and policemen stood in grim anticipation watching two men in a flat-bottomed fishing boat struggle to pull a body from the water. While one held the collar behind the neck, the other placed a blunt-edged grappling hook underneath the torso.

Once they had the body secured to the side of the boat, a police officer on the bank pulled a rope drawing the craft to the side of the creek bed. Another used a grappling hook to haul the corpse onto the path.

The dead man lay like a slumbering walrus. Water seeped from his soggy overcoat and trousers staining the concrete a darker gray. The back of his head shone with blood mixed with water and something yellow and pink. The left arm had landed under his body when they hauled him out. The other arm lay splayed out in front of his face with the palm down so that it covered his features.

The police weren't letting anyone pass the yellow tape, so I scrambled up the hill and made my way to the bridge where more onlookers had gathered for a better view. I wedged in between a woman carrying a baby in a backpack and a young man holding a briefcase under his arm. Like everyone else, they stood motionless, mouths slightly open, staring silently at the corpse.

I recognized the detective in charge.

Underneath a pork-pie hat too small for his head, Lieutenant Detective Buford Higgins was six feet of muscle going to fat in late middle age. His broad Irish face featured a bushy mustache that one rarely sees these days outside Durango and a smashed nose that bespoke an active career in law enforcement.

During the Corretti bribery trial in my salad days as a trial lawyer, I made a fool of him on the witness stand. He wasn't the only cop who didn't appreciate my methods of cross-examination, but Lieutenant Higgins had a memory longer than most.

I watched with the others as he carefully shifted the corpse's head back and forth, poking the wound with a pencil, then turning the body onto its back. That's when I recognized the horribly bloated face of my colleague.

One doesn't make the connection easily between the living and the dead under those circumstances, but it was Gareth all right. He wore the same ugly paisley tie from the night before, and nobody else in Kansas City would have been wearing a heavy overcoat on a warm summer night. An oily black substance still clung to his lower lip and chin. At least what was left of his lip. There are fish in the creek, after all, and he had been there all night.

It appeared he had been struck by a hard object and was shoved or fell into the water to drown. I was about to go down to report what I knew about Hughes's final night on earth when the thought occurred to me that I was probably the next-to-last person to see him alive and that, as witnessed by a hundred or so people in Fitzpatrick's Pub, it wasn't under the most genial of circumstances.

It didn't help my nerves knowing that Higgins would be in charge of the investigation. While that big ol' country boy hadn't been much on the witness stand, he was a persistent and instinctive homicide detective who could marshal a small army of investigators. Two of them were probably making their way to the bars on the Plaza and in Westport to see if anything untoward had occurred the night before.

I was already practicing my alibi when a flurry of new activity away from the corpse caught my attention. A cop had found something in the bushes next to the stone parapet twenty feet upstream.

The object looked like a baseball bat flattened by a steamroller, but I recognized it as an Irish hurling stick used for Gaelic Athletic Association games, just like the one given to me on a rugby tour to Ireland. I kept mine under the counter at the bookstore to wield in the unlikely event a robber was stupid enough to think my daily sales worth stealing.

When the cop handed it to Higgins, I saw the broad ash covered with dried blood and bits of hair and flesh. I noticed something else as well, something that caused a nuclear mushroom to cloud my brain.

For several seconds I stared stupidly ahead, my eyebrows scrunched together as if miming Richard Nixon, while I muttered "Jesus H. Christ" over and over.

The hurley had alternating strips of black-and-white tape at the grip and the stamped crest of the Cross Keys Gaelic Athletic Club above them.

I had put that tape on in the fall of 1994 when I captained the KC Blues on a tour to Ireland. During an off day in Dublin, we traded rugby balls for hurling sticks and nearly beat the locals at their national game. The hurley didn't say *Property of Michael W. Bevan, Esquire*, but it might as well have.

Before backing away from the low railing, I studied the scene unfolding below.

The body, having been photographed from every angle, was placed on a gurney and covered by a white blanket. A man in a jumpsuit tagged the hurling stick with a yellow identification card, wrapped it in a clear plastic bag, and made his way up the stone steps to a police van parked on Ward Parkway. The ambulance attendants unlocked the wheels of the gurney and then pushed it up the ramp.

As the grim procession moved through the throng of bystanders on the bridge, I whispered a parting prayer for Gareth's soul; the only funeral my fellow bookman was going to get.

The door of the ambulance closed and I returned my gaze to the creek bed to find the squirrel-like eyes of Higgins staring up at me.

I nodded, he nodded back, and, with a thready smile, returned to his job, leaving me with the feeling that my brain had just been x-rayed.

He couldn't have connected me with that hurling stick so soon, but it worried me enough not to take further notice of the tanned and limber girls by the tennis courts as I began the run home.

Chapter 9

I t took less than ten minutes to cover the final mile and a half to my house, a compact bungalow built in 1923 when the Arts & Craft style was all the rage.

There were three main rooms on each of the two floors and an open porch on the west side. A wall of french doors in the living room looked onto a garden that featured a small pond. The backyard extended sixty feet to where the detached single-car garage sat unobtrusively, its sides covered by a profusion of honeysuckle that my wife, Carol, had planted our first day living there.

We bought the place shortly after my discharge from the Marine Corps for seventy thousand when we didn't have much money. It was to be our starter home, but we became so attached to it that we never considered moving. Instead, we spent any money that would have gone to a more expensive house by filling it with Stickley furniture, mica-shaded lamps, and oriental rugs.

If there was one positive thing my daughter and I still shared, it was affection for that old place.

After feeding my cat, I took a shower, put on a pair of khaki hiking shorts and a black knit tennis shirt, fixed toast and juice, and went outside to sit and think by the garden.

I'm not one to meet trouble halfway, but the events had unsettled me enough that I needed to hold the glass in both hands while I took stock of the recent developments.

The South African at the auction must have realized Hughes had stolen the Colette and killed him for it. Did he do it on orders of his employer, this Martin Quist creep?

Could there have been something even more important about the book than its remarkable provenance?

How—and why—did the murderer think it a good idea to borrow my hurling stick?

Was it pure revenge for my running the auction price to over his employer's limit and getting him into trouble? Or was there another reason for their setting me up as their patsy?

Finally, there was the surprising last-second bid by Richard Atwood. Who would entrust a guy like that to bid such a large amount on their behalf?

There were a lot of questions I needed answered. And fast. But I needed a lawyer first. I gulped the juice, tossed the toast onto the grass for the birds, and drove my Jeep three miles to Kansas.

CROSSING STATE LINE Road at Sixty-First Street, I entered a real estate agent's paradise of Tudor mansions, Spanish haciendas, and columned colonials; all fronted by yards slightly smaller than the Azores.

Tim Winter lived in a more modest Cotswold variety nestled on a two-acre corner lot. What the house lacked in size was more than made up for in its tasteful design and serene location next to a willow-graced pond.

Even if he hadn't become one of the best lawyers in Kansas City, I would have been walking up the path to his door that early Sunday afternoon to see his wife. I needed an understanding friend and Alice Winter, of all my acquaintances, came closest.

Soft-spoken, calm and unprepossessing, she was a tall, shapely woman with a face just this side of beautiful that radiated a restrained emotional power. In Europe she would have passed for an aristocrat by her bearing alone, but her natural dignity and gentle nature belied a bitter ennui that only I ever seemed to notice.

Alice and I had grown up next door and been the best of pals. As a child, she had comforted me when life with my parents disintegrated. At fifteen, we initiated each other in the intimacies of physical love. After our junior year of high school, I moved in with my grandparents across town and we drifted apart.

It was lonely at first trying to get along in a sometimes unpredictable world without her, but I soon got used to it, even finding myself relieved at my newfound independence.

I'm not sure she was ever able to say the same thing about me.

I went off to the University of Iowa and she

attended Stephens College in Columbia, Missouri. We continued to see each other during summer breaks. Shortly after I graduated law school, but before leaving for the Marines, we even discussed getting married.

A year later, I fell in love with Carol, the daughter of a British Royal Marine exchange officer at Camp Lejeune. I didn't have the courage to telephone Alice that I had found my future wife. Instead, I wrote her a breezy letter that began with a description of the weather in North Carolina and ended with "Oh, by the way…"

It took her several months to respond, but the letter that finally arrived oozed with thoughtful wishes for the "lucky English girl" and just the right touch of wistfulness at our having grown apart. She added in a postscript that she and Tim Winter were to be wed in the spring of that year and regretted she would be unable to attend my wedding. I never received an invitation to hers.

By the standards of middle-American society, the Winters enjoyed a comfortable marriage, due mostly to Tim's successful career and the pride they shared in their son. Happiness was another matter. Beneath the veneer of conjugal harmony, a darkness of spirit lurked within her, and I couldn't help but feel I was partially to blame.

I knocked on the door and moments later, Alice appeared, inviting me in with a smothering hug.

"Is Tim home?" I asked, pulling away.

"He and Mark are training at the high school. They're running the stadium stairs with rocks in their backpacks. If you ask me, the rocks are in their heads."

"Which mountain is it this time?"

"McKinley," she sighed. "I wish he wasn't taking

our boy. Colorado fourteeners are one thing, but the highest peak in North America is a whole different matter for a high school kid."

"Tim would burrow to hell if he set his mind to it."

"So would Mark," she said with reluctant pride. "Both of them bore easily, I suppose. Their joint response to my concern is that Tim's father escorted him up Aconcagua when he was Mark's age—as if the actions of that abusive shit justified anything."

We went into her kitchen, a large airy space where copper pots hung from iron hooks on thick wooden beams and checkered paper from the Ralph Lauren catalog covered the walls. Swaths of dried basil, recently plucked from the garden, were spread out on a five-by-ten-foot island in the center of the room. Thin slices of ham and swiss cheese rested on a cutting board next to a jar of imported mustard and a loaf of bread.

"Do you want something to eat?" she asked. "I thought the boys would be home by now and lunch is just sitting here."

"Sure."

Alice prepared sandwiches for both of us, cutting the crust off the bread before applying mustard, ham, and cheese.

"Why cut the crust?" I said as we sat at a small table in an alcove of the kitchen.

"Why?"

"Yeah. Carol used to do that. I could never understand it. What's wrong with the crust?"

She shrugged. "I don't know why we do it. Maybe it's one of those little signs of affection to show we love you."

"'Loved', you mean."

"I didn't mean it in the past tense."

"Aren't you going to eat?" I asked.

She shook her head and reached for a glass of milk. The drink left a white ring above her upper lip. Without a word, I wiped it off with a napkin.

"You used to do that when we were kids," Alice said. "You could be so sweet when you and Kenny Shannon weren't tormenting the nuns. That time you tied Sister Theresa's shoelaces together during the christening of my little sister, for instance."

"That was Shannon."

"Maybe. But you put him up to it."

"And we both paid the price: sentenced to two years' duty as altar boys. I haven't been to an early mass since."

"Fifteen years later you were the only lay person asked to speak at Monsignor's funeral."

"That's only because it was the old guy's last chance to torment me."

We ate in silence and then Alice put down her sandwich.

"Are you seeing anyone now?"

"Nobody special."

"Lucy Danton was nice. I liked her."

"So did I, but never got past the liking stage. A little too much Junior League."

"So you prefer barmaids to blue bloods now."

"Let's not get personal."

"What about that gal at The Peanut you always talk about?"

"Peg Flynn? She's not the marrying kind. Or so she tells me every time I propose."

Alice smiled. She'd heard all the excuses before.

"You're going to wake up someday and find your-self a very lonely old man."

"Gee, thanks for the reminder."

"So," she said, leaning back in her chair. "What brings you to this little piece of heaven? Got some moldy old books for Tim to peruse?"

"Not this time. I'm in a jam."

"Somebody pregnant?"

She asked it as if I were a sixteen-year-old girl.

"Not on my account, as far as I know. A colleague of mine was murdered last night. The police are going to think I did it. Earlier, I got in a fight with the victim at a bar."

She stared at me, uncomprehending for a moment, then made a vague motion with her hand for me to keep silent and stood up. She walked over to the refrigerator, opened it, and drank some orange juice straight from the container. She put the box back but continued to stand with her back to me for a few moments, fiddling with the magnets that held family snapshots on the door.

She turned around, smiled faintly, and said: "I don't want to be called as a witness to any admissions against your self-interest. Save the specifics for Tim."

"I'm innocent."

"I assumed as much."

"You've always been a trusting soul, Alice."

"Not necessarily. I just happen to be your very, very good friend."

Things got quiet until she brought up something we'd never discussed on any of the occasions when we had found ourselves alone.

"Do you know why Carol insisted that the two of you come home that night?"

"It wasn't my idea," I said quickly, caught off guard. "Tulsa's three hundred miles from here and Highway 169 is treacherous at night. Drunk as I was, I knew that much. The team was staying at the Ramada Inn. I'd paid for a room, but she had to get back. It seemed so important to her and I was too sloshed to talk her out of it."

Alice turned away, putting her hands to her face.

I got up from the table to put my arms around her. "What's the matter?"

"You know perfectly well," she said softly. "My baby shower was the next day. She couldn't miss your damn rugby match knowing how much it meant to you, but she wasn't going to miss my party either. Goddamn it all."

We stood clutching each other like we were in love. But when Alice brushed my lips with hers, I pulled back.

She shot me a peculiar look; a spiteful glint similar to the one I'd seen long ago when I introduced her to Carol. Just as quickly, it dissolved into a gentle glaze of regret and acceptance. We weren't in love, it seemed to say. We were merely partners in grief.

Still, I might have returned her kiss for old time's sake if her husband hadn't pulled into the driveway. We dabbed our eyes, straightened our clothes, moved into the living room, and practiced smiling.

Chapter 10

Tim Winter was my age and just as fit, but his restless eyes and stress-lined forehead made him appear a decade older.

Whether in his study, in a court of law, or on top of Mount Kenya, he presented a rugged, somewhat damaged look; a veteran linebacker eager to start the next series of downs despite a long history of injuries.

This particular morning, he wore rubber-soled hiking boots, khaki trousers, and a knit shirt soaked with sweat. A towel hung around his neck like a water-logged boa constrictor.

He greeted me with what passed for a smile and shook my hand. He had a wrestler's grip, but I gave as good as I got until both our hands turned white.

He released first.

"You're too damn competitive, Bevan," he said.

When Alice stifled a laugh, he looked at her as if surprised.

"One of these days I'll take you on a climb," he said, looking back to me.

79

"And afterward, we'll attend the Pope's wedding," I answered, dredging up Ronan Gill's line.

"How're sales at the bookstore?"

"Grand. You should come by more often."

"Of course. Let me know when you get something I'd be interested in."

"I'll be sure to do that," I said, stung by the putdown of my stock.

He was a knowledgeable collector, and while he had put up the seed money for Riverrun Books, he had yet to find anything to match his refined tastes there.

A young man with the buoyant friendliness of a golden retriever and wearing a T-shirt with the Greek letters of Phi Delta Theta fraternity entered the room. His face and manner displayed an attractive combination of confidence and civility. He was deeply tanned and his long brown hair bound in the back by a rubber band had bits of red in it from the sun.

He kissed his mother on the cheek then turned to me, extending his hand.

"Hello, Mr. Bevan."

"Hi, Mark. How's college?"

"It's great. I've decided to major in English literature."

"Followed by law school?"

The room temperature plunged fifteen degrees.

"I don't think so," he said, glancing briefly at his father, who returned the look with a face that might have done a dried carp credit.

"Time will tell," Alice interjected diplomatically.

"I took the rocks out of the packs and put them by the pond," Mark said to his father. "Will we need them next week?"

"No," Tim said, rubbing his lower back. "We'll do

some weightlifting instead. It does no good to practice suffering."

"It wasn't suffering. It was training."

"I suppose that's how it seems from your end of the age spectrum."

Mark shrugged his broad shoulders and excused himself.

"He's a fine boy," I said.

The Winters nodded simultaneously. Their unabashed pride and love for their son was one of the couple's more endearing qualities. I suspected it was also the glue that kept their marriage intact.

"What brings you here?" Tim asked.

"A legal question. Could we discuss it in your study?"

Winter looked at his wife with a pained look. "Will you excuse us, Alice?"

"Sure, but I'm putting away lunch."

"Don't," I said. "This won't take long."

She said something about the Pope's wedding and waltzed into the kitchen.

"Any desire to return to the law?" Tim asked over his shoulder while leading me up a winding staircase to his second-floor office. "Bill Evans was just appointed to the state disciplinary board. He asked about you at a bar luncheon last week and said he thought a majority would look favorably upon a motion to reinstate you."

"Sorry, not interested. I've gotten used to running a business where people leave their problems outside the door. Anyway, it appears you've done all right by my former clients."

"I admit it's added considerable spice to my practice," Tim said, grinning. "I leave the tits-and-ass trade to others, however. Alice insists."

"Smart girl. How is everything with you guys? Still madly in love?"

"She's a fine woman," he said and left it at that.

The room he ushered me into was on the second level of a three-story turret where I half expected to find Virginia Woolf scribbling in a corner. An elk antler chandelier hung from the center of the high ceiling, casting a dusky light that was good for atmosphere, but not much else.

Blood-red drapes bordered a multi-paned window featuring the Winter family crest—a serpent impaled by a lance and the rather odd motto *De Mal Me Paists*, which, if my old French was correct, translated to *I Feed on Evil*.

Floor-to-ceiling walnut bookshelves filled with beautifully bound volumes relating to mountaineering, nineteenth century whaling and exploration covered a ten-foot section of the concave brick wall. In the last century, they would have been covered with law books, but attorneys no longer needed them with the advent of laptops and Westlaw.

I sat on a worn leather couch while Tim settled behind the desk in a high-backed chair. He looked at his manicured fingernails and then at me.

"Now, what's your problem?"

"How did you know I have a problem?"

"It's Sunday afternoon and the Yankees are in town for a doubleheader. You decided to miss that for a little chat with me. I figure it's some kind of trouble. Is it Anne?"

"Not this time. She's put herself into another unfortunate situation, but I'm into something far worse. I need your services, partner. There's been a murder."

Winter sighed and looked at me indifferently as if he heard such announcements every day. His hands worked the towel back and forth across the back of his neck.

"Are you a suspect?"

"I will be."

"Hmmm. What happened to place you in this predicament?"

"I attended an auction down at River Market yesterday where some remarkable books were offered."

Tim leaned forward. My possible indictment for murder didn't seem to pique his interest, but the mention of rare books did.

"Whose collection was it?"

"It wasn't announced. The owner wanted it kept private, I suppose because of the erotica."

"Erotica?"

"Yes. Not the trashy stuff. Lovely Shunga prints and early twentieth-century European illustrated works. It included a book by Colette."

"The French writer? Which book?"

"Are you familiar with *L'Ingenue Libertine*?"

"Of course," Tim said, slightly offended that I could question his expertise. "In 1922, it established her as not only a scandalous young lady but a distinguished prose stylist as well. The novel makes flagellation seem rather charming."

"Is the book rare?"

"Not particularly. She had already become famous with the publication of *Claudine a L'Ecole* in 1900 and then the three *Claudine* sequels. Still, you won't find many first editions of *L'Ingenue* in this neck of the woods. In Paris or Berlin, a fine copy can be found for a hundred euros or more. Colette certainly held nothing back in declaring that women have a right to an orgasm whether it satisfies the male or not. The illustrations by Charles Laborde are delightfully risqué."

The lawyer fiddled with his thumbs before adding with a touch of envy, "I suppose you bought it for a pittance."

"It wasn't for me to own," I said, moving my chair closer to his desk. "There was considerable competition, and I didn't get it, but not for want of trying. The front-end paper contained an inscription on the title page to Sylvia Beach from Colette, followed by an intimate note written to Sylvia by Hemingway."

Tim's eyes shone like shiny black buttons.

"How intimate?"

"I only saw it briefly, but it made clear that Sylvia and Ernest had shared more than a love of literature."

He whistled softly. "If it's the real thing, the inscription alone may be worth tens of thousands. Any chance the buyer will let us have a peek?"

"Not a chance. The man who left the sale with it in his possession was Gareth Hughes. He stole it before the winning bidder knew what had happened."

"Good Lord. Hughes, you say?" Tim looked puzzled as he tried to place the face with the name.

"You must have met him at some point. He was a Welshman who focused on contemporary firsts. He didn't have an open shop."

"Oh, yes, that rather large, unkempt fellow. Welsh, you say? I mistook his accent for a speech impediment. He tried to sell me a battered third edition of the *Ethnological Albums of the Pacific Islands* and made a scene when I showed no interest. I had a couple of associates escort him from the building. Tell me more."

"Gareth enjoyed it for less than a day. If he thought it important enough to steal, someone else thought it worth killing for."

"So Hughes is the victim?"

"I'm afraid so. The police are going to think I had something to do with it."

Tim tugged at his ear. "You'd best tell me why a jury shouldn't think that as well."

I related that I had witnessed Hughes steal the Colette at the auction, then confronted him that evening at Fitzpatrick's where we attempted to settle our differences with fists among spilled pints of stout.

"Lovely. What happened afterward? Please tell me you kissed and made up in front of all those bystanders."

"Actually, we did calm down and reconcile, but it was on the sidewalk after we'd been kicked out of the joint. He told me the winning bidder was named Rolf Kramm and that he was an associate of a millionaire named Quist."

"Did Hughes mention why the book was so important to him?"

"It's pretty obvious, isn't it, when you consider that inscription? He also admitted stealing an early Hemingway edition and something about a Dr. Guffey not wanting a man like Quist to possess the book. He seemed to hint there was more to this than the Colette."

Tim jerked his head up sharply.

"What Hemingway book?" he asked, putting down his pen.

"It was *in our time*. Title in small caps. Inscribed to Guffey by Hemingway."

Tim hunched forward and when he spoke again, his voice was very dry and serious.

"Have you ever heard of Dr. Don Carlos Guffey?"

"Should I? He sounds like an Irish Mexican chiropractor."

"Good god, no! Guffey was an obstetrician in Kansas City who delivered two of Ernest Hemingway's sons—Patrick in 1928 and Gregory four years later—by Cesarean section. It wasn't all that common a procedure in those days, used only when the mother or child's life was truly at risk. It's likely that Hem borrowed those harrowing experiences for Catherine Barkley's death scene in *A Farewell to Arms*. Dr. Guffey was one of the few close acquaintants to remain on good terms with him.

"Collectors were always knocking at Hemingway's door, and tradition has it that the door was rigidly closed if they sought more than a signature. But to his special friends, of which the good doctor was near the top, he went out of his way to enhance their collections. Guffey was the recipient of letters, signed first editions and even a partial manuscript of *Death in the Afternoon*."

"I assume he died years ago," I said. "What happened to his collection?"

"It was sold at auction by Parke-Bernet Galleries in 1958. My father happened to have been there. Hemingway was ill—in two short years, he would kill himself—but I'm surprised neither he nor Mary nor his sons attempted to reclaim some of his past."

"What were the titles?"

"Practically everything from *Three Stories and Ten Poems* published in 1924 to the *Esquire* magazine stories and piles of letters. The *Afternoon* manuscript went for thirteen thousand. God only knows what it would go for if the JFK Library ever let loose of it now."

"What about the *in our time*?"

"It was his second published work after *Three Stories* and went for under three thousand dollars, but today it's considered a major Hemingway rarity. Only a hundred seventy copies of the original Three Mountains Press version were printed because of a disfiguring watermark in the paper used by the original French printer. Plus, with the long inscription to the man who delivered Hemingway's sons, you have a remarkable connection to his personal life. It's completely unique. A simple signed Hemingway copy goes for over sixty thousand, but this particular one would fetch a quarter million today."

"I suppose the Kennedy has it."

"Not this one. Dad sat in the row behind the man with the winning bid at the Parke-Bernet sale. Captain Louis Henry Cohn got it for nine hundred dollars. He had known Hemingway since 1930, became his first bibliographer, and, like Guffey, was one of the premier collectors of his works. After Cohn's death in the mid-eighties, his wife sold everything to the University of Delaware. It should still be there, locked away in a clam-shell box far from the eyes of anyone but researchers. One never knows, however. The university might have needed money for a new tennis court and sold the thing."

Tim picked up his pen and became a lawyer again.

"We can check on it, but, for now, we have to assume Hughes was killed only for the Colette and its unique Hemingway inscription. You said that Hughes mentioned that a man named Quist was Kramm's boss. Would that happen to be Martin Quist?"

"Yes. Do you know him?"

Tim hesitated, but only enough to put down his pen and pick up a letter opener in the shape of a miniature Bowie knife. He ran it ever so gently across the palm of his hand as he spoke.

"Unfortunately, I do. He's a member of the Stable Club. His father had dealings with my father when they were in the oil and gas business. When I was a child and the Quists visited Kansas City, my mother forbade me to play with him, if that tells you anything. The family still operates out of a little burg twenty miles north of Salina and run the county like earls in a fourteenth-century fiefdom. They sent Martin back east for school, but I understand it didn't take."

"Did Exeter expel him for playing with matches and torturing cats?"

"Actually, it was St. George's Academy in Newport. He probably wet the bed as well. The family shipped him to a place in Southwest France that was part prep school, part prison. By the looks of him, he picked up some culture and jet-set refinement along the way. He went to Brown, got a degree in art appreciation or some damn thing, then spent time in New York and Paris where he still keeps apartments. He moved here five years ago in order to keep an eye on the family holdings and still maintain a distance from his siblings whom he loathes. I understand the feeling is mutual."

"Where does he live?"

"In the old Haliburton pile of bricks and marble. You could see it from here except for those blasted trees. He likes to throw lavish parties. The wife and I are never invited. I've done rather well, but apparently not well enough to rate an invitation. Alice wouldn't go anyway. Like my mother, she thinks he's a very naughty boy."

"He's a friend of Bob Langston," I said.

"So I've heard. Martin was always starstruck. The word around the country club is that he's hurting for money, having invested in a couple of dreadful horror flicks that went directly to DVD. He recouped some of the loss by backing a series of porn films, but that was the last straw for his relatives.

"It's one thing to gamble on speculative oil and gas ventures, quite another to risk the family fortune on gang-bang films. His brother and sister have obtained a temporary order freezing a major share of the family assets. Ted Garvin from the Hastings, Flynn & Cordish firm is representing them at a probate hearing set for next month."

"But the Langston movie is legit."

Tim nodded. "Quist will use that evidence at the hearing. But he's running out of money in the mean-time because his trust fund assets are restricted to basic necessities pending Judge Taylor's ruling. It's chicken or the egg time for him.

"He needs money to ramp up production on the Jesse James flick and thereby provide evidence of his intent to produce a legitimate enterprise, but the money to produce it is vanishing. He must have had a conniption fit when Kramm told him what it cost for those books at the auction."

"Yeah," I said. "Poor Rolf."

Tim Winter leaned forward, resting his elbows on the leather-topped desk. "No, Mike. Given Martin Quist's propensity to never forgive an insult to his pocketbook, I rather think it is poor *you*."

Pretending to laugh, I said, "Quist tried to take

Langston to lunch at the Stable Club, but they were refused service. I didn't know the 'Barn' had gotten so stuffy as to not let film stars wallow up to the trough."

"That wasn't the reason. Quist was banned indefinitely for fondling the tennis pro's wife at last year's Christmas party."

"Lovely. Did you hear how Langston hooked up with him?"

"According to Ted Garvin, Quist lost all credibility in Hollywood years ago but was willing to gamble what was left of his fortune on Langston's dream for a comeback. Long Bob was equally desperate. I can't think of any other reason for even that reprobate actor to get involved with such a shit."

"That reprobate," I said glumly, "is sleeping with my daughter."

Tim Winter's eyelids fluttered, but he didn't offer an apology. Nor did he look surprised. He lay down his glasses and got up from behind the desk.

"You know how this business works, Mike. Even if you whacked Gareth Hughes and tossed him into Brush Creek, I'll do my best to defend you. He was a big man, a quarrelsome man. Self-defense is a major option to consider. Lack of intent to kill gets you a lesser offense."

I looked up at my former law partner and suddenly didn't like that he had a thriving practice, a fine house, a charming wife, and a son who, by all indications, didn't have a drug problem. And I particularly didn't like recognizing that there was a time when I was just as distrustful and condescending to people who had been in the same spot I now found myself.

Tim leaned against the side of the bookcase,

narrowing his eyes a little. He put the point of the letter opener under his chin and scratched a follicle.

"What else do you have to tell me? You're holding something back."

I gazed at the leather-bound books on the shelves behind him, then pretended to study the Kazakh carpet with its hexagonal patterns of navy blue and gold.

"The police found a hurling stick close to Gareth's body," I finally said. "My hurling stick. His blood and pieces of his skull were attached to it."

"I assume you were going to mention that sometime in our conversation?"

"We were having so much fun talking about books, it slipped my mind."

"Uh-huh. Get me a list of your staff and any regular customers who might have had access to the stick."

"All right."

We looked at each other silently for a moment before I said with more than a tad of irritation: "I'm innocent, Tim."

He raised his chin a fraction and smiled faintly.

"Of course you are. We'll visit Lieutenant Higgins tomorrow morning to put his suspicious mind at rest. I'll call to keep them from picking you up today should they be so inclined. Ten a.m. all right?"

Alice was still in the kitchen making a new set of sandwiches when I let myself out. I said goodbye to her, but she made it a point not to notice.

Chapter 11

I t was noon by the time I returned to Riverrun. Phyllida was listing books for sale on the Internet. The shop was quiet except for a few browsers in the history section, but soon the post-brunch crowd from Sharp's Café would be flooding in. I looked underneath the counter for my hurling stick.

It wasn't there, of course.

I moved my laptop to a table in the far corner of the store to log in. BiblioFind confirmed what Tim had told me. Most of the earlier inscribed Hemingway firsts were listed in the mid-to-upper five figures, but Printers Row Rare Books in Chicago offered the only one with a previously owned Dr. Guffey provenance: a first edition, first printing of *Three Stories & Ten Poems*. Printers Row was asking $225,000.

If what Tim had said was true, the Kansas City physician's copy of *in our time* was even more desirable, but the odds were close to nil that another Guffey-owned book would appear on the private market.

It was enough of a miracle that Printers Row had

92

kept *Three Poems* from the ravenous clutches of the JFK Library in Boston, let alone the Ransome Center at the University of Texas. Individual collectors, no matter how wealthy, were finding it increasingly difficult to compete with such well-endowed institutions. The upside, however, for private owners was that prices on those items still on the open market increased exponentially with each passing year.

According to Tim, Louis Henry Cohn had bought the Guffey *in our time* at the Parke-Bernet auction in 1958 and Cohn's widow sold their rare book collection to the University of Delaware in 1985. I checked on the Internet for the catalog listing of the school's library holdings. It confirmed that the slender twenty-seven-page book remained there.

So much for Gareth Hughes's hint that someone locally might have it.

Except.

For all his faults, it wasn't like the Welshman to mislead when it came to books. As the day wore on and the regular customers began to pile into my store, I became more convinced that Gareth believed the slender volume that was in the front rank of twentieth-century literary rarities had somehow become available. I was also certain that if he didn't have it on the night of his death, he knew who did.

I returned to the counter and called the University of Delaware's Special Collections Library. Half an hour and three library assistants later, I was finally connected to the main curator.

"That particular volume isn't here," Professor Wilson Traynor, MFA, LLB, PhD, said.

"Is it on loan?"

"You might say that. It's been missing for ten years."

I gawked at the phone in my hand.

"Did you investigate?" I managed to ask once my stomach stopped rumbling.

"Of course. Only five people that week had access to the book according to our sign-in sheet, but our security procedure was practically non-existent in those more trusting times. The librarians rarely asked people for identification before letting them go into the stacks. There could have been a dozen more that we don't know about."

"Do you recall the names you had?"

I heard the shuffling of notes as he cleared his throat. Obviously, I'd dredged up a very sore subject for Professor Traynor.

"Three graduate students—Mary Evans, David Steinman, and Janet Wiglesworth. The great Hemingway bibliographer, Audrey Hanneman, was another visitor and then a private collector named George Land. All were questioned and cleared by the police. The assistant district attorney rather snidely advised me that the actual thief wasn't likely to sign his real name."

"A pity," I said.

"You will let us know should you hear of its where-abouts, won't you?"

I promised I would, but the promise didn't come easy. I put the telephone in its cradle and stared into space. I must not have been smiling.

"Yo, boss, what's the sorry look for?" It was Weston, concerned for my well-being again.

"Something's come up," I said to him and Phyllida.

"I'll need your help running the shop until I can work it out."

"I have a dental appointment Thursday," Phyllida said. "You'd better be back by then, or you'll be looking for someone else to type these book descriptions."

"Ah, goin' to show a leg on us again, Skip?"

"I've given it some thought, Weston. Gareth Hughes turned up dead in Brush Creek this morning, following a night when half of Kansas City's Irish community saw us trading fists at Fitzpatrick's."

"Heavens," Phyllida said. "That *is* a bother." An eyebrow arched, her chin jutted out, but for all the surprise she exhibited, I might as well have told her the price of milk had gone up a nickel. "Have you talked to the police?"

"I'll talk to them soon enough."

I paused, took a breath and continued my story.

"I'd been on my jog when I saw them fish him out of the water. Someone crushed the back of his head. The police found my hurling stick in the bushes a few yards away."

They answered this revelation with silence and cold slate eyes.

"I had nothing to do with Gareth's death," I said acidly.

Instead of a sympathetic nod, Weston pretended to be a deaf mute. Phyllida tried to sell a crocodile smile.

"Think hard, folks. Who's handled the thing recently?"

I might as well have asked them to name the capital of Rajasthan.

"Didn't you show it to that New Zealand couple around Thanksgiving?" Phyllida finally offered.

"And you took it down to the St. Patrick's Day parade last March," Weston added. "Otherwise, it just sat there, worthless as a drunk penguin. Was you shot away last night?"

"I'd had a few, but not enough to make me crazy."

I took money out of petty cash, stuffed it in my wallet then looked back at them.

"I didn't do it, drunk or sober, but Lieutenant Higgins will have questions that I don't have answers for yet. I need time to investigate this on my own before the police come calling. It may take a couple of days."

Phyllida chewed on her lip for a moment before glancing at Weston. He took that as a cue to begin cleaning the espresso machine.

"Okay," Phyllida finally answered. "How can we get in touch with you?"

"Leave a message with Peg Flynn at The Peanut."

When they went back to their duties, I picked up the phone. My first call was to Richard Atwood, only to learn from his mother that he had left her a note saying he'd gone to parts unknown on a Greyhound bus that morning.

I then called Colonel Bender, the auctioneer at the River Market warehouse, who remembered me with good feelings. I took the chance that the police hadn't contacted him yet and that he still appreciated my volunteering to help take the books to Kramm's car, not to mention jacking up the bidding beyond his wildest dreams.

We discussed the Royals' draft prospects for next season, the weather, and a few other things before I felt comfortable enough to ask whose estate provided the books for the auction.

"They was George Land's books," Colonel Bender said. "He died years ago, but his widow only recently decided to sell. She still lives at the house, 3618 Belleview Avenue."

The colonel even gave me her phone number, but I didn't use it. Granddad Bevan hadn't brought me up this way, but I decided to make an unannounced visit to a stranger's home.

I went to the restroom in the rear of the shop, splashed some cold water on my face and headed for the back door, nearly colliding with Josie Majansik as she entered.

"Whoa, big fella! Where're you headed in such a hurry?"

"I'm going for a sandwich."

"Mind if I join you? The newspaper's buying."

"No thanks. Gotta go."

"Something's bothering you," she said with a tug on my elbow that I thought meant she actually cared for me. "Can I be of any help?"

"No, but thanks. I need to handle this alone."

"Here," she said, pulling a business card from her wallet. It was bent at the corners and slightly smudged. "Just in case you change your mind. I understand you had an argument with the late Gareth Hughes last night. It's the talk of the newsroom."

I took the card and read, "Josephine A. Majansik. Reporter, *Brush Creek Gumbo*," followed by a street and internet address, a cell phone number and the logo "*A Progressive Peoples' Potpourri.*" It was on one of those flimsy #5 cardboard things printed off a computer.

"Where's the union bug?" I teased.

"It's an alternative weekly," she said defensively. "Not the campaign headquarters of the Democratic

Party. My publisher can't afford embossed lettering, let alone living wages."

"And children are starving in Sudan. It's a cruel world, Josie. I'm sorry I can't give you a scoop."

"Mike, that's not…"

But I didn't stop to hear the rest and left the building feeling empty as a church on Monday morning.

After pulling out of the parking lot, I drove onto Brookside Boulevard where the first vehicle approaching in the opposite lane was owned by the Kansas City Police Department. It glided slowly past me, the officers within it obviously looking for the address of a charming used bookstore. I didn't see much of a future in the rearview mirror, so I kept driving to a section of the city named after the martyred patron saint of lovers.

Chapter 12

I crossed over Brush Creek on the Main Street bridge and took a left on Westport Road, passing a row of neighborhood taverns, tattoo parlors, and coffee bars until I got to Southwest Trafficway.

After a couple of miles heading north on that gritty, pot-holed thoroughfare, I made an illegal left turn into the Valentine District, a leafy area where Kansas City's lumber magnates and grain traders had lived in baronial splendor a century ago. The fine old homes were mostly inhabited by urban pioneers, energetic young professionals willing to live close to shabbier neighborhoods as a trade-off for the old-world charm and quality workmanship one doesn't often find these days.

I parked the Jeep on Belleview directly in front of Thomas Hart Benton's former house and art studio and walked across the street onto the edge of the Land property. The house sat on a rise overlooking a dry creek bed where the debris of a recent flash flood lay lodged against a stone bridge.

Tendrils of ivy meandered around the windows and chimneys like a monstrous octopus. A sizable number of slate tiles on the roof had become loose and fallen onto the untrimmed bushes below. It was mid-summer but the dead leaves of several winters lay in the eaves and gutters. A copper drainpipe hung precariously off the brick front, a loose tin brace the only thing keeping it from collapsing to the ground.

A fence comprised of rusted iron spears topped by pointy fleurs-de-lis guarded the property. Finding the front gate locked, I squeezed through a gap where several rods had rusted away, then stepped across the cobblestones of a circular driveway.

A Bentley S1 Continental, its chassis splotched with bird droppings, squatted on flattened tires under a towering sycamore. At the opposite edge of the driveway, in stark contrast to the Gothic setting, was a spotless, late-model Nissan Sentra. The Kansas plates on it suggested I wasn't the only visitor.

I flattened my thumb against the porcelain doorbell only to watch it spring from its casing. The brass knocker worked better. Three solid knocks echoed in the chamber beyond the door and soon I heard the clacking of high heels on a wood floor, followed by the sliding of a bolt.

Because of the outside condition of the house, I expected to be greeted by a bedraggled crone, but the tall, elegantly dressed woman who opened the door didn't look anything like Dickens's Miss Haversham. Her silver hair, intricately braided like a Swiss milkmaid's, was as silken as a girl's. When she tilted her head in a questioning look, her hazel eyes caught the glint of sunrays seeping past the highest leaves.

She was a beauty, nothing less, and if she had more

than a few crows' feet around those almond-shaped eyes, it didn't matter—they just spelled character. She wore a wraparound tweed skirt that stopped above her knees and a matching jacket over a cream-colored blouse. The top two buttons were undone, exposing lightly tanned breasts that I suspect had never nursed a baby.

"Hullo," she said. "Who are you?"

"I'm Michael Bevan."

She offered a puzzled smile.

"I'm sorry for barging in when you have guests," I said, nodding toward the Nissan. "But it's important that I see you."

"How did you get past the gate?"

"It was partly open."

She furrowed her brow skeptically, but sizing me up again, decided to let it pass.

"You say your name is Bevan?"

"Yes, Mrs. Land."

"I knew a Malachy Bevan once; a dear man who was police chief long ago. Any relation?"

"He was my grandfather."

Her face brightened.

"Well, for goodness' sake, you should have called first. Do come in. My other visitor is currently engaged."

From the vestibule, we entered a wide hallway with parquet flooring. Mahogany banisters led in long, wavy curves to the second floor. It was a grand house, but the first floor was devoid of furniture or paintings.

"I've had to sell most everything," she said in a matter-of-fact tone. "There is still the Bentley and a few things upstairs. I should have enough to live on for a while and then I'll sell the place."

I followed her up the broad staircase to the second floor and down a hallway to a room at the west end of the house. A fireplace, big enough to park a Hummer in, anchored the eastern wall. A parade of windows offered a broad view of the wooded park to the north.

The auctioneer's gavel had not intruded in this part of the home where a Shakazi rug covered most of the hardwood floor and a pair of Art Deco chairs bordered a Louis XV four-poster bed. The fireplace mantel held small tokens of foreign visits: a pair of brass bookends in the shape of Indian elephants, a tiny ceramic incense holder with Arabic markings, a Ming vase, and a silver tennis trophy etched with the words *1st Place St. Tropez 1961.*

A handsomely framed poster from the late nineteenth century hung on the south wall. It portrayed a full-bosomed beauty on a swing, her shapely legs kicking high toward a beaming sun, a glass of champagne in one hand while the other clutched the rope. Beneath her, leaning expectantly against the trunk of the tree, leered a satyr, his eyes captured either by the sparkling glass or the charms beneath the spread petticoats of the woman.

The viewer cannot be certain. I suppose that was the point.

"Do you like it?" she asked.

"Yes, very much."

"It's by Jacques Paleologue, known by his signature 'Pal.' He produced some of the finest posters during the fin de siècle and his studio printed Toulouse Lautrec's work. Something like this would have been pasted to a kiosk in front of the Paris Opera House or on the side of a pissoir near the Folies-Bergeres. I like them because they weren't meant for a salon or museum and yet they are extraordinarily beautiful."

She sat in one of the chairs and motioned for me to do the same. Between us was a hot plate with tea brewing in a pot.

"Please call me Beatrice, Mr. Bevan," she said as she pulled out a calendar book. "Let's see. I believe I had you scheduled for eleven tomorrow morning."

"I'm afraid not. I didn't make an appointment."

She frowned ever so slightly. "You didn't? Oh, dear. I'm afraid such discourtesies, no matter how small, can sometimes create rather large problems. I don't mean to offend."

"No, no. I'm sorry about this. I had to make sure that…"

"Yes, Mr. Bevan?"

"…that you would not avoid me."

"Why on earth would I want to avoid meeting such a handsome young man?"

"Given the nature of my visit, you might. I have some rather difficult questions to ask."

"Questions?" Her composure slipped a little. "Have you followed in the footsteps of your grandfather? Are you a policeman?"

"On the contrary, ma'am. The police are probably looking for me at this moment."

"How interesting," she said dryly. "You haven't killed anyone, have you? I should be very upset if that were the case."

"No, but circumstances have placed me in a most uncomfortable position."

"I see. Well, actually I don't see at all. What can I do for you? I thought you had other reasons for coming here."

She smiled most becomingly, but there was such sadness in her voice that I couldn't go immediately to my questions.

"If I may say so, Mrs. Land, you are a lovely woman."

She touched my hand in tender gratitude.

"Thank you, young man, but it's not really true anymore. What you see is an attractive illusion. I'm as fragile as a Wedgwood teacup now. There," she said, pointing at a silver-framed photograph of a fashion model stepping from an old twin-propeller airplane, a small handbag in one hand and a tennis racket in the other. The beauty wore a sleeveless khaki blouse strategically unbuttoned to display a string of pearls that hung from neck to sternum. "That is the woman I was before old age and poverty intruded."

I nodded appreciatively. The model in that photo seemed vibrant and was stunningly beautiful, but her face was tinged with the arrogance of accustomed comfort and compliments too easily captured.

"A woman of my age cannot compete with the costume of youth," she continued wistfully. "But I don't envy these young girls of today. In my time, a man swooned at a glimpse of knee. You could play them for all it was worth and sex became an exciting game. Nowadays, what is there to be gained when all one's cards are face up on the table?"

She crossed her legs, showing a shapely calf and ankle.

Who was I to disagree? She was certainly making my temperature rise despite having twenty-five years on me. But that wasn't what I was there for, as I reminded myself twice before starting the interrogation.

"I'm a book dealer, and I'm looking for information about the books you had auctioned by Colonel Bender."

"You were at the sale?"

"Yes. I was outbid for your books. Were you aware of their worth?"

"Oh, I had some idea what George paid for them fifteen years ago. It didn't seem all that much at the time; certainly nothing like we paid for our paintings or pieces of Lalique. I suppose some had charming illustrations, but most of the words were in French or German, and I never could fully appreciate the Japanese prints, brilliant as they were. Given their lewd subject matter, it's not as if I could have framed them and put them over the downstairs mantel for George's business associates to ogle."

She hesitated, fixing her eyes on me as playfulness brightened her face like a child's, only not so innocent. "Are you the grimacing Samurai type?"

I responded by picking a peacock feather off the table and studied it as if it were the most interesting thing in the world.

"No, I suppose not," she said with a coquettish frown. "At any rate, the price paid at the auction was a pleasant surprise. After all those years, I just wanted them out of the house. My husband used them to enhance his libido in the days before Viagra."

She looked at me slyly again, tilting her head and then laughing.

"I shouldn't think you need much prompting, Mr. Bevan."

I coughed, laid down the feather, and studied the wall. But her eyes weren't letting go without an answer.

"I suppose not, Mrs. Land."

"Beatrice."

"Who?"

"Call me Beatrice. Of the *Inferno*. Dante's genius has always comforted me. In my declining years, I find him even more relevant." Her thoughts seemed to drift away and she spoke as if I wasn't in the room. "There is no greater grief than to remember days of joy when misery is at hand."

I shuffled my feet until her eyes focused on me again.

"Sorry, my dear, what was it you wanted?"

"Was there anything about his collection that was unusual?"

"Besides being erotic, you mean?"

"Yes."

"Not really," she said, arranging a lacquered pin in her braided hair. "It bothered me that he didn't take better care of some of them. He'd write notes in the margins with a pencil, scribbling things even on the illustrations. I complained that we'd never get a decent price because of the markings, but George didn't care because he never intended for them to be sold. I suppose it never occurred to him that he might die before me either."

"Did anyone contact you about the books shortly after his death?"

She nodded and was about to say more when she cocked her head and stared past me in the direction of the opposite wall from where a soft scratching sound was coming.

I followed her gaze to the faint outline of a closed door that I had not noticed at first because it was covered in the same wallpaper as the rest of the room. Only a keyhole above a small doorknob indicated its purpose. Suddenly, she stood, reached into a drawer next to the bed and pulled out a key attached to a royal blue tassel.

Swinging the tassel slowly back and forth as if weighing a decision, she glanced again at the door and back to me, putting a finger to her lips. I had the uncomfortable feeling that the owner of the Nissan was lurking on the other side, spying on our conversation.

As she slowly crept toward the door, the scratching became louder until it culminated in a whimpering, high-pitched male voice that nearly sent me flying out the window.

Chapter 13

I began to ask what the hell was going on when she turned to me and said, "It's my noon appointment. He'll hush if we don't pay him attention."

She returned to her chair as if nothing strange had occurred and after putting the key in her lap, proceeded to answer my earlier question.

"A pair of vultures swooped in within hours after my husband's funeral, offering saccharine condolences and obsequious pleas to look at the books."

"Who were they?" I asked, trying to ignore the bleating voice in the other room.

"The first to call was an odiferous fellow with course manners and an accent that could only have come from the slag heaps of South Wales."

"Gareth Hughes."

"That sounds right. Since I wasn't aware at the time that my husband had left me practically destitute, I told him in no uncertain terms that I wasn't interested in his money."

"And the other dealer?" I shouted over the hysterics emerging from the adjacent room.

Beatrice hesitated, played with the tassel, and frowned vaguely. She stood up, walked to the closed door and tapped on it until the noise softened to a whimper. Satisfied, she turned her attention back to me.

"Phyllida Law," she said with undisguised bitterness. "It was before her bookstore burned. For years she helped George build his collection."

"Including the erotica?"

"Especially that! But don't be naïve, dear boy. Books weren't the only thing she helped him with."

She lowered her chin. "I suppose you know her, being in the book trade?"

"Until now, I thought I did. Phyllida works for me."

She stared at me as if I had pissed on her oriental rug. Just as quickly the coldness evaporated.

"You have my sympathies, Mr. Bevan. It goes without saying that I refused to sell that slattern my books at any price. After her store burned, she couldn't have paid for them anyway."

The door behind her began to rattle.

"I'm afraid I'm going to have to get back to work," she said apologetically. "It's the only means left for supplementing my income, you see."

"I've just a few more questions, Mrs. Land. Please."

"All right, but you'll have to excuse me for a moment. I'll be back in a jiff."

She used the tasseled key to open the door, and for an instant, I saw a pale-arsed elderly man skip across the room in full retreat, followed by the sound of several rapid swats against bare flesh. After a minute, the moans ceased, and in the ensuing silence, Beatrice Land returned, softly closing the door behind her. She held in her left hand a supple leather cord, no more than twenty inches long, to which small black beads were attached on the end.

If the man had been a collie, I would have congratulated my host on her training methods but suggested that a dog biscuit might do just as well next time.

Instead, I just sat there with my jaw hanging against my chest like an unemployed marionette and prayed there wasn't going to be a second act.

"Please try not to be judgmental, Mr. Bevan," she said, settling into the chair. "The gentleman has lost his sexual capabilities for the most part, so it takes a bit of playfulness to bring him around. Now, you wished to question me further?"

She looked at me, all innocent anticipation, and, after quelling the urge to ask the name of the lunatic asylum I happened to have wandered into, got on with the matter at hand.

"What sort of things did your husband jot in the books?"

"Varying methods of sexual acts that George gleaned from our participation in a rather unique social group. He would try a position described in the book and rate it according to the satisfaction he— always he—" She sighed. "Derived from performing it. If there were other people involved, he might include their names and level of performance. Sometimes he wrote their telephone numbers."

"Why did he bother?"

"For future reference, silly boy. There were quite a few people involved, after all."

"Are you referring to a particular sex club in Kansas City?"

Mrs. Land's face flushed and her tongue flicked out to play with her lips. She put her tongue back in to smile at me and brushed her foot against my ankle.

Her eyelids fluttered but remained open. "How would I know about such things? I'm over seventy years old, for God's sake."

I just smiled. If it hadn't been for "dog boy" in the next room, I might have retracted the question.

She returned my smile, confirming my suspicion.

"Many years ago, George accompanied me when I had a modeling assignment in Paris. One night we were invited to a dinner party by the president of the Societe des Anciens Livres at his home on the Place de Augustine. George's reputation as a bibliophile was well known. He was quite handsome as well and every bit as charming as our host. The other guests were the crème de la crème of Parisian society, and we spent hours after dinner in scintillating conversations. At some point, the party, I'm not sure how to this day, evolved into a daring group experience."

"You mean an orgy?"

Beatrice shot me a pained look.

"I'm not boring you with this, am I?" she said.

I gazed at a photo on the mantel of a handsome couple in their early forties and tried to imagine them locked in an acrobatic embrace with the Baron de Plessis, Madame Jourdan, and a supporting cast.

"No," I said. "Please continue."

"So delighted were we by our sexual awakening that we shared our experiences with friends when we got home. Most were so shocked they cut us off their Christmas lists. But two or three couples didn't, and that became the nucleus of the New Moon Society. It eventually grew to fifty participants, give or take a few of the voyeur variety."

"Why New Moon?"

"The double entendre was unintended, I assure you. George came up with the name one moonlit night during our first bacchanal. Apparently, he'd never heard of the disgusting college boys' habit of sticking their bare bottoms out of car windows.

"No matter, the name stuck. Not everyone in the group played our games, but most did at one time or another. We were forced to retreat a bit in the '80s— too many younger folks wanting in on the act. Despite their lovely bodies, they were considerably freer with drugs, and that simply wasn't our style. Nor was the ghastly music they insisted on playing."

"Was Martin Quist a member?"

Beatrice's smile evaporated.

"Yes, he came along much later, but I prefer to forget him. Not our kind at all. He was very young when we knew him and very uncouth."

She hesitated for a moment. "No, uncouth isn't quite accurate. I should say 'pathologically deviant' better fits his ilk. My husband considered him dangerous, and whenever Quist appeared at a party, George always encouraged me to slip away by a side door. Eventually, I tired of the shenanigans and quit going to the functions entirely."

"And George?"

"Unfortunately, he stayed in somewhat longer. Two years longer."

"Why so long?"

"Why? For the varied experiences, of course.

Different men and women. Wilder games. Sex is addictive as any drug. When the prescribed doses get heavier, one gets hooked for more."

"Did your husband ever talk about a more detailed list or photographs he might have kept?"

She stopped brushing my ankle with her foot. The tongue came out again, but it was as dry as her lips, and after a moment, it returned to where it belonged.

"Please, Mr. Bevan, tell me again that you are not a policeman. You don't seem the type at all; not with such sensitive brown eyes."

I told her again.

"What is it exactly that has landed you in trouble?"

"I was in the wrong place, wrong time."

"Haven't we all?"

"What about the names?"

"George kept a very detailed list. Actually, two of them, one labeled 'A,' the other 'B.' I think there were compromising Polaroid photos as well. The A team were high society types who had money and influence. He wasn't much interested in the B list as it consisted of lesser types—runaways and other vulnerable kids."

"Why did your husband think he needed to document everything?"

"For leverage, of course. George planned to use it only in self-defense should anyone threaten his business interests. He was a highway contractor, among other things, and highly leveraged men like him are always magnets for litigation. Believe me, having that list paid off when competitors threatened to sue George's company for price fixing."

"Do you know what happened to the lists?"

"They disappeared a long time ago," she said.

"Some think the current district attorney has them and is using them for his own political purposes. He's certainly venal enough to do it."

"Denton Crowell?"

"Yes. Do you know him?"

"Vaguely," I said with a thin smile. I didn't mention that the senatorial candidate had successfully lobbied for my disbarment years earlier.

"At any rate," she said. "That's just wild speculation. I don't know what became of them."

"Could they have been hidden in one of the books presented at the auction?"

"Perhaps. You see, I didn't give the matter much thought after he died. I wasn't interested in such materials. They were George's 'pact with the devil' kind of thing, not mine."

"Do you recall——"

But my words were interrupted by new howls from the next room, bringing the interview to a close.

"Won't you stay longer, Mr. Bevan?" she said as we both stood up. "I haven't performed before an audience in quite a while, and your presence has gotten me rather worked up."

"Perhaps some other time," I stammered.

"Oh," she said sorrowfully. "All right then."

She led me down the stairs and to the front entrance.

I was about to walk out when she said, "You were going to ask if I knew what book might have contained the lists."

"I was."

"My husband's favorite novel was by a French hussy."

"Colette?"

"Yes, that was the name. Does that help?"

"It does, Mrs. Land."

"Please," she said, offering her cheek for a farewell kiss. "Call me Beatrice."

Chapter 14

I left the Land property the way I entered. There were still plenty of hours of daylight and, despite his recent high tailing out of town, I decided to drop by Richard Atwood's place to see if he'd left any hints as to whom he'd done the bidding for at the auction.

He lived on Strawberry Hill across the Kaw River in Kansas City, Kansas, in a carriage house behind his mother's place. I'd met her in my shop before and, unlike Richard, she wasn't a bad sort. I thought that even with Richard gone she wouldn't object to allowing a fellow bookman to look at his stock.

On the way over, I mentally sorted through what Beatrice had said and tried to understand how it applied to my situation. Her late husband, George Land, had created and maintained a detailed list of a significant number of prominent persons' sexual activities—information that could wreak havoc on the social structure of the city if it were to become public, let alone the reputations of all those involved.

There were photographs as well. George Land kept the documents close to his vest to protect himself, but in someone else's hands—someone like Martin Quist—the sucker list would be blackmail gold.

I had handled the Colette only briefly, but other than the revelations of Hemingway's affair with Sylvia Beach, I perceived nothing to indicate it contained any lists. On the other hand, I knew books could be a convenient and effective source for hiding things.

A portly man in his late sixties once brought into Riverrun a second edition of an eighteenth-century aviary book by Cuvier with a lovely leather binding and a beautiful etching on the frontispiece. Without checking beyond the first few pages, I offered seventy-five dollars, a sum that surprised and pleased him.

The next day an agitated woman on the sunny side of forty showed up demanding the return of the book. Immediately upon receiving it, she opened to a back chapter where a two-inch square section in the center pages had been cut out with a razor. Nestled in the little makeshift box was a twenty-carat diamond that she had kept hidden from her husband.

"My insurance policy," she explained as she popped the gem into her purse. "You can keep the book."

So it was no stretch for me to believe the Colette hid something important within it that had nothing to do with its literary value. Obviously, it couldn't have contained a comprehensive list, let alone photographs. But it could easily hide a flat key within its bindings.

Quist was willing to pay sixty thousand and possibly more for George Land's books. For a knowledgeable collector with sufficient capital and foreknowledge of the legitimacy of the items listed, that was a more than a reasonable figure. If the provenance proved accurate, just the two books Gareth had lifted were worth a cool half million. But my instinct was that Quist had no concept of the collection's importance to the antiquarian trade.

He simply wanted whatever item that a book or books within the collection contained that would lead him to the lists and photographs. Had he known at the time of the auction that it was in the Colette, he would have instructed Kramm to bid only for it.

This was all speculation, however. The only things certain were that Gareth had been murdered with my hurling stick and the two books he had stolen at the auction were missing.

So what else was new?

After crossing the bridge on I-70, I drove up the hill past a row of boarded-up Catholic churches.

Poles, Croatians, Serbs, and Ukrainians had settled on Strawberry Hill at the tail-end of the nineteenth century when Eastern European immigrants were willing to take on work in the slaughterhouses that even the bog Irish refused to do. Men and women labored fifteen hours a day, six days a week, in the alluvial valley between the Kaw and Missouri rivers known as the "West Bottoms."

How they managed the time to have children, let alone raise them, is anyone's guess. But they did, averaging eight or more to a family and living long enough to see a great many of their grandchildren go on to college with the help of the G.I. Bill.

Three generations later, the stockyards had moved to western Kansas towns like Garden City and Dodge, and the only people willing to work in what were now euphemistically called "meat processing plants" were Mexican immigrants.

That left the Bottoms a hollowed-out no-man's-land of weed-patched fields, decaying buildings, and the once-vibrant hill above it an urban wasteland. The great-grandchildren of the original Eastern Europeans had taken their college degrees to flee Strawberry Hill for the suburban cupcake land of Johnson County, but Mrs. Atwood and her son weren't part of that migration.

She was pulling weeds in her front yard when I pulled up in the Jeep. A tiny woman, she wore a plain housedress, white cotton socks, and old combat boots. There was no indication that she had ever been an attractive woman. Her auburn hair had turned a mottled gray and her dark eyes, sunk deeply into her gaunt face, seemed locked in a perpetual squint. The skin sagged over her entire body as if she had once weighed considerably more. She had a hard little mouth that tried to smile when I approached her.

"Afternoon, Mrs. Atwood."

"Howdy, Mr. Bevan. I told ya on the phone that Dickey's gone away on the bus."

"Yes, ma'am. I was wondering, though, if I might look at his stock. He'd told me he had some local history stuff I'd be interested in."

"Can't it wait 'til he comes back?"

"That depends. I'm not always in the mood to buy. Do you expect him soon?"

"He didn't say where he was going or when he'd be back."

"He hasn't called you?"

"He only left a note."

"I'd really like to see some of those books he

mentioned. Obviously, I'd expect you to come in with me."

She dropped her weeding tools and pulled out her key chain. "No need for that. I'll give you fifteen minutes to look around."

I followed her through a gate into a tire-strewn backyard and to the carriage house where her son lived and stored his inventory. She unlocked the door for me, then returned to her weeds.

It was a clammy fifteen degrees warmer inside than in the fresh air. An air conditioner was lodged in the window but it didn't show signs of having worked for years. An old Apple computer sat on a desk cluttered with notebooks and pens. A musty odor filled the room.

Some people not familiar with the care of books think that smell is charming. It simply means some of the inventory suffers from mildew, rendering it value-less. If not tossed out, it eventually contaminates the rest of the stock.

The walls of the room, including the window spaces, were covered with cheap floor-to-ceiling book-shelves whose one-by-ten-inch pine planks sagged in the center under the weight of the volumes. Catalogs and journals spread out everywhere—on shelves, crammed in niches, piled in boxes on the floor. There was order in some sections, chaos in others where books piled in stacks several feet high had toppled over.

It seemed hopeless that I was going to find a hint as to where Richard had gone or for whom he had bid at the auction.

I went through the items on his desk but found only notes he intended to copy onto the computer for listing with the web services. I turned my attention to the shelves.

Richard was no different than most booksellers in one respect. He found it hard to throw any book away, no matter how common. Some important titles were mixed among the majority of negligible ones. He had three shelves devoted to the works of Jack London, but they were not in particularly good condition.

I noticed another area dominated by British Isles subjects and pulled out a slender book of a play titled *Cathleen ni Houlihan* by William Butler Yeats and Lady Augusta Gregory. I moved it closer to the lamp on the table and confirmed what I'd suspected for a long time.

My original pencil code marking of #4114 had been erased, but the indentation was still visible. He'd obviously stolen it from Riverrun along with a number of other Irish literary volumes. They were lined up together. Yeats, A.E., Sean O'Casey, Oliver St. John Gogarty, John Millington Synge, a fourth edition of James Joyce's *Ulysses*. None of them firsts, but six personal favorites that I'd kept in my shop, bought long ago on my rugby trip to Ireland before I ever thought of owning a bookstore.

I pulled them from the shelf and placed them in a stack on the desk next to the computer. Then I wrote a note for Richard and put it in one of his envelopes.

Continuing my search toward the rear of the house, I smelled something sweet, but not flower sweet. A rotten tomato lay next to a half-eaten ham sandwich on a paper plate set on a windowsill. Flies buzzed over and on the mess. Close to the window was a half-opened door, behind which ascended a narrow staircase.

"Dick lives up there."

I jumped half a foot in the air, startled by Mrs. Atwood's sudden return.

Before I could say anything, she said, "I don't think he'd care for you pokin' around his private place. It's time you git. You been here longer than a quarter hour."

"I understand," I said, following her back to the desk.

"You gonna buy these?" she asked, pointing to the pile of my Irish books.

"These are rightfully mine, Mrs. Atwood." I handed her the envelope. "The note explains to Richard that I retrieved them in your presence."

She stepped forward so that her eyes were just under my chin. "Are you accusing my Dickey of being a crook?"

"Take it how you want," I said, stepping past her and gathering the books in my arms. "They left my store without being paid for. I suspect there are a few more that Richard has been keeping in trust for me and other dealers. I'll want to discuss it with him when he returns."

"You people think you can walk all over him, just because he's missing an arm and never had your advantages. He's nobody's fool, my Dickey. He'll get you for taking advantage of me and stealing his books."

"Just make sure he gets my message," I said over my shoulder as I headed for the door.

The late afternoon breezes coming off the junction of the two rivers cooled the clammy sweat on my forehead, but it couldn't erase that cloying sweet smell I'd picked up by the staircase. I was pretty certain the stink didn't belong to the sandwich.

———

BACK AT MY HOUSE, I saw the light of my answering machine blinking. The recording belonged to Tim Winter.

"The meeting with Detective Higgins is confirmed for tomorrow morning," the message said. "Please try to come up with a meaningful alibi by then."

Chapter 15

Monday, June 28

T he next morning, I avoided the fourteen traffic lights on Main by taking Gillham Road, cruised past Children's Mercy Hospital, and turned onto Grand Boulevard into the heart of the city where I got stuck in traffic behind a slow-moving cement truck.

Kansas City's once shabby and lifeless downtown had changed dramatically for the better in the past decade. The Sprint Arena and the equally sparkling Power & Light entertainment district of bars and restaurants had brought new life to the area, while the iconic Performing Arts Center designed by Moshe Safdie reaffirmed the city's long-standing commitment to culture.

But the police station at Twelfth and Locust, a ten-story concrete slab erected in the 1930s during the reign of Boss Tom Pendergast, looked like the boil on the face of a pretty lady. I knew the place well enough from my lawyer days but never cottoned to that kind of environment where even the bantering between cops, bail bondsmen, and attorneys seemed as hard and sharp as the furniture.

I parked in the underground lot and took the steps to the second floor. Once there, I passed a stark waiting room where witnesses and victims sat for hours before being interviewed. All too often, these already nervous citizens found themselves crossing paths with the suspects they were helping to indict.

Displayed on the dull wood paneling outside the room were photographic portraits of Kansas City's police chiefs dating back to the days when the Mooney brothers, Bat Masterson and Cole Younger roamed the city's streets. With the progression of time, the handlebar mustaches of the lawmen had given way to trimmed beards and finally to clean-shaved faces, but the steely-eyed glares that brooked no-nonsense remained constant.

I took a moment to study my grandfather's severe, chiseled face that hung four frames from the end. His salt and pepper hair that dipped in a widow's peak above bushy eyebrows was clipped in the flattop style of the fifties.

He had rescued me when I was a frightened mess of an adolescent and I came to trust everything he had to say, especially his dictum to respect oneself. Most of my good qualities came from that man and remembering that Beatrice Land knew him, perhaps a few of my ornerier ones as well.

After touching his picture for luck, I walked on, passing the sex lab with its earnest, mostly female minions and the bail bond area where sullen clerks listlessly stamped subpoenas and stuffed them into envelopes. In the marble hallway, while waiting for an elevator, a formerly petite and bouncy court reporter who had put on thirty pounds remembered me fondly from the old days and asked if I had seen the previous night's *American Idol* contest.

I took the ancient lift to the seventh floor, feeling twenty years older than I had before entering the building.

The doors opened to a noisy room filled with fresh arrests and stale lawyers. The walls were stained by decades of cigarette smoke. I nodded at a couple of familiar faces as I made my way to the desk sergeant's counter that was manned by a hefty female with a face hard and brown as a walnut.

"Good to see you, Aretta."

In response to my greeting, the sergeant blew her nose on a frayed cotton handkerchief that might have been white once.

"We almost went looking for you, baby," she said, putting away the rag and reaching into a two-pound plastic jar of Tootsie Rolls. "Sign right here and don't think of goin' anywhere. You're already five minutes late."

I scrawled my name on the desk blotter while she popped the chocolate into her mouth and fished for another one before ringing Higgins.

"Okay," she said. "First office down the hall on the right."

"I expect my lawyer will be arriving soon."

"Mr. Winter's already there."

The linoleum corridor smelled of bug spray and liniment. At a door marked 704, I knocked and let myself in. Higgins, his huge hands clasped behind his head, leaned backward in a swivel chair behind a steel desk that was old when Kennedy was president. He didn't bother to get up.

"Howdy, Bevan," he said in a surprisingly soft baritone. "How'd your run go yesterday?"

"I've had better, but not many as interesting."

"I'll say. Have a seat, brother."

I took the chair he pointed at and nodded at Tim Winter, who stood in a corner between two filing cabinets. My lawyer had taken his jacket off and it lay in the crook of his right arm. He returned my greeting with a silent nod of his own then went back to studying the venetian blinds.

Higgins's office was probably the only one in the building that didn't have a computer. Doodles of airplanes and boats covered a calendar desk pad. An electric Olivetti typewriter sat on top of a cardboard box next to a windowsill. Beyond the window was a fine view of the county jail.

The air conditioning was turned up full blast, causing the window shades to rattle, but Higgins still found it necessary to dab his brow with a blue bandanna. The only decoration consisted of three citations for bravery framed in black plastic on the wall and, on the desk, a photo of Charlton Heston shaking Higgins's hand at an NRA convention.

"You both know the Miranda rule better 'n me," the detective began. "Want me to read it?"

"Get on with it, Buford," Winter answered. "What do you have?"

Higgins's country smile faded. He didn't like familiarity on the job and he didn't like Tim Winter.

I'm not sure how he felt about me. I'd been pretty rough on him when I had him on the witness stand in years gone by, but my questions had always been direct and I'd never gone out of my way to embarrass him. He had accomplished that feat by himself by positively identifying an undercover cop as the defendant Corretti.

Still, he seemed uncomfortable with me in the room. Maybe it was because his normally pale skin was badly sunburned from the previous morning's work on Brush Creek.

"I'm the one who asks the questions in this office, Mr. Winter. If you prefer, we can go down to the interrogation room, turn on the tape recorder, and Sgt. Reeder will assist me in questioning your client for ten billable hours. I don't give a rat's ass if he pleads the Fifth to every question."

"Certainly, Detective," Tim said, calming down. "My client will be happy to cooperate, but it would help if you explained why we are here."

After a moment's silence, Higgins leaned forward, spreading his hands on the desk. A manila file disappeared under them.

"All right," he said slowly to me, studiously ignoring my advocate. "You probably know this much since you came upon us pulling the body from the creek. Hughes was unconscious when he went into the water. He drowned as a result, but not before someone took his wallet and keys. We have plenty of folks who witnessed your altercation with him in Fitzpatrick's. A lot of bad words were exchanged, he tried to belt you, you smacked him, and the two of you were thrown out. As far as we know, you were the last person to be seen with him."

"Lots of people walk between the Plaza and Brush Creek," Tim said. "Without corroborating evidence to place Mike near the water Saturday night, you don't have enough to book him."

Higgins rubbed his hog jaw of a chin. He scratched his ear, investigated a hangnail, and adjusted his necktie, a paisley thing four inches wide clamped to his shirt by a gold-plated tie clasp in the form of an M-14 rifle. Then he reached down and from under the desk, brought up the hurling stick. It was wrapped in plastic with a yellow exhibit tag stapled to it.

His gunmetal eyes studied me as he put the thing on top of his desk so that the etched words *Cross Keys GAA* stared up at me.

"Why don't you ask your lawyer friend how we spell 'corroboration,' Bevan? I believe it's s-i-g-n-a-t-u-r-e c-a-r-d. And don't bother denying it belongs to you. One of my investigating officers was on the same rugby tour when the boys on the Dublin team gave it to you."

"Murphy?" I asked.

"Nah, it was Quinn. But Murphy remembered, too."

I studied the photograph of Charlton Heston while Tim muttered something about posting bail.

Higgins quickly interrupted him.

"Don't worry, counselor. I'm not booking your boy today."

Winter and I exchanged looks.

"To be honest, Bevan," Higgins continued. "I don't think you did this. You'd had a few drinks, but the witnesses in the bar said you weren't drunk. Nobody sober and with half a brain kills another after that kind of scene, then tosses the body where it's sure to be found by the first jogger of the day."

The detective got up to stretch his legs behind the desk, slowly swinging the hurley back and forth. "No, it doesn't make sense. A lot of people had access to that stick while it was in your shop. We've already talked to your staff and regular customers. I'm not going to take you in. Not yet, anyway. I suggest you not leave town for a while."

I thanked him for the entertainment and got up to leave.

Higgins let me get my hand on the doorknob before asking another question.

"What happened after you left Hughes outside Fitzpatrick's?"

"I drove home."

"Straight home?"

"Yeah, my cat was hungry. Feel free to subpoena her."

Higgins failed to see the humor.

"My boys will be talking to your employees some more. Do you know anyone who's taken a sudden dislike to you? Customers, old clients, girlfriends?"

"No, Lieutenant." I was getting tired of holding the doorknob.

"Anything else I should know about? You look like you know something I should know."

"If I seem a little nervous, it's because I'm not used to being a suspect in a murder case."

"We call them 'a person of interest' now," Higgins said helpfully. Then he walked over to me and lightly tapped my chest with the hurley. "If somebody is trying to place the rap on you, I'm one of the few people in a position to save your ass—Mr. Winter notwithstanding. But, brother, you gotta be square with me."

"If I think of anything else, you'll be the first to know."

It wasn't a total lie. I was, however, withholding information about the auction and the books Hughes stole. The only motive I could think of for someone to kill him. I planned to tell Higgins soon enough about that and my suspicions regarding Quist, but there were a few questions I needed answering first. Foremost among them was why anyone would want to set me up.

I knew something else, too, and that was to trust very few people serving the public in Denton Crowell's district, even if they had been friends of Charlton Heston.

"You do that, Bevan. I didn't like you much when you were lawyering, but that's only because you were good at keeping your scumbag clients out of prison. You always played an honest hand. District Attorney Crowell doesn't have the same high regard for you, however. Understand?"

I understood, all right. In the elevator, I asked Tim if he was supporting Crowell's campaign.

He smiled at me calmly. "You and I have always disagreed politically, Mike. I don't personally care for the man, but he's my party's choice."

After leaving the police station, we walked in silence to the parking lot. Tim lit a cigar while I opened the door of the Jeep.

"Crowell's going to be our next senator," he said. "It doesn't hurt to be on his good side."

"There's no good side to that guy," I said, climbing behind the wheel.

Winter shrugged, took a long drag on his cigar, and

said, "So why didn't you mention Quist and the auction?"

"I'm going to poke around a bit more, then I'll get back to you and we can both try to figure out what else to tell the police."

"I hope," he said, blinking through the cigar smoke, "that you don't intend to solve this yourself."

"What do you think of Higgins, Tim? I always considered him an honest cop, but things can change."

"Buford's the same as he ever was, but Crowell is putting the squeeze on the department these days. Voters in St. Louis, Springfield, and the sticks don't know much about him and he's been looking for a big trial to raise his appeal statewide for the Senate race. He may have that case in you—no unseemly gang war stuff, no corporate bigwigs to piss off, just a nice juicy murder suspect who used to be a prominent criminal lawyer."

"I'll try not to oblige him," I said, putting the car in reverse.

By THE TIME I returned to my house, all thoughts were again of my daughter. I had to tell her what was going on, not because I expected any sympathy from her, but because I didn't want her to hear it first on the news.

More importantly, I wanted to warn her about Martin Quist.

I called Laura Dowell, the production assistant whose number Anne had left for me, wondering whether many other fathers had to call an intermediary to speak to their children.

A young woman's voice answered. It sounded like she had half a pack of gum in her mouth.

"I'm Anne Bevan's father. Please have her call me as soon as possible."

"Sorry, she's not available. They're shooting scenes in Porton this week."

"Right, thanks."

"I wouldn't go up there if I were you," she said. It sounded like the girl was losing the battle with the chewing gum.

"Why not?"

"They've started filming, and she's under a lot of pressure. Besides, she doesn't want to see you."

"What reason is she using now?"

"It's difficult for her, sir." Smack.

"Look, Laura, I must talk to her about something very important. It has nothing to do with Bob Langston."

"Be careful," the girl said. "You could lose her."

"What do you mean?"

"I mean, she really does not like you. After all,"— smack—"you killed her mother." Smack, smack. "Didn't you?" Smack. Smack. Smack.

Chapter 16

P orton, Missouri, population twelve hundred, lies on the eastern side of the Missouri River at a bend twenty-five miles north of Kansas City. Hardwood forests and tobacco fields cover the surrounding hills. Since 1841 the McCormick Distillery has employed a third of the populace. The people are civil, prosperous, and happy in their semi-isolation. The downtown buildings were built prior to the Civil War from native limestone, and one can still find an old-fashioned pharmacy, hardware store, and fine arts theater nestled among its quaint houses.

The best places to eat and drink, however, are a block east of Main Street on a rise overlooking a vine-yard. The Derby Restaurant is a lovely antebellum place specializing in fried chicken.

Next to it is O'Malley's, a classic Irish pub, most of which lies thirty feet below ground in a stone-arched cavern. It was originally built in 1846 to store local wines, tobacco leaves, and spirits that would be loaded onto steamboats bound for ports downstream.

At midweek O'Malley's packs in bluegrass fans to hear local and regional talent perform, but most Fridays and Saturdays, the Irish bands come to play and the seats are filled with officers and wives from the nearby Army war college at Fort Leavenworth.

The Jesse James movie crew was shooting a scene in the subterranean tavern. I knew that the set would be closed to the public, but I had called ahead to Tony Collins, the owner of the bar, and he walked me past the security guard without a problem.

At the end of a winding stone stairway, I entered another world.

Generators buzzed, carpenters hammered, and the growl of power saws ricocheted off the stone walls. Production assistants glided through the sets, carrying papers, dodging carpenters, costume ladies and makeup men, speaking softly into wires, listening intently to instructions through the headsets, their bright young eyes blinking furiously, their lips alternately pursing and smiling wistfully with confusion and consternation and wonderment at the whole crazy, manic, creative process of making a movie.

Bearded actors in floppy cowboy hats and bandoliers played cards in clusters of two and four while those with speaking parts reviewed scripts in the shadows of cameras and sound booms. I was leaning against a klieg light, pretending to be interested in a wrangler's poker hand, when Anne entered from an adjoining room.

A young man with the winsome features and long blond locks that teenage girls and aging actresses love followed close behind her, mouthing words from a script that sagged between his fingers.

My daughter wore a pair of faded blue denim

overalls and a soft pink T-shirt. Earphones hung around her neck like a Celtic torque. She looked so full of enthusiasm and purpose that I suddenly regretted my visit and might have backed out of the bustling room if the set had not closed behind me.

"Listen up," Bob Langston said from a dark corner where he had been sitting unnoticed by me. "We'll start shooting in a few minutes, and I want no repeat of yesterday, understand? No dropped notebooks, no rustling of skirts; absolute quiet or you're outta here. Not just off the set. Out of work. Got it?"

While he scanned the room, I snuck quietly toward Anne and the actor who had found refuge behind a stone column in order to rehearse his lines.

"'Yew ben gon' a mightee lon' time, Jesse," the actor recited in a whisper.

"Not long enough," Anne read from the script in response.

Frowning, she lowered the paper.

"Mark, don't overdo the hillbilly accent."

"Okay. How's this? 'You've been gon'…'"

I recognized the actor then. He was Drew Arondale, former Billabong surfing champion and current soap opera hunk. In the daytime drama, he played a Navy SEAL named Chad Herring.

"Excuse me," I said, stepping out into the dim light.

"Oh my god," Anne uttered. "What are you doing here?" "

"Sorry. It's important, or I wouldn't have come."

Drew Arondale looked annoyed. "Anne, I'm on in two minutes."

"Practice by yourself," she said. "Don't forget to enunciate."

"What's 'enunerate' mean?"

"Oh, Mark," she said, letting her British accent slip. "Just bloody well do it."

She turned to me, her face flushed with consternation.

"He surfs sixty-foot monsters off the Maui coast with ease but ask him to memorize a script and he turns to jelly. How did you get in?"

"I know the bartender."

"It figures."

"Anne, I'm in some trouble. I wanted to tell you before you see it on the news."

"What sort of trouble? Money?"

"If only."

Suddenly a command from a bullhorn silenced me and everyone else in the subterranean chamber.

"QUIET, EVERYONE. QUIET ON THE SET."

Drew Arondale moved to his mark next to Everett Turner, the actor playing Jesse James, while Bob Langston left his chair to study the angles a final time.

"Looks good," he said after several adjustments. "Let's try to do it in one take. Ready, Mark? Everett?"

Both nodded.

Langston moved to a position behind the main camera.

"Roll it."

"You have been gone an awful long time, Jesse. Perhaps if you…"

"HOLD IT! HOLD IT! CUT!! For chrissakes, Arondale, what the fuck are you doing? You sound like a Sausalito hairdresser."

"Just trying to sound authentic, Bob."

"Well, you're doing a shit-poor job of being a Missouri bushwhacker. Try it again, lad."

It wasn't warm in that cellar, but the sweat was rolling down surfer boy's neck when he uttered his lines again.

"Ewe shore hav' been gon' a long time…"

"CUT," Langston snarled, glaring at the Apollo of the Beach.

"A 'ewe,' Mr. Arondale, is a female sheep. How did a female sheep get in my movie?"

"Sorry, Bob. I'm still trying to get my character down. I thought I had it, but Anne, uh, Miss Bevan, thought I should try it differently and then she got called away, so I couldn't prepare properly."

"What the hell are you talking about? 'She got called away'? I don't pay you to blow lines when the rest of us are ready to roll."

"But she and I were interrupted when we were practicing," Arondale whined. "I only needed a few more minutes."

"A few more minutes?" Langston exploded. "You've had that script for two weeks. Why don't you take off a fucking day? A week? No, on second thought, take a year. You're off the movie."

He turned to his assistant director.

"Burt, get that stand-in to play this role. It's only a few lines and he's got the accent."

"Boss," the very practical-looking assistant director said. "We're talking about ten million housewives and another twenty million teenyboppers who don't care whether Mr. Arondale sounds like Liberace or a caveman."

"You can't do this," Drew Arondale proclaimed. "I got a contract. It'll cost you plenty."

Then he pointed at me. "There's the dude who

caused this problem, Bob. He's the one who stopped my rehearsing."

I began my retreat when the eyes of that small universe turned upon me, but before I reached the stairs, Langston did something that forced me to stay.

Turning to my daughter, he said, "If I was going to fire anybody's ass today, it should be yours."

He hesitated just long enough for the actors and crew to watch Anne squirm. Then, allowing a broad smile to grace his crooked, charismatic face, he said, "But I won't. You're too damn gorgeous. Now, let's get back to work. That means you as well, Arondale."

There were scatterings of nervous laughter. A muscle-bound set wrangler with the face of a Kaw River catfish grabbed my elbow and suggested it was time for me to leave. I had cooled off just enough to consider doing it when Langston looked at me with a smirk that said, *"I'll do with her as I please."*

Still staring at me, Langston mouthed a cigar grotesquely, then pulled it out and yelled, "Roll." That's when I jerked my arm from the grasp of my escort and ran to within spitting distance of the comeback kid.

"Don't you ever talk to her like that again, you son of a bitch."

"She deserved it," Langston growled. "Now, get off my set."

I lunged for him, but two security guards and Jesse James held me back.

"Stop it, Father!" I heard Anne cry just as somebody rabbit-punched me in the kidney.

"I'm so sorry, Bob," she added, watching one of the grips do a nice job of stretching my arms behind my back.

Long Bob allowed himself another smile, this time one of magnanimity. Then, in a way that recalled his stirring portrayal of General Butler in *Apache Midnight* when he allowed the Chiricahua women and children to depart camp before slaughtering their warriors, he said, "Of course, I understand, Anne. But next time, let's try to keep personal matters off the set."

He turned to me. "If you'll excuse us, Bevan, we have a motion picture to film."

I agreed to leave peacefully only because Anne whispered that I could call her later, but that didn't stop the security boys from hauling me up the stairs and tossing me out of O'Malley's saloon. I careened into a post and fell into a horse trough that had been placed there as a prop. I pulled myself out, shook the water off, and limped to my Jeep, harboring dark thoughts.

Damn, if it wasn't just like in the movies.

Chapter 17

I left a message for Anne early that evening. She returned the call two hours later. There were no apologies, no thank you's for coming to her aid.

"What was so important that you had to crash the set and threaten my job?"

"I suspect Martin Quist murdered a colleague of mine last Friday night. Langston may be involved as well, and I don't want you caught in the crossfire."

"The TV news report said that you were seen brawling with the man shortly before his death. Is that true?"

"Yes. And you might as well know if you haven't already heard, the murder weapon was a hurling stick I brought back from Ireland."

"Jesus."

"I've been set up, Anne. You have to believe me."

"Why should I?"

"Because your life could be at risk as well."

"What evidence have you that Martin, let alone Bob, had anything to do with the murder?"

"Quist desperately wanted a particular book in order to blackmail people, some very important people."

"A book? What kind of book?"

"It doesn't matter what kind. It's what might be contained in it."

"How do you know he's so desperate to have it?"

"His man outbid me for that and other books at an auction."

"Oh, for God's sake. His man? Have you lost your mind?"

"It's complicated, honey. You've got to understand."

"I understand all right. I'm not ready to believe you killed someone, but now I know you'd say anything to get me to break up with Bob. How dare you accuse Martin Quist of murder. That's so sick."

"How long have you known him?"

"Bob introduced us three months ago, long enough to know how kind and generous he can be. In whose house do you think Bob and I have been sleeping the last two days?"

I waited long enough for my saliva ducts to unjam.

"Just come home. I'm really afraid for you."

"Why this? Why now?" she cried. "Can't we have a bit of normalcy in our lives?"

"I didn't ask for this particular nightmare, Anne. And when it comes to pushing the envelope of normalcy, I'm not the one sleeping with the best customer the Betty Ford Clinic ever housed."

I never mean to say stupid things, but it always seems to happen at the worst possible moments.

"*You're* the one in trouble, Father. Not Martin, not

Bob, and certainly not me. Just leave us alone and fight your own fucking battles."

In the brief silence that followed, I heard another voice in the background. It belonged to Bob Langston.

"There, there, that's all right, baby."

He must have been holding her. His voice was very clear.

Then one of them hung up the telephone.

I stared at the telephone receiver for a long time after that.

Deep-rooted acrimony between father and daughter is unnatural. It plays against all the laws of familial harmony. The lesions it creates aren't the normal cuts and bruises that friends or even spouses inflict on each other. Those tend to heal easily with a gift or an apology.

But the gulf between Anne and me was going to require considerably more. Like a split in the skin that resists closing, we'd spent too many of her formative years apart and didn't share enough material to help the healing. I wasn't ready to give up, however. Somehow we had to find a way to stop walking over each other with cleats.

I walked zombie-like into the kitchen, poured a couple shots of whiskey and drained it with shaking hands. Weston Preston called such alcoholic impulses "elbow crookers."

With those cautionary words ringing in my brain, I put the bottle down and settled on the couch in front of the empty fireplace and fell asleep.

An hour or so passed before I realized that the doorbell was ringing. I let it ring for a few minutes more, but the caller had obviously noticed my Jeep in the driveway and wasn't about to leave.

I staggered to the door and opened it to find Josie Majansik shifting from one foot to the other, tape recorder in one hand and writing pad in the other. She studied my face for an instant and, without a word, took me by the arm and led me back to the couch.

"I looked for you at the bookstore," she said, pulling a coverlet over my legs. "Then checked downtown at the police desk. The sergeant said you'd been released after giving a statement. I figured you'd be here."

"To get a story."

"Yes. No sense in lying."

"Did you get it?"

"Not anything I plan to use. Not now."

"Thanks."

I caught a scent of basil and ginger between her breasts.

"I still plan to cover the murder case, whether you figure in it or not."

"I wasn't thanking you for killing a story. I'm glad you came by to see me, for whatever reason."

She took my hands in hers. "What was she like anyway?"

"Who?"

"Your ex-whatever."

"You presume an awful lot."

"Well, something makes you act the way you do."

"She isn't an 'ex.'"

"Then what is she?"

"Someone you would have liked to know."

"Still in love with her, huh?"

"You might say that."

Josie looked around the darkened room.

"You got any candles?"

144

"In a drawer by the refrigerator. Upper shelf, next to the flashlight."

She went into the kitchen and returned with a candle last used ten Christmases ago, a screw-top bottle of wine, and two paper cups.

"That's one empty kitchen," she said, lighting the candle.

"You didn't see the week's supply of cat food."

"I suppose you're the kind who eats out a lot. No need to plan for tomorrow. Live one day at a time and to hell with the future."

"Mind if I borrow that line for my family crest?"

"Is that why she left you?"

"You really want to know."

"I think you'd better tell me since I plan to stay here tonight."

"All right," I said, pouring the wine. "A long time ago I met this English girl."

Chapter 18

Tuesday, June 29

I awoke alone. The furies of the day before and the mattress gymnastics of the night that followed had left me with a monstrous headache. The sun streamed through the side windows, however, promising another pretty day.

I made my way to the bathroom. A shower and two aspirin had me feeling better and in the hallway the aroma of coffee greeted me. Somewhere, probably in the kitchen close to the coffee maker, Josie was singing off-key to a song by Mick Hucknall of Simply Red.

I put on a pair of white cotton shorts and walked downstairs. She stood at the kitchen counter, her back to me, wearing my charcoal gray XXL-sized Riverrun Books T-shirt.

The last line of James Joyce's *Ulysses* stamped on the shirt was like an invitation: "...and yes I said yes I will

Yes." The shirt went all the way down to the back of her thighs, but her shapely, muscled calves were enough to excite me. She picked up three eggs in quick succession, cracking them expertly, and dropped them into a bowl.

"Good morning," I said.

She turned around, whisk in hand and gave me a beautiful smile. "And good morning to you, sunshine. I hope you like scrambled eggs."

"I do."

"Good. Would you make some orange juice?"

"Sure."

I took a can out of the refrigerator and as I stirred the juice, Josie beat the eggs while howling "Holdin' Back the Years." My laughter didn't faze her in the least.

"Tragic, isn't it?" she said. "I have the voice of a frog with tonsillitis. Oh, well. Can't be helped." She went back to croaking and whisking and adding a touch of milk to the eggs.

We ate breakfast on the brick patio, watching cardinals and blue jays fight for places at the bird-feeders.

"Thanks for last night," she said.

"The pleasure was all mine."

"Not necessarily. As a wise old Argentinean once said, 'It takes two to tango.' You're a good lover."

"What a relief."

"You don't kiss so good though."

"Blame it on chapped lips."

"Don't get me wrong," she said. "You're good at the mechanics, but no fire."

"At my age, one has to be careful not to overheat the system."

She reached over to brush a piece of toast off my chin. "I don't bite, Michael."

"Really? I seem to recall otherwise."

"Never mind that!"

"If you haven't noticed by now, I'm ancient enough to be…"

"My older brother?"

"Something like that."

"You don't really believe you're too old for me, do you?" she said. "I crossed the big three-oh two years ago."

"My god, you're almost as old as Madonna!"

"Spare me."

"I had a friend my age who dated a girl younger than you," I said, taking the last bite of scrambled eggs. "The only thing they had in common was neither had heard of Cold Play. Trying to relate to things from opposite points of the age spectrum can get embarrassing."

"If not exhausting."

"Yeah, that, too."

"Well, I'm not too young for you, big fella."

"Say what? Hearing's getting a bit iffy."

"Be serious."

"No, let's not."

She leaned back in the Adirondack chair and pulled off her T-shirt, the only garment she happened to wear that morning.

Brown nipples highlighted her firm breasts. She opened her legs just enough to show a tuft of dark curls.

"Well, come on, Methuselah," she said, pointing to my shorts and shirt. "Take those things off. Or do you need help?"

She led me back upstairs where we did some more horizontal exercises.

Afterward, Josie said she needed to go to her newspaper office. But first we took a shower together and that started the whole thing over again. It was half past noon before I made it to Riverrun Books.

▭

PHYLLIDA WAS HUNCHED over the computer typing descriptions of books at a champion pace.

"Well, if it isn't the prodigal son," she said without looking up.

I wondered if there was ever a moment when the lady wasn't annoyed.

"Looks like you been in a needle-fight," the lunatic Weston Preston added.

I puzzled over that, wondering if he somehow could tell I'd spent the morning in amorous activities.

"You been to the hoosegow yet?" The barista was anything but subtle. "The cops have been askin' us all kinds of things. I'm sorta surprised to see you here, if ya don't mind my sayin' so."

"Why is that?" I asked with a wire-thin smile.

"Now, I'm not saying you linked your everlastin' soul with Cain to slay the Welshman. But we all know you two got along about as good as a mama hen and a black snake."

"No one got along with Mr. Hughes," Phyllida said in a surprise defense of me.

"Most def'nitly," Weston quickly added. "I just thought the brass badges held suspects for more than a day."

I considered asking Weston what *he* had been doing

the night of the murder, but decided to pass, knowing the answer would be something like "at home in the forecastle, jerking the cat's jib."

"Jus' what was your alibi, boss?"

"The one I gave the police and that's all you need to know. Also, I'm not a suspect but rather a 'person of interest,' according to Detective Higgins. There's quite a difference."

"Sure, boss. If you say so."

Fortunately, customers lined up at the coffee counter to pry Weston away from me, and a customer entered the shop carrying grocery bags filled with books to trade. The email orders started flooding in and it was back to work for the three of us. The ecstasies of the previous evening and this morning were nearly, but not quite, forgotten in the rush to get small things done.

As the day progressed, however, my subconscious worked overtime trying to put more pieces together as to who, besides Quist, had a motive to kill Gareth Hughes. The books he'd stolen at the auction were extremely valuable in and of themselves. A quarter million each if the inscriptions and the provenance were valid.

But Beatrice had made pretty clear there was something else to be gleaned from the Colette—information worth a million or more in blackmail capital.

Try as I might to consider others' motives, it all pointed to Martin Quist who needed money to finance Langston's movie and needed it fast. His Afrikaner henchman would have had little trouble dispatching even a man as big as Gareth. But my fumbled explanation to Anne showed that I needed more information, and the only way to do that was to get close to the only suspect I had.

As it happened, I didn't have to wait long.

The telephone rang.

"Riverrun Books," I answered.

"My name is Martin Quist, Mr. Bevan. I should like very much to speak to you. Will you be at your store for a while?"

I wasn't quite ready for this, but the voice sounded so civil it was impossible to not agree to talk.

"Sure," I said. "Come over. Do you mind my asking what this is about?"

"Not at all. We'll discuss your health. Whether you prefer living to dying; matters of that nature."

Chapter 19

Half an hour later, the Lincoln Continental I remembered from the auction parked in front of Riverrun. Rolf Kramm got out from behind the wheel and opened the rear passenger door. The man for whom it was opened said something to Kramm, then stepped out as if descending the passenger ramp of the Queen Mary.

Martin Quist was of average height and carried himself with the lean, elastic look of an Ivy-League middleweight boxer. Perhaps a year or two shy of forty, he had a receding chin and a broad forehead topped by ginger-colored hair. His tanned skin was the color of a medieval parchment. He wore a beautifully cut cream-colored suit, a white shirt, and a crimson and navy rep tie.

I couldn't imagine who his barber might be.

Kansas City haircutters have names like Hank or Manny and their specialty is the Harrison Ford farm boy look, cowlicks being especially popular.

Not for this fellow, though. His trim styling with the

sides brushed back was that of a Chicago advertising executive or a British cabinet minister. He exuded such convivial confidence that I began to think I had misjudged him.

That impression faded as he came closer. Rimless glasses fronting watery gray eyes caught the glare of the sun and sent it back at me. His smile that had seemed so pleasant at a distance was now a thin line, behind which tiny teeth showed like the silver fittings on a coffin.

Because he carried a book in his right hand, I shook his left. It was small, but the grip was surprisingly powerful and he held it long enough so that I was the one disconnecting the exchange.

"Hello, Bevan. Shall we sit out here? It's such a lovely day."

"Sure. Would you like coffee? A soft drink?"

"No, but thank you. Thank you very much indeed."

His thin lips parted enough to let the words slip out. Then he pressed them tightly together again so that it was difficult to hear just what he had said. He seemed to know that he made it difficult to understand him and it was obvious he preferred it that way.

He placed a book of photography by Cindy Sherman on the green bistro table as we settled across from each other. Crossing his right leg over his left knee, he gave a tug at his trouser cuff. He sat back and silently studied me for a while, enjoying my unease.

"You're a handsome fellow," he finally said.

Thoroughly caught off guard, I blushed like a first-grade communicant.

"Don't be embarrassed by compliments," Quist said with the slightest condescension. "I only mention

153

it because I see where your daughter gets her firm jaw. Surely the blond hair, high cheekbones, and extraordinary figure were gifts from her mother."

"Leave the personals alone," I said.

Quist lifted his chin and lowered his eyes. The sides of his mouth twitched as if a school of minnows were trapped inside his gums. Only briefly did I see the tiny teeth when he spoke again through that tight smile.

"No offense intended, Bevan. I only meant to praise your child. Anne is charming, utterly captivating as well as beautiful. You must be very proud of her. I know Bob Langston is. He introduced us last winter in Aspen. 'How do you like my little rabbit?' he said. They are staying with me during filming, you know. It's quite cozy."

I tried to look deadpan. I must not have tried hard enough, because Quist's tongue caressed his upper lip before speaking again.

"Well, well, you do care. That's not the impression one gets in talking to your daughter. Does it bother you that an aged movie star has stolen her heart? Or that the poor girl has an addiction to drugs?"

For a moment, I considered introducing my fist to his esophagus. Instead, I asked, "How's Langston's picture coming along?"

He placed a hand on the table and studied the tips of its manicured fingers before looking up with a sleepy expression.

"It's not *his* film, Mr. Bevan. I happen to be the producer. We've had some misunderstandings, to be sure."

"You mean he owes you money."

"Yes. Quite a lot, as a matter of fact. I've been supporting him for some time now, in the style to which he'd like to be re-accustomed. He's really quite talented when kept on a short lease."

"What do you want from me?"

"The book by Mademoiselle Colette; the one stolen by Mr. Hughes. A friend of yours kindly advised my associate, Mr. Kramm, of the theft."

"Richard Atwood?"

"I believe that was the gentleman's name."

"I don't have it."

Quist sighed. "Then who does?"

"I was under the impression that you did. After all, your man killed Gerald."

Quist smirked. He was a natural smirker.

"That's not the way I do things. Dumping people in the creek as if I had a message to send someone? Who would I wish to impress? Given time, I would have searched Mr. Hughes's apartment and, failing to locate the book, would have extracted the necessary information from him. Rolf, after all, is quite effective with an electric drill. He prefers a Bosch but must make do with a Black & Decker here. When in Rome…"

He looked at his watch then waved a pinkie finger at Kramm, who leaned with folded arms against the Lincoln.

"I wasn't aware that the Colette was missing from the sale," Quist said, looking back at me. "Until after Hughes's unfortunate demise."

"I suggest you ask the cops where it is."

"I have. They found many books, many lovely, expensive books in your colleague's hovel, but not the Colette."

"I didn't kill him," I said mechanically.

"Of course you didn't," Quist said. "You had less

of a reason than I. But someone set you up, and you have the best motive to determine who it was. I suspect the police think the same thing, or you wouldn't be sitting here."

He opened the Cindy Sherman book and casually turned the pages before continuing.

"I don't care who performed the deed, Bevan. I simply want what is lawfully mine. Get it for me. Please." He stopped flipping pages and gave me his full attention. "Then we can be friends."

"Like Bob Langston and you are friends?"

Martin Quist nodded, looking faintly amused. "Deliver the Colette to me, and I shan't trouble you or yours." He hesitated before adding wearily, "I hope we understand each other."

I understood all right. I knew that if Martin Quist wanted you, he would get you. I also knew that happiness is nothing more than a case of settled nerves and that it was going to be a while before I found it again.

"I'll be going now," he said, rising languidly. "You may keep the Cindy Sherman work. It's listing for a hundred or so on the Internet."

We didn't bother shaking hands again. He walked to the Lincoln while I remained at the table tapping a drum solo on the metal top.

After the car pulled away, I opened the book to a place marked by a yellow Post-it. The photograph showed a model, probably Cindy Sherman herself, lying face up on the ground, legs splayed apart, her head swathed in black cloth so that only one glassy eye remained visible. A milk-white breast spilled from the black gown. A dart lay embedded in the flesh an inch or two above the nipple.

I went into the store and placed a call to the

production assistant on the Jesse James movie. Laura Dowell answered on the fourth ring. She thought Anne was on the set but wasn't sure and said they were only taking calls from Los Angeles today on orders from Langston. She gave me the number anyway and I called. Nobody answered. I gave Miss Dowell the telephone number of The Peanut and told her that if I wasn't at home or the bookstore she could reach me by leaving a message with Pegeen Flynn.

I hung up just as Phyllida approached me with a sheet of Internet sales statistics.

"You're shaking," she said.

It was true. My hands trembled as if I had Parkinson's. I took the papers from her and pretended to look at them.

Phyllida tapped my shoulder. "Why don't you go home? Weston and I can take care of things here."

I nodded, said something about the Alibris sales being lower than AbeBooks's numbers, and pushed away from the desk.

"Phyll, I heard that you helped George Land build his book collection."

She turned her head a little to look at me. A streak of red spread across her cheeks.

When she didn't respond, I said, "You also tried to buy them back from his widow shortly after he died."

Her eyes hardened. "That was a long time ago when I had my own store. She wouldn't sell."

The telephone rang before she could finish. She quickly picked it up, grateful for the interruption.

"For you," she said, covering the mouthpiece. "It isn't Anne."

"Take a message."

Phyllida repeated what I said to the caller, listened

to the response then looked back at me. "Best take it," she said, handing me the phone.

"Bevan here."

"Thank God I caught you," Josie Majansik said breathlessly. "Richard Atwood's body was found by his mother in his carriage house. His throat had been cut. District Attorney Crowell has ordered the police to arrest you."

I remembered the sickly-sweet smell and realized it came from his room upstairs. Richard had never taken that bus and he wasn't the author of that note.

"I don't plan on waiting for them to arrest me," I told Josie. "Quist was just here. He insisted he didn't have Hughes killed but implied he would harm Anne if I don't find the stolen book for him."

In the brief silence that followed, I heard her fingernails tapping nervously at the other end of the line.

"Get over to my place," Josie ordered. "Right now. Don't risk driving your Jeep. I'm on the west side of the Plaza, behind the Benton Grill. The Rousseau-Cezanne Apartments at four-twenty West Forty-Eighth, number fourteen, first floor."

"Got it," I said, jotting the address on a dollar bill.

"I'll be waiting on the steps."

I hung up but kept my hand on the telephone until the shaking stopped. Slowly a cold anger replaced the anxiety as adrenaline began to take over.

"I'm going back to the police station," I said to Phyllida. Lying was getting easier. "More questioning, I'm afraid."

"Good luck," she said.

As I turned to leave, she took my hand and quietly added, "Forgive me for bristling at your questions about the Lands' books. George was a friend and my best customer. Beatrice resented me, actually thinking I'd had an affair with her husband."

"Did you know it was the Land collection that sold at the auction yesterday?"

She returned my stare with a steady gleam.

"I figured as much," she said. "Are you going to be all right?"

"Not really."

"No shit," Weston Preston said from behind his coffee bar. "You're lookin' real wonky, boss. Maybe you done rollicked around with too many fillies lately. It might help to get an oil change in your vee-hickle. It's at twenty thousand miles and you know what they say?"

I didn't know what "they" say and didn't bother listening to the rest of his blather. I thought of telling him to "kill his own snakes," an Ozark term for minding your own business, but I was too busy counting a wad of twenties pulled from the overnight cash box. I folded ten of them into my front pocket and added five tens to my wallet before leaving through the back door.

A twenty-minute jog through three miles of leafy back-street neighborhoods brought me to Josie's apartment building. If I'd known what I would learn there, I might have kept on running until reaching St. Louis.

Chapter 20

I turned the corner onto Forty-Eighth Street and saw Josie standing on the front steps of her apartment building. She wore a white cotton blouse, tan skirt, and a face as cheerful as a funeral. I hesitated before crossing the street in order to signal my presence when an old man in a walker crept up behind me.

"Who are you waving at?" he demanded.

"No one in particular," I said, bending over as if searching for something on the sidewalk. "I dropped my keys and...ah, here they are."

He didn't believe a word.

"I wouldn't mess with that one," he said, inclining his head toward Josie. "She's trouble. I can tell."

I had the feeling that any attractive woman born after the Korean War meant trouble to him. He shuffled toward the entrance of the Rousseau-Cezanne Apartments while I fiddled with the keys in my pocket and whistled "Zip-A-Dee-Doo-Dah." Once he had crawled up the steps, the old man nodded in my direction and whispered in Josie's ear. Finally, the door closed behind him and Josie motioned for me to come in.

"What did he say?" I asked when we were inside.

"He said you were trouble."

Josie's apartment smelled of herbal candles and popcorn oil. The living room was dimly lit by a table lamp that rested on a plastic milk crate. A television set with a sixteen-inch screen and a VCR player on top sat like an afterthought in a dark corner. The west wall was a series of pane-glass windows that looked out upon the courtyard, but the blinds were partially drawn, letting in slivers of daylight and not much of a view. Piles of paperback books lay scattered on a radiator. A worn sofa, partially covered by a moth-eaten horse blanket, lay against the east wall opposite the windows. Next to the sofa, a three-legged end table supported a telephone and an empty bottle of beer.

This disheveled nest didn't match the woman I thought I knew. It was as if we had entered a rent-by-the-hour motel room and she was too embarrassed to admit it.

"Nice digs," I said.

"Yeah, sure. I had no choice but to keep the previous owner's furnishings. My salary doesn't allow for luxuries. Help yourself to a beer and then we'll go over some things. I need to get back to work soon."

I stepped into the kitchen, flicked a cockroach off a hot plate, and opened the refrigerator. It was a Kelvinator manufactured before the invention of automatic defrosting. I took out a bottle and took a long pull of semi-warm Pabst Blue Ribbon.

"Your fridge needs Freon," I said.

"And my car needs transmission fluid and I could

use new heels on my damn shoes. Got any other advice, Mr. Fix-It, or shall we get down to business?"

"Sorry, I didn't mean to critique your living quarters."

Her face softened.

"Forget it, Mike. I've had a bad day, that's all. Nothing like yours though."

She tilted her head toward another room. "My office is in there, but don't get any ideas."

I followed her into the bedroom which wasn't much of an improvement from the living room.

A card table with a laptop computer on it stood in the corner, a king-size bed covered by a sheet, but no bedspread, another three-legged nightstand crowned by a lamp with a cracked plastic shade. On the windowsill behind the bed was an ashtray full of cigarette butts.

"I didn't know you smoked," I said.

"I don't."

She picked up the laptop and sat on the edge of the bed, then looked up at me with a tired, expression-less gaze.

"I like you, Mike. Maybe even more than that. But I'm an out-of-town girl with a shitty-paying job and little chance of advancement. I'll be leaving one of these days, probably sooner than later. I'm willing to help you, but you must realize I have my own life, such as it is, and I'm not looking for advice on housekeeping or anything else. And let's get it out of the way before you ask: you aren't the only boy I've kissed."

The ringing of the telephone interrupted our happy talk. Josie rushed into the living room to answer it, mumbled a few words, and returned with her cheeks looking rosier than before.

"Who was that?"

"My editor. I can't stay long."

"How did he know you were home?"

"I work from here a lot of the time. Any more questions?"

"No. Sorry. I'm getting paranoid."

"Given the circumstances, that's understandable," she said quietly.

I looked at our reflection in the full-length mirror hanging on the ceiling above the bed.

"Your office is, uh, unique."

Josie managed a smile. "The landlord evicted the previous occupant for soliciting male prostitutes. He never got around to taking the mirror down and now I'm used to it. Take off your shoes and relax."

She sat next to me again.

I told her about going over to Richard Atwood's house, seeing his mother, poking around the cluttered library and taking the books he had stolen from my shop.

"Do you think his body was upstairs while you were there?"

"Looking back on it, I'm pretty sure it was. I smelled just a hint of something cloyingly sweet. Bodies beginning to putrefy smell that way."

"How do you know that?"

"First Iraq War."

"I thought you were just a military lawyer."

"Every Marine's considered a rifleman, even JAGs. I handled my share of patrols outside the Green Zone."

"Tell me about Gareth Hughes," she said, opening the laptop. "Who was he?"

"A colleague of mine in the book trade. He grew

up in Wales, worked on a sheep station in Australia, then as a forester in New Zealand before coming to the States. While knocking about the country working odd construction jobs, he would buy books from thrift stores in his off hours and sell them to local bookshops for a profit. By the time he settled in Kansas City, he'd become knowledgeable enough about rare books to make a living at it."

"Who were his friends, his enemies?"

"None that I can recall, except for me. I was a bit of both."

"Great. Now we're getting nowhere."

"Thanks for taking me in."

"You're welcome. Please concentrate."

"That's easy for you to say with that damn mirror above us."

She put the computer aside and stood up. Just as quickly, I pulled her down.

"Okay," I said, handing the laptop back to her. "Gareth stole two books that collectors would pay a great deal for. One was by a sexual pioneering French woman named Colette that contained a very personal inscription by Sylvia Beach and Ernest Hemingway. It's the kind of thing to keep members of the literary tea society hot in the britches. He also took an extremely rare Hemingway first edition titled *in our time*."

"What are they worth?"

"Together, maybe half a million dollars. If the economy ever improves, possibly more. I suppose that's plenty enough for certain people to kill for, but murder isn't the means one expects from bibliophiles."

"Well?" she said, tapping her fingers on the laptop. "Go on."

"I don't think Gareth died because of a book, but for what was concealed in one. The killer wanted a list in order to blackmail some of the most powerful people in this town."

"Where were the names written?"

"Not sure. According to Beatrice, the widow of George Land who put the books up for auction, they might have been written in the margins of the Colette where her husband had described the sexual preferences of their friends. But Beatrice also mentioned that he had kept a much more detailed list that included compromising photos."

"Were these 'friends' business acquaintances as well?"

"I suppose so. Probably a politician or two as well. And let us not forget the clergy."

"Hughes must have had the book when he was attacked," Josie said. She removed a shoe to rub her right foot.

"Perhaps. He was wearing an overcoat even though it was a warm evening. It had deep inside pockets, handy for concealing stolen books. I always made him take it off when he was in my shop. But I can't believe Hughes would walk into a bar in that condition lugging something that rare."

"Do you think he left them at his apartment?"

She kept rubbing that foot. It was small and delicate, and her toenails were painted a bright pink.

"He didn't have anywhere else to put them."

"Sounds reasonable. Tell me about Weston Preston and Phyllida Law. Loyal to the firm, are they?"

I leaned back on the bed and stared up at the mirror. Noticing that my widow's peak seemed more defined, I added male pattern baldness to my list of worries.

"They helped to put my life back together," I said, scratching the back of my head. "They work for next-to-nothing to make my bookstore a success."

"I think you had something to do with that, too, Mike. Just tell me a bit more about them."

"After getting out of the Merchant Marine, Weston raced motorcycles, worked as a janitor at the Art Institute, did other odd jobs, and learned to make coffee. He tends to live in an alternative universe at times, but I can't complain about his work ethic. Kids enjoy his goofiness, and so do most of the mothers. When there are no coffee customers, he shelves books, cleans the bathroom, answers the phone, helps my customers, and lends an occasional hand to little old ladies trying to cross Brookside Boulevard. This place is as much his life as it is mine."

"He lives alone?"

"He's divorced with two grown daughters whom he never sees. Their mother's been in once or twice to harangue him. He's always looking for love but plays the forlorn fool too much to find anyone who takes him seriously."

"Then there's Phyllida."

"Right. She could run the place and probably thinks she should. Her husband was an architect and apparently quite accomplished. After he died of a heart attack, she used his life insurance to open an antiquarian bookstore. She traveled the country and Europe buying fine books and solidified her reputation by becoming an officer in the Antiquarian Bookdealers Association of America. Then she lost everything in a fire. She's not a happy person these days. George Land had been a customer of hers. According to Beatrice, Phyllida and George were lovers. Phyllida denies it."

"Do you think she and Weston have anything going between them?"

"Get serious, Josie."

I got up from the bed, walked over to the windowsill, and dumped the cigarette ashes into a wastebasket. Stuff like that bothers me. Without turning around, I said, "I saw you interviewing Edward Worth in the shop not long ago. How well do you know the guy?"

When I looked back, she was standing by the bedroom door with hands on hips and a half-smile that wasn't a smile.

"Enough to wish he didn't smoke."

I looked at the ashtray.

"Does that mean what I think it does?"

"As long as we're concerned, Michael, it's none of your business what I do outside that bookstore of yours."

"If you say so. '*Uisce fe talamh.*'"

"What?"

"It's an old Irish phrase meaning 'water under the ground.' My grandfather was fond of using it to describe secret currents, hidden matters. But it really is absurd to think that goofball barista and Phyllida could be involved."

"Every peach has a stone," she said, slipping her shoe back on. "A favorite phrase of *my* grandfather."

"Ahh, the wisdom of our elders. You planning to go somewhere?"

"Yeah, I've got to go down to the *Gumbo* to finish a story."

"Does that mean I can stay here?"

She picked up her notebook. "For another day, but only if you behave."

"Thanks, Josie. I have another favor to ask. I need to know how my daughter is doing. A production assistant on the set named Laura Dowell may have heard from her. Would you check for me?"

"You can't call Anne yourself?"

"She and Langston are Quist's house guests. We're not communicating these days."

I gave her Laura's telephone number.

"I'll check it out," she said. "Now, get some sleep."

"Okay, but first why don't you tell me what your editor really told you on the telephone."

She looked at me warily.

"It wasn't my editor, but a confidential source. It doesn't matter who."

"And what did this person have to say that made you blush?"

"It's why I have to go now and find more information. It's also why I've decided to let you hide out here another day."

She checked the top button on her blouse and then looked back at me. "He said the police found Gareth Hughes's wallet. It was in a bag under the passenger seat of your Jeep Cherokee."

"You didn't plan on telling me?" I said once I'd unrolled my tongue from my throat.

"There's nothing you can do right now. Just get some sleep. You're going to need it. I'll find out what I can and get back to you."

"Jesus."

"You poor guy," she said after a chaste kiss. "I'm not going to let you down. And somehow, someway, I'm going to bring you and Anne together again."

After she left, I slept for about two hours before the nightmares caught up with me.

I stepped into the living room, grabbed a paperback by Herman Hesse off the radiator, sat on the sofa, and started to read about a man who thinks he's a wolf. Seven pages later, the narrator was getting right to the heart of all humanity. That's when I reached for what was left of my beer and saw a notepad lying next to the telephone.

Obviously, Josie had an artistic bent. The pad was covered with charming drawings of fairies, goblins, and flowers, along with telephone numbers and cryptic notes. Intrigued by the doodles, I flipped the pages and saw what I wasn't supposed to see. Next to a willowy drawing of an Arthurian knight was the name *Eddie Worth*. Below it were the initials *M.Q.* followed by a telephone number.

I called the number and a woman who identified herself as the housekeeper said that Mr. Quist was not in at the moment.

"I was hoping to get a message to Mr. Quist or Ms. Majansik," I said.

There was no hesitation at the other end at the mention of the names. The woman's voice even lost its matter of fact, frigid tone.

"We don't expect her back until tomorrow's party. If you care to leave your name and number, I'll be happy to tell Mr. Quist."

"The name's Toby Bing," I lied. "I'm from out of town and can't leave a number, but I'll see them at the party. Is it set for eight p.m. still?"

"Some guests will be arriving earlier, Mr. Bing, but, you know, things never heat up before ten."

"Right! How could I forget? And the real action doesn't start until midnight."

The maid giggled. "I guess you've been to one of these before."

"Only once, and it was a while ago. On second thought, I think I'll surprise Martin and Josie. Would you mind not mentioning that I called?"

"Sure. And don't forget your mask, Mr. Bing."

"Pardon?"

"You know, for the black-and-white masked ball. It's going to be awfully exciting with Mr. Langston being here."

"Will you be wearing a mask as well?"

"Oh, no. I'll be serving the guests. But I get to wear a costume."

"What might that be?"

"A French maid's outfit."

"Lovely," I said. "Can't wait to see it."

"Oh, Mr. Bing." She giggled. "There won't be much of it to see."

Chapter 21

Well, well, well. Caesar may have had Brutus, but Josephine Majansik had to rank right up there in the treachery department. Trusting soul that I am, how was I to know that the object of my affections was sharpening her claws the whole time? Just when I was getting used to falling in love again, too.

My nerves settled down after a few minutes, morphing into a cold calm enhanced by an edge of sharp bitterness and aroused curiosity. Looking at the seedy apartment with clearer eyes, I saw it as nothing more than a hooker's playpen, a place for a few drinks followed by a roll in the hay and a wad of twenty-dollar bills discretely dropped in a basket by the front door.

In her bedroom closet, I discovered a stack of hard-core videos under a pile of *People* magazines. One of the tapes had no label and wasn't marked as if it were an amateur homemade job. I put it in the VCR and watched with sick apprehension as grainy black-

and-white images crackled across the screen. The opening shot presented the back of a woman with short dark hair walking into a dimly lit room where she casually disrobed. The compact body seemed achingly familiar as she lay face down on a bed.

Any hope I'd held that the performer wasn't Josie evaporated when her face filled the screen with an absurd expression that slowly morphed from complacent restfulness to fear. I couldn't help noticing that her talent as an actress matched her inability to carry a tune.

Possibly the only thing worse than the subject matter and Josie's role in it was the abysmal editing that changed focus and even color tone with every scene shift. It was bad, *Plan 9 From Outer Space* bad, and when the camera focused on two men standing at the door in white cotton briefs and dark socks ready to pounce, I would have laughed if I'd been watching this travesty at a fraternity house a quarter century earlier.

One of the men was lean and swarthy. The other, not nearly so lean and pale as a February moon, wore his long greasy brown hair in a ponytail. They walked stiffly toward the bed as if taking directions. The swarthy one was the first to leap into action, pinning his supposed victim down before straddling her head with his knees. She pretended to struggle, but the man tightened his grip to stop her resistance. The beanpole with a ponytail stripped off his shorts and stood rampant for a moment before joining in. Close-ups of the sickening climactic scene looped over and over until the camera zoomed in on a close-up of Josie's tear-stained face. The tape ended on that sad note, all the more terrible because her final look of anguish was not in the least bit convincing.

I pulled another beer from the refrigerator and chugged it without leaving the kitchen. Two beers later, I was thinking clearly again and dialed the *Brush Creek Gumbo*.

"I'd like to speak to Josie Majansik," I said to the receptionist.

"Who is that again, sir?"

"Majansik. A reporter who's been there six months."

"One moment, please," she said.

I heard the shuffling of papers at the other end.

"Don't you have the number of her extension on your computer?" I asked.

"No, sir, she's not in the computer. Oh, wait a minute."

More paper shuffling.

"Yes, here it is on this other sheet. She's on special assignment with the police beat."

She connected the number for me, but all I got was Josie's recorded voice message. On a hunch, I asked for an old law client at the paper who covered the music scene.

Jason Harper was up against a deadline but took the call when he heard my name. Years ago, when fresh out of J-school and working as an impoverished stringer for the daily newspaper, he'd accumulated ten parking tickets within a three-month period while covering concerts downtown and in Westport. I got them thrown out for no fee and gained a friend for life.

"What's up, Mike?"

"I'm looking for one of your colleagues at the *Gumbo* named Josie Majansik?"

"Never heard of her."

"I heard she was working the police beat."

"What police beat? We're a weekly alternative. The only things we write about are sex, rock n' roll, and the latest inanities of the city council."

My next question was interrupted by the clicking of high-heeled shoes on the tiled hallway outside. Hanging up the phone, I snatched an ice pick from a drawer in the kitchen and rushed to the door. A man and a woman were quietly arguing on the other side of it. The muscles in my forearms tensed when I heard the jangling of keys, but just as quickly relaxed when it became apparent the couple intended to enter the apartment next door.

I plopped down on the bed after grabbing another beer and tried to imagine what Josie intended to do upon her return. Given what I'd seen so far, the odds were good that Rolf Kramm would be with her to dispatch me. I looked at the ice pick that I'd laid on the floor next to me. Most likely, she would enter first. In that event, I would shove her aside and go for Kramm's throat. But then what? If she were to pull a weapon on me, would I use the pick on her as well? No need to worry about that if she had a gun. It would be too late for me anyway.

On the other hand, she might be alone, still confident of my naiveté and planning to string me along in the hope of gaining more information for Quist. If that were the case, I might try to play along. But she would see through me soon enough. All I knew for sure was that when Josie returned, with or without Kramm, the result was going to be ugly if I remained in the apartment.

The clanging, bonging, whooping cacophony of a car alarm outside the bedroom window suddenly interrupted these depressing thoughts. After an eternity of waiting for it to stop, I went into the bathroom to let out some of the beer.

Great revelations have been known to come to men at such moments. And so it was with me.

While standing over the toilet, my mind buzzed with thoughts of that particular alarm. It was better than thinking about a lifetime prison sentence, Josie's double-dealing and my daughter's dalliance with some very unsavory characters.

I wondered what set it off. Would it turn itself off eventually or go on indefinitely until the owner returned or the battery died?

I remembered how my Jeep's alarm had shattered the Saturday morning peace in Brookside and how Weston Preston had reminded me that there was a second key in a magnet box under the front wheelbase. Weston knew how to get in my vehicle which I always locked. No one else did.

And what had he told me just before leaving the shop today? One of those mindless admonitions I generally ignored. But this was about the "vee-hickle" needing an oil change. "Twenty thousand miles," he had said, meaning he'd recently seen my odometer.

"Jesus," I said aloud after connecting the dots. Weston killed Gareth Hughes then set me up by putting the victim's wallet in my Jeep.

Another revelation quickly followed. Other than a talent for auto mechanics and making cappuccinos, the lamebrain barista didn't have the gumption to do this without the backing of my only other employee, Phyllida Law.

Josie was straight with me about one thing—the couple, as mismatched as Two Buck Chuck in a Steuben crystal decanter, actually did seem to have something going between them. I still couldn't believe that in Phyllida's case it was love, but I didn't doubt that Weston would do anything for her, even go so far as to commit murder.

I left Josie's apartment with a thousand thoughts jumping up in front of me, feeling unable to handle any of them. Still, I had enough sense to use my cell phone to call Pegeen Flynn at The Peanut.

"I need your help," I said when she answered.

"Boy, I'll say. You're all over the news."

"I know who set me up, Peg. I need to borrow your car."

"Ah, jeez, Mikey, let the cops handle this, will ya? You're gonna get yourself shot. Whether it's the cops or the bad guys, it won't matter. They all want a piece of you now."

"Still driving the old Saab?"

"Yeah, and what of it?"

"Nothing of it. Maybe I'll talk your boss into paying you more if I get out of this mess."

"That'll be the day."

"You don't think I have a chance?"

"Maybe. You'll just never get that cheap bastard to give me a raise."

"Maybe you won't need it. Maybe I'll marry you and you can live off me."

There was a nervous laugh at the other end of the line.

"I keep telling you, boyo, I'm not the marryin' kind."

"More's the pity."

"I'll put the key under the mat. There's half a tank of gas in it."

"Thanks, Pegeen. One other thing. A reporter

named Josie Majansik knows I might contact you. Don't talk to her. She's not on my side. Not anymore."

"Understood. Take care and please try not to get the car shot full of holes. It's paid for."

I ran an easy mile from Josie's apartment to The Peanut parking lot where three pickup trucks, a couple of Harleys, and a 1992 Saab convertible waited for their owners. After leaning against a telephone pole for no other reason than to gather myself, I walked to the Saab and climbed in. Pegeen had set back the driver's seat to accommodate me. The considerate act meant a lot. Too bad she wasn't the marryin' kind.

The Saab started up after I pumped the accelerator a few times and headed onto Main Street for Midtown and a chat with Weston as the sun dipped under the horizon.

Chapter 22

Weston Preston lived a block north of Thirty-Ninth Street in a three-story firetrap.

I parked Pegeen's car around the corner and walked past a twenty-four-hour laundromat with no customers, a liquor store that specialized in forty-ounce malt liquor, and a purple-painted shack with a starry sign on the porch that promised someone inside would read my fortune for "$10, 24/7, holidays included!"

The entrance to Weston's palace had a buzzer lock, but not wanting to announce my arrival, I waited downstairs for someone to come out.

After a few minutes, a slender girl wearing a keffiyeh draped around her shoulders bounded down the stairs, fumbling for keys that dangled on her purse. I nodded a greeting as she held the door open for me, her comely face smiling shyly as we edged past each other.

Weston's name and apartment number were listed on the postbox in the lobby. I walked quietly up the uncarpeted staircase to the second floor and Apartment 2C. The overhead bulb nearest his door had burned out so that the only illumination came from another one at the far end of the hall where someone in a kitchen was having a love affair with garlic and onions.

I heard movement within his apartment, but when I knocked, there was no response, just more of the shuffling noise and then quiet. I knocked again.

"Let me in, Weston. It's Mike Bevan."

No answer.

The door was one of those cheap composite things the landlord must have bought on sale at Home Depot. I steadied myself, placing weight on my right leg, and raised the left one preparatory to knocking the door off its hinges. I must have looked like a Doberman Pincher about to relieve itself when someone opened it without my help.

The apartment was dark, with a low-wattage light coming from somewhere to the right.

"Good timing," I said as I lowered my kicking leg and, gaining my balance, stepped inside. My eyes were still getting used to the dimness when I noticed the long, bony face of Rolf Kramm instead of my hundred-fifty-five-pound coffee barista standing in front of me. I instinctively threw a straight right, very fast and well sprung, but he stepped inside it, fast, cool and clever, and delivered a roundhouse to the left side of my head that sent me sprawling to the floor.

I reached for the doorknob to pull myself up, but a hard chop to the back of my neck ended that business. An instant later, I was kissing the shag carpet with Kramm on top of me, trying to disconnect my spine.

Just when I felt the big Afrikaner would succeed,

his weight shifted from my lower back to my shoulders. I felt a gun barrel nudge against my right ear. Turning my head slightly, I saw the hard face staring at me with the expression of a deadpan comedian.

"We will now get up."

I didn't argue, but I was in no hurry until he tapped the gun against my skull.

"Move in there; to the kitchen."

I followed his orders, gingerly stepping over empty wine bottles, Fritos wrappers, and a dozen other things Weston hadn't bothered to pick up that week.

A bare bulb flickered above a Formica-topped table. Next to it, a hook that had once held a flower basket now supported the rope that, in turn, supported much of Weston Preston by his scrawny neck.

The rayon cord tied in a slipknot had expanded his jugular veins to the size of Vienna sausages. His hands were tied behind him, and a dish towel had been stuffed in his mouth. He trembled precariously on tiptoes atop the rattling table. Adding to the surrealistic scene, the light created a shadow that covered his distorted face from nose to brow, giving it the hollow-eyed cast of a skull.

"Look who has joined us," Kramm said, tugging on Weston's belt, setting his shaking legs further off balance. "You will now have a witness to your execution."

Unintelligible noises gurgled through the towel.

"Why do this?" I said with disgust.

"Because he has something to tell me," Kramm said, jerking the rope so that it cut deeper into the pale skin above the Adam's apple. The added pain caused Weston to open his swollen eyelids, revealing a spider's web of broken capillaries.

"You understand now what you must do to live?" Kramm said as he withdrew the gag.

Weston stared emptily at his tormentor. Although his eyes remained open, I wasn't entirely sure that he was conscious because the shaking stopped.

He had shown courage holding out this far, I'll give him that. But as tough and stubborn as the old sailor was proving, I knew he wasn't going to sacrifice his life, given the slim chance Rolf Kramm would keep his end of the bargain.

Kramm released his grip. Weston sucked air back into his lungs. His legs began to tremble again.

The South African stepped back from the table to sit on a kitchen chair. He pointed the gun at my sternum, surveying me as Weston danced for his life.

"He will talk," he said. "They always do."

"Did Richard Atwood?"

"Who?"

"The one-armed man whose throat you cut."

"Oh, yes. No resistance whatsoever when I showed him the box cutter. Couldn't get him to shut up."

"You killed him anyway?"

"Force of habit," Kramm said tonelessly. He prodded Weston's crotch with the gun. The barista's startled response nearly caused the table to tip. "When Mr. Quist heard the weapon came from your store, he suspected that this worm killed Hughes on your behalf. Was he correct in thinking that?"

"Possibly," I said. "It doesn't matter anyway. The police know I'm here."

Kramm's tongue, thick and gray as a garden slug, caressed the corner of his mouth. He pulled on his cauliflower ear and said, "I don't believe you. It's not to your advantage to have told them."

He settled back in his chair to contemplate something. A few moments later, he ended his thoughts with a grin that displayed a silver right incisor. He looked at me and said over the racket caused by Weston's dancing, "It will please me to kill you. Your reckless bidding forced me to spend considerably more than I had been instructed. Much of the difference came from my wages."

"Well, hell, Rolf, if that's your only problem with me, consider this: I'll cover your loss, up to forty grand, mind you, no more, and you keep it quiet that I paid Weston here to knock off Hughes. No questions asked. We'll pretend I never came here."

What the hell, it was only money.

Kramm displayed a ruptured grin that I took for a "no."

I tried reason then. "Kill me and you'll have to answer to Quist for going beyond his orders. People are going to ask a lot of questions."

"Mr. Quist won't mind. He hates you almost as much as that movie man."

"What's his problem with Langston?" I asked over the rattling sounds on the table. "I thought they were pals."

I didn't particularly care to know, but it never hurts to stall when you're facing the end.

"He angered Mr. Quist enough that forgiveness is no longer an option."

"How?"

"Langston insisted that he stop supplying drugs to your daughter, even threatening to stop working on the movie. Such insolence has its price."

I said nothing. What he said was enough to

unfreeze the larynx of any father, but I never so much blinked or twitched a muscle.

"I cain't hold much longer," Weston moaned. "The gammons are cramping."

"Then talk while you still can."

"I will. Jes' git me down."

Kramm pulled the chord tighter. "The list. Where is it?"

"In a storage box," Weston groaned. "Close to the ticket counter at Union Station."

"Whose box? What number?"

"George Land owned it! I don't know the number. It's embossed on the key."

"Where's the key now?"

"With Phyllida Law. It was wedged in the backboard of some French book like she said it would be. It wasn't on Hughes when I smacked him down, but I took his apartment key and wallet before shoving him into the crick. She told me to put the wallet in Michael's Jeep while she searched the apartment to find it.

"Please, Mr. Kramm, get some thieving hooks and cut me down. You can have the books and all the rest. Just leave us to have the store. That's all she really wants. That and me."

"Soon enough."

A peculiar stillness came over Kramm's face.

I must have made a sudden move then. Either that or Kramm decided he was tired of me watching his cat-on-mouse play. The next thing I felt was the butt of his gun smashing the side of my head above my right ear that sent a white-hot message through my skull.

I dropped to my knees, clawing at the point of the pain that had centered behind my eyeballs. There followed another blow and a worse pain, accompanied by a pale light that turned blue and gray.

After what seemed like an eternity, but must have only been seconds, I looked up through a blood-red haze to watch Kramm stuff the towel back into Weston's mouth and casually knock the table out from under him.

The Afrikaner had laid out as good a cue for action as I was going to get. My legs were rubbery and my head felt like ball bearings were ricocheting between my ears, but somehow I got into a crouch and lunged into Kramm hard enough to bring him down. He'd been enjoying the spectacle of Weston's flailing legs too much to notice me, but now the real fight began and I knew enough to not give away the advantage of surprise.

I could never have bested him in a fair fight, even if fully conscious. The only thing for it was to get the gun that he had dropped when I surprised him.

The weapon seemed to slide into my hand of its own accord. I shoved it under Kramm's chin, pulled the trigger, heard a deafening explosion, and felt the impact reverberate all the way to my elbow. The bullet entered the bottom of his jaw cleanly and exited the top of his head very uncleanly. The slippery mess of blood and brains caused a lot of trouble for me as I jumped to my feet and tried to support Weston Preston's weight.

His legs were still jerking, but I was able to get my head between them and, by standing straight up, relieved the pressure on his neck. His bowels had loosened and the stench was horrific. I reached over my head and pulled the towel out of his mouth, allowing him to suck in a quart or two of oxygen.

I stood for a few seconds, gathering my strength while contemplating how to get him down. The only option was to lower him as gently as possible, letting him hang while I got a knife to cut the rope. Except for an involuntary twitch, he'd gone completely limp, so there was no hope that he would support himself if I were to set up the table under him.

I bent my knees slowly until the rope was taut again. He jerked violently with the return of the terrible pressure, but it meant he was still alive. I pulled open three kitchen drawers before finding a serrated steak knife.

Setting up the table Kramm had knocked over, I climbed onto it, holding up Weston's weight with my right arm while sawing the loose rope with my left. After a long minute, the rope snapped and the barista sank onto the table, sputtering profanities while farting to high heaven.

When he started blubbering about my saving him from ol' split foot's domain, I told him to shut up. When he begged me to find the key to the handcuffs, I told him I had better things to do, like dialing the police station. It didn't take long for Higgins to get on the line.

"Good evening, Lieutenant."

"Where the hell are you, Bevan?"

"At Weston Preston's apartment. My former employee has a few things he'd like to tell you."

I put the telephone to Weston's mouth so he could tell his story the second time that evening, only this time without a rope around his neck while dancing the fandango.

"I hadn't meant to kill him," Weston said in the midst of a crying jag. "I followed him from the bar meaning to knock him out and take his key. He didn't just go out the first time I knocked him. He started to get up, so I had to clack him with it a couple more times to protect myself and then he rolled over into the water. He was a big man, Lieutenant. It was self-defense. You gotta believe me."

Following that creative argument, I made sure he mentioned that he and Phyllida did all this with the intent of setting me up in order to take over my bookstore.

"I suggest you bring a clean-up service with you, Buford," I said after retrieving the telephone. "Thanks to me, a South African corpse is leaking blood and other matter on the kitchen linoleum. Kramm admitted killing Atwood as well, but you'll just have to take my word for it. I didn't have much choice in the matter. If you haven't traced the call by now, you can find Weston Preston and the late Rolf Kramm at five-three-four Madison, just off Thirty-Ninth Street, Apartment Two C."

"You'd best be there as well, Bevan."

"Sorry, I need to attend to some other necessities. I'll be in touch."

"Now wait just a damn minute," Higgins said evenly. "Josie Majansik isn't one of them. She's an FBI agent working undercover. Early in the investigation, Edward Worth agreed to be the sucker bait in the blackmail setup. Josie did her part to convince Quist that her rich boyfriend was prime for the taking. Because your daughter is wrapped up in this mess, maybe you'd like to help us."

That got my attention.

"What can I do?"

"First, meet me at Phyllida Law's house. It's on

Rosewood, over by the Nelson-Atkins Museum. Know the area?"

"Yes."

"While I sneak into the back of her house, you ring her doorbell and greet her with the news that you know she had Weston kill Hughes for the book. Pretend you want to cut a deal and let her do the rest of the talking."

"What if she doesn't want to talk? What if she decides to answer my intrusion with a gun? After all, I'm the alleged killer of two men who's gone on the lam."

"I doubt that the old broad has ever touched a firearm. If she does have one and knows how to use it, I'll be there to identify your remains. I might even recommend you for a medal."

"Well, if you put it that way."

After hanging up, I used the hanging rope to secure Weston to a radiator in the living room and tied a scarf around his mouth. I didn't want him disturbing the neighbors before the cops arrived.

I went into the bathroom to wash off the blood and filth. The face in the mirror looked better than it should have after such a beating. There were bruise marks on either side of my head and my lower lip was split, but the internal stuff didn't seem too bad.

I left the apartment and found cover behind a lilac bush to watch an unmarked car and a hazmat van pull silently into the apartment parking lot. Rather than greet them, I slipped into Pegeen's Saab and eased it onto Thirty-Ninth Street heading for Phyllida Law's house five miles away.

Chapter 23

I turned left at the corner of Forty-Eighth and Rockhill Road to a row of identical cottages in an area referred to by those who live west of it as East Berlin. It wasn't in the inner city, but it was on the cusp, and that meant it was the last stop for white middle-class widows and divorcees hanging by their polished fingernails to live in a "decent" neighborhood.

The homes had been built of native stone at the end of the nineteenth century on orders from William Rockhill Nelson, the founder of the *Kansas City Star* to house his blue-collar employees.

For two generations, pressmen and their families had lived contentedly in the subsidized houses along Brush Creek. But after World War II came the white flight to the suburbs and the block of limestone dwellings survived the wrecking ball only because *The Star* used its influence to list them on the National Register of Historic Places.

Rejected by African Americans as too small and by

upwardly mobile young whites as too close "to the line," the block held a tenuous middle zone between the races.

A light shone through a side window of 1524 Rosewood Place. I waited for Higgins's car to pass and watched it park half a block down the street. After a couple of heartbeats, I got out of the Saab and walked across a brown patch of lawn where two days' worth of newspapers lay untouched. A wicker mail basket next to the door groaned under the weight of uncollected junk mail and bills. When I rang the doorbell, it chimed something from a Mahler symphony.

Phyllida, or rather a soused version of her, greeted me in a silk bathrobe that was all red except for a pair of gold Chinese dragons running down the sides.

Elegance gone bad is never pretty but seeing her in this condition for the first time was downright depressing. Her face was as gray as bone china before being glazed. Thinning hair, released from the confines of the bun, looked as if it had been tossed by an eggbeater and hung down to her shoulders in tangled rivulets streaked with shards of gray over patches of scalp. Eyeliner had missed its mark on one eye. Her lipstick forgot a lip. She wore a pair of pink slippers where the toes had been cut out to make room for bunions. She looked like Walter Matthau in drag.

I'd expected her to be rattled at seeing me, but I guessed wrong.

"Welcome to Rosewood," she said as if I'd come to Buckingham Palace. "Wanna drink?"

"No, thanks."

"To what do I owe the pleasure?"

"I think you know."

"Really?" A mocking smile.

She motioned me to enter. "I don't wish to disappoint you, but I haven't the foggiest notion what has brought you here. Come in and sit yourself down."

I hate arguing with drunks, especially when I'm the sober one, so I held my tongue and followed her into a living room that looked like a set from The House of Usher, minus the charm. She sat on a worn chintz sofa covered with Kilim pillows, and I settled into an armchair spotted by cigarette burns and wine stains. Framed steel engravings of Samuel Johnson, Montaigne, and Dickens hung in black and gray clumps on the walls.

There's no denying that Phyllida's love of books and literature was genuine. Handsome leather-bound volumes of the classics and crisp-jacketed moderns stood in ordered rows on sturdy oak shelves throughout the room. An elephant folio titled *The Thousand Buddhas* by Sir Aurel Stein covered half of a library table by the front window. Glancing into the adjoining dining room, I saw hundreds more volumes.

Under different circumstances, I would have instinctively read the titles, run my fingers over the bindings, and pulled out a book or two that interested me. But there wasn't time and I'd already spotted what I had come for.

The coffee table had been made from an old ship's hatch cover. A passport and *Fodor's Guide to Europe* lay on a corner with a computer-generated airline ticket sticking out of the book. Next to those items was a cocktail glass half full, a bottle of vodka half empty, a key to a storage box, and an accordion file with a dozen or so typed pages stacked within it. On the top of the file rested *L'Ingenue Libertine* by Colette and a thin morocco slipcase containing a slender volume of the Hemingway *in our time*.

"Going somewhere, Phyll?" I asked.

She picked up her drink and slowly swished it from side to side.

"I've thought of visiting Europe," she said, putting the glass to her lips.

"Plan on taking Weston?"

She downed her drink, wiped her mouth with the sleeve of her silk bathrobe, and in a clotted voice sniggered, "Why on earth would I? He's served his purpose. Can you imagine that Ozark rooster engaging my clients in Paris? Dear God, the horror!"

"He nearly died to keep your secret from a man who would have liked nothing more than to kill you. I think you owe him some consideration."

She shrugged. "The infatuated idiot also backed half the amount of my bid at Bender's auction. But he's past forgiving. If he had kept his mouth shut, you wouldn't be here. I suppose you are prepared to bargain with me."

"Perhaps."

While she poured herself another vodka, I picked up the slipcase and gently removed the *in our time* published by Three Mountain Press. I opened to the first page of the Rives handmade paper and read the inscription that began, "Dear Dr. Guffey."

This book was printed and published by Bill Bird who had bought an old hand press and set it up on the Isle Saint Louis in Paris. It came out later than it should because I introduced Bill to Ezra Pound and Ezra suggested a series of books— 'There'll be me and old Ford and Bill Williams and Eliot and Lewis, etc.' *and some others Ezra said* 'and we'll call it* *an inquest into the state of English prose. Lewis and Ezra had five titles—Bill said, 'What about Hem?'*

    'Hem's will come sixth,' Ezra said. So when they were all printed and this one finally gotten out it was later than the Three Stories and 10 poems although Bill had the manuscript long before MacAlmon had the other set up—Ernest

I placed the book back into the case and set it on the table. It was nice to have held it, even if only for a little while.

"It's over, Phyllida. You conspired with Weston to kill Gareth Hughes in order to get the Colette and the secret documents George Land had kept hidden."

She leaned back on the sofa with half-closed eyes and a derisive look. Her fingers curled like claws around her drink.

"Do tell, Michael."

"You knew Beatrice would have to put George Land's collection up for sale. After she refused to accept your offer after his death, you realized she'd never voluntarily sell it to you. As his lover, you knew better than she how troubled George's finances had become with the collapse of his construction business that led to his heart attack. Beatrice didn't realize the gold mine that his books represented, let alone the potential blackmail value of the New Moon Society list. To her, the books were just scraps of paper. You waited patiently to regain what you thought to be rightfully yours, scrimping to put aside wages that one day could be used to regain the collection. When you learned Beatrice had put them up for auction with Herl Bender, you sent Richard Atwood to bid for them with your savings. Only you didn't count on me being there. And certainly not Martin Quist's man."

"It *did* make for an inconvenience."

"But all was not lost when Atwood reported that he had seen Gareth Hughes steal the Colette and the *in our time*. It even saved what you might have spent had your fifty thousand been the high bid. All you had to do was steal them from the thief."

Phyllida eyed me with the bleak disapproval of a mother superior for an altar boy who had failed to memorize his catechisms.

"There was a time early on," she said, "that I might have suggested we pool our resources and acquire the collection for the shop. But I knew you would balk at taking advantages of George's list and photos in order to substantially improve our opportunity. It wouldn't do for me to have a partner with burdensome scruples."

"Thanks for the compliment."

She wet a finger with her tongue and rubbed it around the rim of the glass until it made a vibrating sound. Two dark spots showed on her cheeks and her voice drawled.

"For all your intelligence, Michael, you're still an amateur when it comes to the book trade. You've always come up short, thinking you know more than you do. Perhaps if you had been born with monetary means, it would have made a difference, but we'll never know. Despite my experience, you never seriously consulted me or even took me on buying trips. Do you realize what we could have done together?"

Phyllida stopped with the finger on the glass routine to push a wandering curl behind the nape of her neck. She looked as worn as her furniture.

"I was just a clerk to you," she continued. "If you want an answer as to why this happened, it simply comes down to that. You were running the bookstore into the ground, catering to bumpkins in the neighborhood who couldn't care less for real treasures. For the sake of my own reputation, I had to take matters into my own hands."

I'd never planned on using Phyllida Law for a future job reference but using my management failings as a motive for murder seemed a trifle bit unfair.

"Did you actually believe you could assume ownership of Riverrun with me out of the way?"

"Of course not. My ambitions are far greater. Anyway, after five years, the business is no closer to a true antiquarian shop than when you started. But thanks to all this," she said, pointing to the items in front of us. "I'll be able to establish a store to rival the finest in Europe."

She put her glass on the coffee table with the overly careful actions of a closet alcoholic. Her eyes fixed dreamily on the passport and the books as if contemplating the pipedream of peddling incunabula to Romanian princes and copper magnates from a select arcade on the Rue de Rivoli.

"Do you really think," I said, interrupting her reverie, "that rare book dealers and collectors would have anything to do with you once word of how you acquired your fortune gets out?"

She gazed at me as if I hadn't learned a thing.

"Don't pretend to be so naïve. It doesn't become you. Bibliophiles won't care. As long as the provenance of the book is real, nothing else matters. Did Arthur Fitch let his conscience guide him when buying *The Faerie Queen* in its original vellum binding from David Rothstein after Kristallnacht? Of course not. He paid the equivalent of a one-way rail ticket to Switzerland for the book and sold it after the war for fifteen thousand dollars. Fitch understood how desperate Rothstein was to get his daughter out of Nazi Germany and paid accordingly."

"I'll take naiveté over that kind of opportunism any day."

"Then you are a fool."

"Maybe. But one thing I'm *not*, Phyllida, is past my prime. You're too old for dreams."

I regret saying it now. Because no matter how battered and lost—indeed, no matter how downright evil—no one deserves hearing they've nothing left but a luckless past, a miserable present and a hopeless future.

In my defense, the words were spoken after she had pulled a snub-nose revolver from behind one of the sofa's silk pillows. It had a pink grip, but that didn't fool me—the two-inch barrel had Smith & Wesson .38 Special written all over it. The five .38 caliber cartridges these beauties packed were enough to stop a three-hundred-pound PCP addict.

If it was what I thought, this hammerless lightweight "ladies' gun" didn't have a safety catch. Just load the rounds and pull the trigger. Simple and very effective. I didn't doubt Phyllida had a round in there for me and four more to spare. So much for Buford's theory that this little ol' book lady wouldn't be packing heat or know how to use it if she did.

"You know nothing," she said bitterly. "I alone built George's fabulous collection. He respected me. He..."

She stared into her drink for a long time, maybe a full minute, before muttering something about love.

"And his wife? Did he respect her as well?"

"That tottering fool?" she said in a voice two clicks past a slur. "Beatrice Land is insane; a nymphomaniac, and God knows what else. George planned to marry me as soon as he could get rid of her. I suggested means other than divorce, but he would have none of it. The poor man was almost as naïve as you. After his construction company failed, our plan was to use his list and his library to finance our new life. He placed the packet and the photos in the storage box at Union Station and inserted the key in the backboard of the Colette, but he suffered his heart attack and died before he could transfer them to me."

Phyllida waited for me to say something, but she'd been waxing voluble in the grip of booze, and I wasn't about to interrupt a tipsy lady with a gun in her hand.

"Beatrice was incapable of comprehending their value, but she wouldn't let me near anything that had been his. I waited years for the collection to become available, putting aside portions of my meager Riverrun salary to one day bid for them.

"When I learned that the sale was to be through that local yahoo, Herl Bender, I rejoiced and sent Richard Atwood over to buy it. He used his cell phone to keep me informed on the bidding, but even with Weston's contribution, I realized it was futile after my offer of fifty thousand was topped. I had no idea there would be competition at such a sleazy auction. Let alone by you."

"And Gareth Hughes, not to mention Martin Quist's South African," I added.

"Yes. Well, they didn't count on Richard seeing Hughes lift the Colette, did they?"

"Cheaters never win and winners never cheat."

"What on earth?"

"Don't mind me, Phyll, go on."

"After Richard informed me of the theft, it was just a matter of setting the trap. I wanted to catch him alone and away from his apartment, so I had Weston place an anonymous call to Hughes telling him you had seen him steal the book and wanted to talk to him about it."

"How did he know to tell Gareth I'd be at Fitzpatrick's?"

"Weston had gone to the shop to collect your hurling stick when he found you still there moping about your daughter's latest insult or some such thing. You told him where you were going; I assume to drink away your troubles. Isn't that what you always do?"

No arguing with that, but I couldn't help adding hypocrisy to Phyllida's list of shortcomings.

"Weston followed him to Fitzpatrick's and witnessed your battle with Hughes," she said, looking faintly amused. "We didn't expect that, but it certainly proved fortuitous. Instead of one or two witnesses remembering seeing you with him, half of Kansas City watched as you beat the daylights out of each other."

She poured another drink and, seeing that it finished the bottle, became agitated. I needed to encourage her narrative if Buford Higgins was going to get a useful confession.

"So, the two of you waited for Gareth to stumble back to his apartment," I said. "When he got to that dark section of the creek near the bridge, you had Weston pounce while you stood look-out. But it took more than surprise and a good clubbing to put the big man down, didn't it?"

"I didn't intend for him to die," she said with an

ounce of actual remorse. "After all, I knew Hughes wasn't going to the police over the loss of books that he had stolen himself that day. I confronted him as he walked home along the creek and demanded that he give me the Colette or I would go to the police. When Hughes threatened to strike me—he really was a most terrible man—Weston emerged from a bush and clubbed him from behind. He didn't have the book on him, but we took the key to his apartment. It was Weston's idea to dump him in the water."

"You found what you wanted in his apartment. As a bonus for a job well done, did you steal the *in our time* from there as well?"

"Of course. I'd have been a fool not to. It lay next to the Colette on the kitchen table, begging to be nabbed."

"But why pin the murder on me?"

"Someone had to have killed him, dear boy. And who better than you who despised the man?"

"That's not true."

"No? I suppose that will remain a matter of conjecture for the prosecutor, a jury, and those ridiculous Irregulars to debate."

There it was. Buford couldn't have asked for a better confession. The only problem was that Phyllida wasn't in an interrogation room at police headquarters. More to the point, as tipsy as she was, she managed to keep the Smith & Wesson aimed at my heart.

She rose unsteadily from the sofa, her bathrobe opening just enough to expose a flaccid breast. With an obscene smile, she casually pulled the top of the robe together with one hand while waving the gun at me with the other.

"I always keep this thing hidden behind my

pillow," she said. "Iffy neighborhood, you know. I've never been able to get the landlord to put bars on the windows. Knowing what I know about you and what you seem to know about me, why did you think I'd let you in this time of night without this insurance?"

She reached for another drink, took a long pull and when she had finished, said, "I'd like you to stand now. And please don't turn around. You're supposed to be attacking me."

My grandfather used to say it doesn't do much good in tight situations to blubber, and I was pretty much used up for salty repartee. So, I just said, "The hell with it! Finish the job."

Although it sounds like I was laughing in the face of death, the brave words weren't meant for Phyllida, but for Buford Higgins, whom I had assumed from our plan was lurking in the shadows ready to drift noise-lessly into the room to my rescue.

He did just that, although none too soon. The problem, as I later learned to my horror, was that the detective had first mistakenly climbed into the bedroom window of the neighbor's house next door. A minor scuffle ensued with the startled husband and wife until Higgins was able to produce his badge and a rather weak explanation.

Once he had the correct address, he easily picked the lock of the back porch door and settled into the dining room about the time Phyllida started jabbering about respect and her love for George Land.

Higgins emerged from behind to wrap his left arm around her chest while grabbing her wrist with his right hand. Even then, she managed to squeeze off a round that drilled a hole in the ceiling and, for all I know, the shake-shingled roof as well.

"Get the damned gun," Buford shouted as Phyllida kicked and screamed like Rosa Kleb in *From Russia With Love*.

I stepped over the table, careful not to bruise my shins, and while the lieutenant struggled with the hundred-and-fifty-pound virago, I pried, with all due consideration for her age and sex, each of her blue-veined fingers from the pretty pink stock. The gun dropped harmlessly on the carpet.

She called me names that would have made my old drill instructor blush, but after my session with Rolf Kramm, I was getting used to handling homicidal malcontents.

"Bevan," Buford Higgins said after securing Phyllida in handcuffs. "Look for something to cover this lady while I call for the posse. And for God's sake, find her a decent pair of shoes."

"Get your hands off me, you fat poltroon!"

"Now, Mrs. Law, we don't want to mess that pretty coiffure of yours, do we?"

By the time I emerged from the bedroom carrying a long cloth coat with a fake fur collar and a pair of Manolos, Phyllida had grown quiet, sequestered between a pair of US Marshals.

"Let's go, ma'am," Buford said while gently placing the coat over her shoulders. "I apologize for upsetting your evening."

Without bending over, she slipped off her slippers and stepped into the stiletto heels as easily as a runway model. Then she departed on the arms of her guards, as regal as the Queen of Hearts and surely just as mad.

Chapter 24

The marshals took Phyllida away in an unmarked gray van. I left the Saab where I'd parked it on Rosewood Place and got in Higgins's car. To my surprise, as we entered the central downtown square, he drove past the Jackson County Jail another two blocks to the federal courthouse.

After parking in the basement garage area designated for federal law enforcement officers, Higgins slipped a card key into the slot of a nondescript door, and we entered a brightly lit chamber inhabited by a bull-necked man wearing a Hawaiian-style short-sleeved shirt with a name tag that said "Joseph Pieklekiewicz." A globe and anchor and the letters USMC were tattooed on his right forearm just above the prosthetic hand that matched his other one.

"Howdy, Gunny," Higgins said as he handed over his weapon for safekeeping.

"Evenin', Lieutenant. Agents Clark and Walsh are waiting for you upstairs."

Despite his prosthetic hands, he handled the gun

expertly, checking that the chamber was empty before putting it in a box with Higgins's card.

"Have they booked Mrs. Law yet?"

"No, sir, they're waiting for you. She's with a matron on the eighth floor getting cleaned up."

"Did hazmat finish cleaning the Preston place?"

"They're still working on it, but they got Kramm's body out without anyone noticing. He's in cold storage at our airport facility. Your friend here created quite a mess."

"What about Preston?"

"Sleeping at the KU Med Center. Knecht and Jennings have babysitting duty."

"Any squawks from the locals?"

"Not a word, sir. Your boys don't know what happened. Walsh handled the noise complaints from the neighbors."

Pieklekiewicz reminded us to sign in, and then we climbed into an elevator barely large enough for the two of us.

Higgins punched the button for the ninth floor.

"Why are the feds involved?" I asked.

"Because the DA's as bent as a tin horseshoe and half the county dances to his and the devil's fiddle. Quist's been pouring cash into Crowell's personal and political bank accounts ever since his first campaign."

"How long have you known about it?"

"A long time. Too long to not have done anything about it until now."

Buford Higgins edged closer to me. I caught a whiff of cheap after-shave lotion. His eyes had a tinge of regret in them.

"I mentioned my misgivings to Major James last year. He listened for half a minute before reminding me that I was thirty-two months shy of qualifying for a full pension."

The elevator door opened and he led me down a hallway bustling with federal marshals and FBI agents dressed alike in blue blazers and gray slacks. The mustached marshals wore six-pointed star badges on their lapels and looked ready to take on the O.K. Corral. I was wondering how the female members of the two agencies differed sartorially when Higgins ushered me into an overheated office that contained a desk, a chair and a couch scattered with magazines.

I shoved a *Sports Illustrated* out of the way and plopped down on the sofa. Higgins sat on the armrest opposite me.

"The situation was affecting morale big time," he said. "But no one had the balls to step forward. Then came that series of missing coeds, when girls from nice families seemed to disappear into thin air. Although the newspapers were demanding action, Crowell showed no sense of urgency.

"I'd gotten to know a federal agent based in this region during an arms qualification course at Quantico and he knew I was square. They'd had their own suspicions about Crowell's ties to Quist but not enough evidence to risk taking on a senatorial candidate until I offered to help."

"So where does Josie Majansik fit in all this?"

"It was the fed's idea to bring her from Ohio to work undercover. She's the best they have for this kind of thing. They got the publisher of the *Gumbo* to give her cover as a freelance reporter. He was more than happy to help after Agent Collins mentioned that the newspaper seemed to have strange bookkeeping practices."

"So much for journalist ethics."

"Since when did publishers have ethics? Anyway, Quist and Crowell have maintained a cozy and profitable relationship over the years, but that association is beginning to wear thin now that the DA has national ambitions."

"Exasperated, no doubt, by Quist's getting cut off from the family largess."

"Yeah, the feds think he's down to his last million dollars."

"And his only option is the blackmail game?"

"You got it. Do you know Eddie Worth?"

"Enough to know he smokes Benson & Hedges and owns half of the Midwest. I hear he plays a good game of golf."

"There's more to our boy than that," Higgins said, telling me what I already knew. "Edward Stuyvesant Worth IV is one of those Skull-and-Bones types who gets expelled from college for screwing the wife of the chancellor, then reforms to become governor or chairman of Goldman Sachs."

"Any bad habits besides sex?"

"Not anymore. He still enjoys wine and cigarettes, but not enough to spoil any rugs."

"And he's your bait to get Quist?"

"Yup. Majansik has played her part beautifully. It took a while, but Quist eventually trusted to go after Worth and she used her charm to reel him in on her own. It wasn't difficult convincing the young stallion to cooperate with us after learning he'd been targeted for blackmail."

"Josie can be very persuasive," I said.

"Yeah," Higgins said with a sidelong glance. "She's not afraid to use the gifts God gave her."

We contemplated the floor for a few seconds, then the detective showed me an invitation card Josie had provided him. The gilt lettering embossed on heavy linen paper read:

Martin Quist and his special guest, Robert Langston, request the honor of your presence at a very intimate black-and-white masked ball…

After citing the time and address, it ended with a postscript:

Leave your inhibitions at home.

"Rest here while I take care of some paperwork," Higgins said. "I need to see if Phyllida has sobered up enough to request an attorney. I'll be back to discuss our plans for Quist's party."

After he left, I stretched out on the couch and picked up *The Missouri Law Journal,* but my concern for Anne was such that even reading the footnotes failed to put me to sleep. I was thinking what damn fools we Bevans were and that there didn't seem much I'd ever be able to do to change that.

It was after one in the morning when Higgins returned. He looked alert as he sat in a chair across from me.

"You awake?"

"Wouldn't you be after reading that tort reform in Missouri lags behind Louisiana?"

"I asked you a question."

I put the magazine down.

"I guess you know that your daughter and Langston have been playing house at Quist's. Majansik and Edward Worth joined them shortly after she left you at her apartment. Since we haven't had a chance to communicate with Josie, she won't know you'll be at the party. It might get complicated."

I got the drift that "complicated" meant "seriously dangerous."

"You still want to do this?" he asked.

"If that was your daughter in there, what would you do?"

"I don't have any girls; just two boys who never grew up to my satisfaction."

He stretched out his legs, scratched his belly, and leaned toward me.

"I hate like hell doin' things this way, but we got no options. It's imperative that Majansik complete her mission. The agents and I aren't going to rush in and arrest Quist and his thugs until Josie finds what she's looking for."

"And what exactly is that?"

Higgins got up from his chair. He stepped over to a window and looked at the lights of the entertainment district below.

"Quist isn't just a blackmailer," he said quietly. "We suspect he's responsible for those three young women who went missing a few months back. I understand your concern for your daughter, but for whatever their reasons, Anne and Langston chose to get involved with this monster. This is the first time one of our agents has been able to get close to his chamber of horrors. I can't allow you to interfere with Majansik's work. You go in on my terms or not at all."

I was shaken by this information but easily managed to nod acceptance of his terms. Taking on Phyllida Law was one thing, but this was a whole different matter with a lot more at stake than a book and a key and the reputations of a few horny socialites.

"What would you have me do?"

"Keep it simple. Sneak in, convince your daughter to leave, and get her out as quietly as possible."

"She won't listen to me. Besides, she'll be with Langston."

Higgins squatted on his haunches in front of me. I noticed that he wore a hearing aid in his left ear and preferred Lavoris for mouthwash.

"We don't know how much Langston is aware of Quist's sadism. For all we know, he may be an enthusiastic participant. We can't take the chance of trusting that he's on the side of the angels."

"My daughter is extremely headstrong. It's going to be difficult convincing her to quietly leave without much of an explanation."

"You don't have to go. In fact, I'd prefer it if you didn't."

"Sure you would, but I've got to try."

"Just worry about yourself and Anne. If you get caught, Quist has a platoon of bruisers even uglier than Kramm."

He stood up. "Now, get some shut eye. You'll want to look your best for the party."

Chapter 25

Wednesday, June 30

The US Marshal who drove me to where I had parked Pegeen's Saab wore a blazer and a six-pointed star badge but didn't have a mustache. Her name was Tina. She was Italian American and was married to the sous chef at a French bistro. She had three adorable nieces and one not-so-adorable nephew, and she absolutely loved NASCAR racing. I learned all this and more in the course of a ten-minute drive to Rosewood Place.

Before going directly to my house, I stopped off at the shop to place a note on the front window stating that Riverrun Books would be closed for a few days due to unforeseen circumstances. I figured that ought to keep the Irregulars in a fine frenzy.

Arriving home just after two a.m., I grabbed the cat under one arm and went into my daughter's old bedroom where I found a photo album Carol had put together when we lived on the Navy Base in Newport.

Curling up on the bed, I stared at pictures reflecting a happier time until dozing off sometime before daybreak.

I slept until noon. Not wishing to be seen by questioning neighbors, let alone the local police, I drove Peg's car twenty miles outside of town to Shawnee Mission Park where I jogged along the lake, consumed two baloney sandwiches and a bag of corn chips, and communed with nature, such as it is in northeast Kansas. I spotted two deer, an owl, and a very mangy raccoon that might have been frothing at the mouth.

On my return to civilization just after five p.m., I took a detour into Mission Hills to survey the Quist mansion. The Roman-style palazzo sat atop a high bluff overlooking the Kansas City Country Club golf course. The only thing modest about the place was the creek that flowed at the base of the hill and even it looked like a medieval moat. Surrounded by cultivated gardens and a forest of mature spruce, maple, and oak, all that was missing was Lake Como.

Caterers and florists were scurrying back and forth between the house and their vans when I pulled up behind a refrigeration truck parked near the front gate. A fog of icy mist streamed out of the open rear hatch where a grizzled hunchback, maybe five feet tall, not quite a hundred fifteen pounds, stood on a metal stool and used iron tongs to lug a three-hundred-pound block of ice onto a cart.

It landed hard.

He said, "Umphh."

A thought occurred. I got out of the Saab to ask him how things were going.

"Just fuckin' peachy," he said. "The shit-for-brains ice ar-teest insisted on carving his Venus de Milo on site with a chisel instead of in the studio with a chain-saw. So I gotta haul this piece of crap up that mountain. His masterpiece is gonna be a melted adolescent by the time he finishes."

"Need some help?"

"You offerin'?"

"Yeah. No charge."

"Name's Harvey."

"Mine's Toby Bing. Glad to meet you."

Harvey's extended hand was as overly large as his head compared to the rest of him. It was like shaking a paint mixer.

"I'll pull, you push," he said.

It took ten minutes in ninety-degree heat to get up the clunky stone path that ended at a large shed attached to the back of the house. I held on to the cart handle so it wouldn't slip down the hill while Harvey tapped his tongs on the gnarled oak door. After a dozen more knocks, a young guy who looked like an assistant manager at Gold's Gym let us in. He pointed toward a gleaming steel table in the center of the room. The surface was a few inches taller than the hunchback.

"Put it on that," the kid said. "I'll lock up after you."

"That all you gonna help us with?" Harvey said.

Gold's Gym looked at him like he'd said something funny. He left through a door opposite the one we came in. From the aromas and clattering noises coming from there, I gathered he'd sought sanctuary in the kitchen.

The oak door wasn't wide enough for the cart, so Harvey used his tongs to lower the ice and drag it along the concrete through the entrance.

I followed him inside. The only light came from the late afternoon sun rays filtering through the door and a pair of curtained windows two feet square. I could see from the cutting shears, steel rods, and shovels hanging neatly on iron hooks that somebody liked to garden; except there were no bags of fertilizer or soil. The shed seemed as clean as any hospital operating room. No paint cans. No lawnmowers. No clay pots. No dirt at all. Not even a container of Round-Up. I touched the blade of a pruning knife. It was sharp as a scalpel.

Harvey had no trouble pulling the block of ice across the smooth floor to the table. Once there, he spit on his hands, worked his giant head back and forth to loosen his neck muscles, and with a grunt, lifted one end of the block up so that it lay against the edge. He moved to the tail end of the block and shoved it onto the steel top.

"Nicely done," I said.

"Piece of cake," the hunchback said. "Uh, I don't suppose you could lift me up there. I got to raise it to a vertical position. Can't have Miss de Milo lying down."

By the time he had the ice standing up, the door connecting the shed to the kitchen opened, and in skittered a slender man, mid-thirties, waving his hands like a fluttering French waiter. He wore a cravat with navy blue polka dots on a white background. Pinned to his white silk shirt was a round button that said *fopdoodle*.

"My god! Where's the rest of it?" he shrieked.

The fifteen minutes it had taken us to get the block from the refrigerated truck to the table had melted from three hundred pounds to the size of a rather large chimpanzee.

"I'll never complete the full torso now," Alphonse

the Ice Artist wailed. "Oh, dear Jesus. Martin's not going to like this. We'll need another block."

"Like hell," Harvey said, jumping off the table. He brandished his tongs toward the man's crotch. "You'd best get to work before all you got left to sculpt is an ear."

Even Alphonse saw the point to that. After he skipped back to the kitchen to get his tools, I sauntered over to one of the windows and unhooked the latch. Then Harvey and I walked out the way we came in before anyone else could impugn our good names. We had the empty cart halfway down the hill when we heard Alphonse's ice-saw sputter into life.

Back at the refrigeration truck, I pocketed the three dollars Harvey offered for helping him. It would have hurt his pride to decline and one never knows when one can use a friend in the ice business.

———

I DROVE HOME, washed down another baloney sandwich with a Diet Coke, took a shower, and after listening to part of a Royals game broadcast, climbed into a tuxedo I hadn't worn for ten years. It was a little tight in the shoulders, but the trousers fit fine.

Higgins picked me up at eight-thirty. A full moon rose as big and orange as a basketball over the trees to the east. We crossed State Line back into the "old money" neighborhood and cruised past Quist's front gate. Where there had been only catering trucks three hours before, the right side of the street in front was now glutted with shining Mercedes, Lexuses, Jaguars, and the occasional Porsche Carrera. Dozens of well-dressed guests were getting out of cars and handing their keys to sweating parking valets. Colored lanterns dangling from the oak trees lining the long circular drive lit their way to the arched entrance of the house.

We drove on for a half mile, dodging sprinting valets and parallel-parked cars until coming to a street that showed no signs of either.

Higgins pulled onto Sixty-Third, shut off the headlights and drove another block west before turning north onto a quiet lane that paralleled Indian Creek on one side and the Kansas City Country Club golf course on the other. He stopped the car opposite the ninth green so that Casa de Quist loomed directly above us. Eerily lit by the rising moon, it looked like the closing credits scene of *Citizen Kane*. Although we were a good distance from the house, we could hear music and high-pitched voices seeping into the night through its open doors and windows.

"Best to go up from here," Higgins said quietly when I got out of the car. "Our men cut off the alarm system this morning, but you're on your own now. And whatever happens, don't screw up our bust, or I'll break whatever bones are left after Quist's boys have a go."

Higgins gave me a thumbs-up, then drove slowly away, lights still off. I crawled through the slats of a country post fence and slid on the slick grass to the edge of the creek. There had been little rain the past month and the water wasn't as high as usual, but it still looked like it would come up to my chest in midstream. I undressed, shorts, shoes and all, and waded across, holding the clothes over my head.

A stone wall eight feet high and two feet thick surrounded the property. After shaking off what water and mud I could, I put my clothes back on and looked for something to help get me over the wall. All I could find was a piece of driftwood a foot thick. I stood on it, got my elbows over the ledge and arm-crabbed my way up, then took a minute to rest on the top of the rough surface to scout the grounds.

A dog barked a short distance away. It was straining on a leash held by a guard moving downhill in a direction slightly to my right. I lay prone on the wall, not sure that I'd been spotted. Balloon-like biceps stretched the sleeves of the dark T-shirt of the man. It was the Gold's Gym boy from the shed. Strapped to his thigh was a Blackhawk tactical drop holster. Sticking out of it was what seemed to be the butt of a Glock 17 similar to those I'd been issued in the Marine Corps.

My first inclination was to drop back to the creek. But retreating, even for a few minutes, meant the end of my helping Anne escape. I felt sure Gold Body wasn't the only guard prowling the grounds and decided to play it out.

While I chewed my lower lip waiting for him to come closer, he jerked the leash to quiet the dog and pulled a cell phone from his pocket. He talked on it for five minutes, long enough that it had to be to a girl-friend, not his boss or another guard. After ringing off, he put the phone in his pocket, pulled out a joint, and lit up. He took a couple of hits of the weed and walked in my direction along the wall until he and Rin Tin Tin were directly below me.

I considered leaping on top of him. The dog would do what it had to do. Fortunately for all of us, the sweet smell of marijuana must have covered my scent. I let my heroic leaping idea pass and, after a few more leisurely drags, he and Rinty walked away.

When I was certain he had disappeared around a corner of the wall, I dropped onto Quist's property. The shed was on the right rear side of the mansion, partially shaded from the floodlight on the roof. I sprinted forty yards uphill to reach the window that I'd unlocked earlier. Panting like an overweight greyhound, I stood on my toes to peer inside.

The room was dark except for a horizontal line of light under the door leading into the kitchen. I pushed open the window, crawled over the sill, and fell in a heap on the concrete floor. I crept up to the kitchen door, but not before slamming my upper thigh into the pointed edge of the steel table that had once held Harvey's block of ice. Only a puddle remained.

I tried the handle to the door and, to my relief, found it unlocked. Clinging to the hope that no one in the kitchen would care about someone entering through the darkened shed, I opened the door a crack. Sweat momentarily clouded my vision, but I could see that the kitchen was full of people in starched white outfits hurrying about their duties. They cut meat, adjusted oven temperatures, spread sauce, and diced vegetables in a noisy, chaotic atmosphere filled with delightful aromas.

At the far end of the large room, I noticed what looked to be an elevator cage. A squat, muscular man stood in front of it with arms crossed. Figuring he wasn't there just to cut carrots, I waited for him to leave the kitchen before making my entrance.

It took ten minutes for him to find something else to do. As soon as I stepped in, however, an obese chef stopped shouting at his minions long enough to demand in a Marseilles accent why a tuxedoed guest had been allowed to enter his terrain.

I answered in the typical French manner—by ignoring him. While he huffed waiting for an answer, I casually plucked a canapé of smoked salmon off a nearby tray table and whistled a Beatles tune before passing through a swinging door into party central.

Chapter 26

I mmediately outside the kitchen on the left was a narrow staircase built in the 1920s, undoubtedly for servants. I went up them, passed through an empty changing room and came out into a hallway crowded with overstuffed chairs. Four masked figures holding candles like extras in a Vincent Price horror flick glided silently past me in the opposite direction. The last in line, a woman, stopped and pointed out the trail of muddy footprints in my wake. She shook her head while I shrugged my shoulders apologetically.

I walked farther down the hall toward the main staircase where the hum of voices and music rose from below. Another masked couple ascended the stairs. I ducked into a dark room before they could notice me. While I waited for them to pass, something on the far wall of the room caught my eye. A faint beam illuminated the photograph of a young woman whose milk-white face was partially covered by a dark hood, lending to it an air of eerie anonymity. The visible side of it appeared devoid of personality. She might have been a mannequin except for the arch in her lip indicating the slightest sense of surprise.

As my eyes became used to the dim lighting, I noticed other photos. All but two were similar in that black hoods partially covered their pale faces. In each, one breast was similarly exposed as if the models had been posed for no other purpose than objects of a voyeur's derision. I studied the eyes of the models, all of which were heavily dilated. The girls must have been drugged when photographed. Except for the last one who I think was dead.

I returned to the hallway.

The couple I had seen coming up the stairs were now humping away in a guest bedroom next door, oblivious to my or anyone else's presence. I stepped inside, grabbing one of their masks and a long scarf that lay among other hastily discarded clothes on a chair.

Back in the hallway, I put on the mask, wrapped the black silk scarf around my shoulders and crept to the top of a circular carved oak staircase that overlooked the main entrance. Any new arrivals who chanced to observe me from below may have thought for a moment they had entered the home of Dracula. Considering Mr. Quist, they wouldn't be far off.

I looked down at the gallery teeming with attractive men and women in their middle-to-late twenties. They laughed and chattered with the familiarity derived from sharing the same private schools and country clubs since childhood. I knew the type, if only from my encounters with their fathers and uncles on high school football fields. They were wimps when it came to us Jesuit punks, always whining how we hit too hard and too late. Circumstances, of course, changed when the playing fields became the social register and financial and professional institutions.

Catholics who graduated Notre Dame, Boston College, or even Marquette and Saint Louis U. had their own kind of economic and political mafia in town, but nothing like these lads and lassies whose golden pedigrees from eastern colleges opened every social and economic door. They were the new elite, scions of the WASP hierarchy just beginning to make their mark in the downtown law firms, banks, and brokerage houses. But, for the most part, they were also very young emotionally. And here was Martin Quist, the pied piper their parents had warned them about, offering a liberating lifestyle, one more sophisticated and daring than they ever thought to find in their stodgy hometown.

An enormous inglenook and Italian marble fireplace filled the north wall of the main hall. A Pre-Raphaelite sculpture portraying Undine hung atop its mantel. It seemed appropriate, given the nature of the gathering, that to the ancient Greeks, Undine was a water nymph who drowned her promiscuous husband with an embrace.

On a marble table in the center of the room stood the ice sculpture of the Venus de Milo, minus the legs. Her truncated waist was surrounded by crepes and turnips cut to look like flower petals. In a nearby corner, I saw the ice artist, tears streaming down his cheeks.

The men wore tuxedos, the women shimmering dresses—more like slips really—that clung to their lithe bodies like lizard skins. Couples lounged around the room on old-fashioned silk davenports, drinking champagne and smoking hashish.

An overly made-up girl dressed in a skimpy maid's outfit cowered near a group of young men who showered her with abusive language, comparing her breasts to cantaloupes and the like. I figured it was the girl I had talked to the day before on the telephone and, on the basis of that tentative bond, considered rescuing her from her tormentors. Fortunately, a butler approached, said something to the men, and stood by her with arms folded until, one by one, they sulked away. The girl pasted on a frozen smile, picked up a tray covered with tooth-picked shrimp, and returned to wandering among the guests.

Sounds of laughter and humming conversations mixed with the strains of Mozart played by a string quartet. Women fluttered about like black-and-white moths, showing off their décolletage, their bare arms, their long legs, inviting the men who shimmered among them to spread their pollen. Virile Adonises and scantily clad Dianas, rented for the occasion from local health clubs, glided through the animated crowd proffering champagne and canapés laid out on round silver platters. Hands flew everywhere, patting shoulders, playfully adjusting each other's masks, brushing against thighs, cupping breasts and crotches.

The swan-like girls and their testosterone-charged counterparts, stimulated by alcohol, drugs, sumptuous food, and the Gatsby-like surroundings, looked primed for whatever revels Martin Quist had planned as the time edged past eleven.

The invitation had indicated that something sexual was in store for them, and because the guest of honor was Hollywood's infamous Long Bob Langston, they must have thought anything short of a Fellini-esque bacchanal would be disappointing.

Two men and a young woman, each glowing with lustful expectation, stopped in front of me on the stairs. The latter, barely dressed in a flowing see-through tunic, nodded pleasantly as I bowed before her like a courtier. They invited me to watch their coupling, but I politely expressed my regrets and descended the staircase looking for an inconspicuous place from which to look for my prodigal daughter.

I wallowed into the throng that filled the main room to overflowing. Not everyone wore the black masks provided at the door, but most did, and the overall sense of anonymity fueled by alcohol, beautiful bodies, and the languid air of unchallenged privilege led to a palpable lack of inhibitions by these ambitious and reasonably intelligent young professionals.

Now that I was among this crowd, it wasn't hard for me to understand why. The scent of expensive perfume and testosterone-charged sweat, combined with the lush surroundings, had a remarkably enticing effect. Given half a chance, pheromones will trump any sense of caution, no matter one's age, and the bulge in my trousers seemed to put paid to that.

I found a seat on a cushioned bench of the inglenook, discretely crossed my legs, and began looking for Anne, and Josie Majansik.

There was no sign of my daughter, but it wasn't difficult spotting the tall Edward Worth who stood under a portrait of a satyr. Josie, partially hidden by a Corinthian post, leaned against it next to him.

I watched as she straightened his bow tie, then reach for two martinis offered on a silver tray by a server clad in leather briefs and nipple rings. After handing Worth one of them, she took a sip and scanned the crowd. It didn't take her long to catch my stare.

A flicker of recognition crossed what I could see of her face, but the eyes behind the mask quickly glazed over as if I was just another piece of decoration. She whispered something to Worth who pretended to laugh rather too hard. A few breaths later, they strolled through opened french doors onto a veranda.

I decided to follow them after spending another minute futilely scanning the crowded room for Anne and Langston. The loggia was open on one side that looked onto the swimming pool. People stood on Tuscany tiles in coveys of three and four, sipping champagne and checking their watches. I saw Worth studying a pair of cavorting swimmers, but Josie had disappeared.

A bell chimed half past the hour and the stately baroque cantata being performed by the quartet abruptly ended, replaced by the wall-shattering bleating of a Kid Cudi recording of "Wild'n Cuz I'm Young." I returned from the loggia to find the room a playground of frenzied dancing.

A statuesque girl, most likely hired by Quist, slipped out of her dress as casually as removing a glove. Her companion put down his drink, neatly folded her dress and led her to the staircase. Another young woman did the same and, like her friend, was carried away by a roguishly laughing boy. A third kicked her shoes into the air and performed a clumsy striptease to the music. Out in the loggia, young men loosened ties and unzipped trousers with the help of strangers.

The bacchanal was beginning, and desperate to find Anne, I entered a semi-darkened room with a billiards table in its center. The heads of several species of African wildlife littered its rosewood walls. Shadows created by the flickering light of candles in glass hurricane lamps gave the illusion that the animals were alive.

A pale, loose-fleshed man, bald as Mount Hood except for a monk's ring of hair about his ears, sat on a zebra skin couch, tapping ashes from his cigar onto the detached palm of a mountain gorilla. The macabre ashtray rested atop a stool made from the lower leg of an elephant in a room where only a beautiful hand-knotted Kurdistan rug seemed to have escaped the hunting knife.

"Well, hello," the man said, patting a spot next to him. "Care to join me in this charming place?"

"No, thanks," I said. "Have you seen a tall girl with blond hair?"

The man pursed his lips. "Dear boy, the house is crawling with such Aryan blue bloods. Anyway, the only statuesque blondes I'm interested in are of another gender."

"She's with an older fellow, a man about my age."

"Ah, you're stalking her," he said with a smile as slippery as a cheap hotel bathtub. "Jealous? Or are you her daddy?"

That thought struck him as so absurd that he laughed until a bit of snot flew from his nose. He quickly pulled out his handkerchief to wipe the mess off his trouser leg.

"Goodbye," I said, turning to leave.

"Come to think of it," he said to my back. "I *did* see such a couple. Not more than a half hour ago. They were hovering about Martin himself. I believe the girl was with that director fellow who makes such abominable moving pictures."

I spun around. "Where were they?"

"They hadn't gone upstairs yet, but it was still early. I must say the girl didn't seem very comfortable. I felt rather sorry for her. Martin and the man were shouting at each other about a film they were making. Dreadfully boring stuff, so I found somewhere else to wander and located this room. They were in the music chamber on this floor, but I shouldn't think they would still be there."

"Thanks," I said.

"Oh, you're so *very* welcome," he twittered with false bonhomie. "Please *do* come back if you're feeling lonely. These parties can be so dull in the beginning and sometimes never properly take off. A few unfortunate events too early, and all mystery and eroticism are lost. Then one might as well be at the Pink Pussycat gazing at a stage full of dancing cocks and vulvas."

The fat man turned around and spoke, jowls twitching with merriment, into a darkened corner.

"Wouldn't you agree, Denny?"

"Most certainly."

The man who said this sat in an oversized armchair next to a cabinet of exotic butterflies pinned to a board. Another person—it was impossible to tell in the darkened space if it was a man or woman—kneeled before him.

I couldn't see "Denny's" face, but I'd heard the voice of Denton Crowell often enough in court to recognize it. I hoped as I slipped into the hall, that the district attorney had been too occupied with the bobbing head in his lap to recognize mine.

It wouldn't have mattered.

I'd barely gone five steps when a beefy fellow dressed in a black turtleneck and jacket tapped me on the shoulder. He hadn't bothered to wear a mask, which was unfortunate because his scarred, wall-eyed face would have looked better hanging on the wall of the room I had just left.

"Mr. Bevan?"

I almost nodded.

"Come with me," he said in a Mexican accent as he grabbed my elbow.

He resembled a bowling ball, as wide as he was tall, which was something like five feet seven inches. When a second thug, also Hispanic but more my size, nudged a sharp point against the base of my spine, I decided to forgo making a scene.

Having come to terms decidedly in my new acquaintances' favor, we marched off, arm in arm, two tall guys and one bowling ball, looking as if we were in a rush to catch a Los Lobos concert.

Chapter 27

They hustled me through the bustling kitchen. The chaos there didn't seem any more controlled than before.

Half a dozen cooks prepared crepes, stuffed venison, and fois gras—the usual stuff one finds at a party if you happen to live in Monaco. Servers rushed past carrying trays of hors d'oeuvres and champagne. A few guests lounged at a table sampling goodies hot out of the oven, much to the annoyance of the chef with the big mustache. Another partier, her back to the rest, stood by the sink drinking a glass of milk and staring out a window, seemingly oblivious to the commotion around her.

At the far end of the kitchen next to the pantry, my guards opened an elevator door and shoved me in. The tall one stayed behind while the bowling ball jumped in with me, binding my hands behind my back with plastic handcuffs.

We descended three stories, maybe four, before

clanking to a stop. The door opened to a tunnel-like chamber that stretched into blue darkness.

"Get out," the Mexican gnome ordered.

"Where are we?"

He laughed mirthlessly. "It won't help you to know."

"Do you do much of this sort of thing?"

"Too much, buddy. If you haven't already guessed, my boss is a very sick motherfucker."

"And you're not?"

"Not like him. But after a dozen years in federal prison, my employment opportunities are rather limited."

I felt the blunt end of something push the base of my spine and stepped out.

Before the door closed, I turned and grinned at him.

"Don't bother offering me money," he said. "I've had prettier folks than you try to buy their way out of this."

I stared at him as if studying an insect.

His eyes got more guarded.

"You're not fooling me a fucking bit, pal. If you ain't scared shitless by now, you oughta be."

He had a point. I felt like guppy bait about to be tossed into a shark tank, but I wasn't about to give him the satisfaction of showing it. I kept the smile, nodded as if he'd just dropped me off at the airport, then turned around and marched into the darkness.

I fought the onset of panic as the noise of the whining motor and straining cable receded above. A putrid odor of decaying animal flesh filled my nostrils. It emanated from both sides, leading me to think that something had been entombed within the walls.

Lacking other options, I continued down the corridor, straining my eyes and steeling my will to face whatever horrors lay ahead. The sound of my footsteps echoed hollowly against the stone walls.

Initially, the ceiling had been only a few inches above my head, adding to my sense of claustrophobia, but the tunnel eventually opened into a large, dimly lit chamber. Recessed lighting displayed patches on the concrete floor that were the color of dried blood. My eyes became accustomed to the semi-darkness, and after taking another twenty or so hesitant steps, I detected a platform no more than a foot off the floor that was carpeted in black. Dark drapes formed a backdrop to the small stage.

Drawing closer, I saw a human figure standing ramrod straight in front of the platform as if bound to something in front of the curtain. Another person kneeled before the other a few yards away. Because they were both clothed in black, they were almost invisible against the backdrop of the drapes. If the standing figure had not twitched, I might not have noticed them at all.

A spotlight suddenly illuminated a poster-size photograph on the wall to my right. It portrayed a woman tightly wrapped in dark fabric similar to the ones I'd seen in the billiards room. Another beam flashed onto a photo of what looked to be the same woman, but with the cowling on her face adjusted to expose an eye. A long slit had been cut in the fabric from chin to navel, exposing white breasts and a flat belly.

A third picture revealed the dark line of a thin red horizontal wound across a slender neck. Dark eyes stared vacantly into the camera. The tip of her tongue, the last evidence of a long scream, protruded from parted lips.

"Smile on our loves," Quist's voice intoned from somewhere in the dark. "And while thou drawest the blue curtains of the sky, scatter thy silver dew on every flower that shuts its sweet eyes in timely sleep. Let thy west wind sleep on the lake; speak silence with thy glimmering eyes and wash the dusk with silver."

A new light came up displaying Martin Quist to the right of the stage. He sat casually atop a small table. His feet dangled an inch or two above the floor. On either side of him were cameras and video equipment. He wore a checkered bow tie with his tuxedo, along with a silly grin and a nine-millimeter machine pistol. The Glock looked like a cannon in his small hands.

"Truth shines brighter when clad in verse," he sighed. "Don't you just love William Blake's poetry?"

"Until just now," I said, not bothering to grin this time, "he was in my top five. Right behind John Lennon."

Quist slid carefully off the table.

"You might as well know," he said, rubbing his gun with a shiny little finger. "I create sublime poetry through the administration of pain. Lovely girls, preferably blond and full-breasted, are my tablets; the camera, my pen."

"What d'ya want to do when you grow up, Marty; write ads for Hooters?"

"Oh, how amusing. A pity that she couldn't hear it."

Against my better instincts, I looked as the spotlight shone on another photograph.

"You're insane," I said, looking back at him.

"Yes, I suppose you're right," he sighed. "People have been telling me that ever since I bit the nipple off my wet nurse, but I simply have a child's soul."

Right, I thought. *And it's in a special jar in the attic.*

Quist motioned with the gun for me to step forward.

"That's close enough," he said after I had moved within fifteen feet of him.

When I stopped, he lowered the gun and continued with his speech.

"I could hardly believe my luck when I learned you had crashed my soiree this evening. Your presence adds such a dimension to the art that I am about to produce that...well, it's indescribable. Thank you, Bevan. Thank you very much indeed."

The little bastard bowed.

"And now," he said, like a barker at the county fair. "On with the show!"

Quist used a clicker to shut off the overhead lights. In their place, a klieg lamp sparked on to reveal a tall, slender woman chained to a post in the center of the raised platform. She was entirely clad in black leather, but the front zipper had been pulled down exposing the top half of her breasts and her throat. A dark cowl covered her face except where holes were cut for the eyes and mouth. A rubber mouth plug stifled her cries. Several strands of strawberry blond hair that had escaped the cowl gleamed in the harsh light.

It took only a moment to recognize my daughter. Her eyes were pools of terrified watchfulness.

Chapter 28

In the shadow of the light a few feet from the stage, Bob Langston kneeled behind a loaded crossbow. Like Anne, he wore the leather outfit head to toe. His hands were secured behind his back with the same type of plastic handcuffs that bound mine. A string attached to the trigger extended to an iron ring embedded in his tongue. The taut line meant that the slightest movement would pull the trigger, hurtling the dart into Anne's exposed throat.

A large Fen-flex camera rested on a tripod behind the unwilling archer. A second string, as taut as the other, ran from the camera to the tongue ring in order to capture on film the exact moment of impalement.

"Once I was informed of your presence," Quist said in his whispery voice. "It took some time for my assistants to set the stage properly. I must say that your daughter gave us more of a fight than Long Bob. We had to resort to a calming drug to get her trussed in the appropriate attire, whereas a gun aimed at his testicles was quite enough to get him to cooperate."

231

Quist sauntered over to Langston, bending down to speak in his ear.

"We could have been such good friends. I provided money for your film when no one else would even think of backing you. But you forgot your obligations when I asked for small favors. I don't take to such treatment kindly."

He kissed his forehead and added: "Isn't that right, Bob?"

The eyes behind the mask stared emptily back at him.

Quist turned to me.

"This has-been wasn't content to ignore my generosity. For the past week, his insults have been the order of the day. I shared my most personal confidences with him, and how does he respond? Not only does he refuse to host my party, he threatens to report my transgressions to the police!"

Quist stared at me with the shining eyes of a man who could sever a man's head with a kitchen knife and butter his bread with it a moment later.

"From the beginning, he refused to take me seriously," he continued. "My ideas meant nothing to him. I intended to merely humiliate him tonight by secretly capturing him on film in the throes of passion with your daughter. The room was prepared, the camera set up, but he refused to make love to her in my house. This aging pig even cursed me for suggesting it. Can you imagine?"

I took three steps forward. Quist aimed the gun at my chest.

"Steady there, Bevan."

Langston groaned.

"Ho, ho!" Quist said gleefully. "The would-be

director finds himself humbled before my camera. He weakens. He shakes. He loses control of his sphincter. Are you ready for action, Long Bob? Then, let the arrow find its way home!"

With Quist's attention focused on Langston, I inched a couple of feet forward until I stood three or four yards to the left of the crossbow. Langston shifted his gaze just enough to make eye contact with me without releasing the dart.

A veteran trial lawyer gave me advice when I was fresh out of law school that seemed appropriate under these circumstances. He said if I ever found myself in a courtroom with a judge whose oars were no longer in the water, the best strategy was to get crazy with him.

There was nothing to lose. My plan of action started with telling the truth.

"Kramm is dead."

Quist looked at me doubtfully.

"It's true, Martin. I shot him in the head. He was torturing Weston Preston, and I put a stop to it, but not before asking a very important question."

His smooth face suddenly became less smooth.

"Just where might this have occurred?"

"Preston's apartment," I said. "The police know everything. They are upstairs at this moment looking for you."

"They never know everything," he scoffed. "And I don't believe you notified the police."

But he knew I wasn't lying about Kramm. There was no way for me to have known that the South African would be in Weston's apartment if I hadn't been there. And there's no way I'd be where I was now if Kramm had survived.

"You certainly are one for surprises," Quist said. "I

had been meaning to chastise the big fellow for his absence here tonight. So, tell me what you said to him."

"I asked him what signals they used for line-outs."

Quist stepped closer. "Come again, Bevan? I don't seem to gather what you're babbling."

"I wanted to know how the Springboks put the rugby ball in play. Surely Kramm must have told you something about the game. It's the national sport of white South Africa."

"I'm afraid football isn't my cup of tea. Bloody boring exercise."

"Mother wouldn't let you play?"

"Something like that," Quist said very softly. "And please don't waste what little time remains for you trying to upset me."

He turned to Langston with mock concern.

"You're hanging on rather longer than I expected. Ah, there now, the old tongue is throbbing again. What a delicious look in those eyes. Fear, anticipation, hatred—so many emotions gleaming in those two little orbs. And just look at Miss Anne with her mouth quivering around that cruel piece of rubber. Delicious!"

I swallowed hard as he walked up to her and caressed her cheek with the front sight of the gun.

"Don't fret, my dear," he cooed. "It's all for the best. With your burgeoning addiction, you'd have died a withered, toothless hag within the year. Best to die in the full bloom of youth and have it captured on film for all eternity."

He sauntered back to Langston.

"You'd best release the dart now, Bob. My guests will begin wondering where I've been and I've scheduled a photo session for no less a personage than Edward Worth."

"The thing about line-outs," I declared as if conducting a clinic in the locker room at Twickenham Stadium. "Is that it takes teamwork between the hooker and the second-row jumper. If the hooker doesn't throw the ball just when his man has begun to leap, odds are strong that the opposing jumper will gain possession."

Quist regarded me over his shoulder. He seemed peeved by the interruption.

"Please, Bevan, you're beginning to…"

"Alabama was the code my team used," I said. "The Chicago Lions used the same one, as I recall."

"Alabama?" Quist asked. "What on earth?"

"It goes like this: Ready…set…California…Texas…AllabaaMA!"

I leaped forward on the last shouted syllable, coming between Anne and the crossbow an instant before Langston released the dart.

Crashing against the stage support, I felt a searing pain in my rib cage that was quickly followed by the stuttering sound of the Glock. I looked back to see Langston, his mouth bloodied from the ring that had torn loose from his tongue, and slammed Quist to the ground with a vicious body check.

The old rugger had acted on my line-out cue perfectly. But while his tackle momentarily stunned Quist, one of the rounds from the machine pistol had struck him high in the chest. Tiny pink bubbles emerged from a round dark hole as Langston thrashed on the floor like a landed fish before going very still.

Quist scrambled to his feet, still holding the Glock.

"So much for that nonsense," he wheezed, taking a

mincing step forward. Very calmly, he fired a single shot into my groin that sent me spiraling to the floor.

I've always wondered why I didn't pass out. Obviously, something to do with endorphins and adrenaline. At any rate, I was way past caring for myself.

"You should know better than to struggle, Bevan. I was prepared to deliver a quick death for all of you had you cooperated. Now look at the mess you've made."

Kneeling beside the inert actor, Quist calmly produced a pair of pliers from a leather satchel, clamped the claws onto Langston's left ear, and with a sudden snap of the wrist, tore it off.

Quist grunted as he tossed the ear to the floor. He approached my daughter, and in a stage whisper, he said to her: "I thought he was playing opossum, but you're wide awake, aren't you, sweetie?"

Anne's eyes seemed to tumble out of their sockets when Quist softly tapped her lips with the opened pliers.

The curtain rippled behind him as a breeze somehow found its way into the underground chamber.

He shifted his gaze toward me. "It's best to start with the tongue, don't you think?"

I responded by shaking as if touched by St. Vitus, letting out a series of howls that would have made a West Virginia snake handler proud.

Quist found my actions amusing.

The edge of the curtain fluttered again, opened for an instant, closed, then opened again. I concentrated on the monster's face, willing him to look at me, continuing to shout and shake because buying time was the only weapon I had left. The hysterics didn't require much acting on my part.

"This has been most entertaining," Quist said as he attempted to fasten the pliers to Anne's lower lip. The rubber plug made it difficult. "But I really must get back to my guests soon."

Because of the commotion I'd been making, he failed to hear the humming of the machinery at the far end of the chamber. Nor did he notice Josie Majansik until she emerged from behind the curtain, butcher knife in one hand and claw hammer in the other, flying at him like an avenging angel.

She underestimated Quist's quickness, however. Instinctively rolling to his left, he wrenched the knife from her and used it to slash the lower part of her calf muscle. She dropped to her knees in agony, but not before slamming the hammer against the back of his skull. It made a thwacking sound like a baseball encountering the business end of Barry Bonds's bat, and Quist crumpled semi-conscious next to her.

I lurched forward, my knees sliding on the widening pool of blood until I was next to them. Bending over, I repeatedly head-butted his face until his nose and cheekbones looked as though they'd greeted a truck. I kicked the gun away from his inert body, then turned my attention to the others.

Josie, her face drained of color, had moved fifteen feet from where Quist now lay sprawled on his back like a corpse. Sitting with her back against an iron post, she clutched her severed Achilles tendon. I crawled over to her. Turning so that my back was to her, I presented my bound wrists.

It must have been excruciating to release the grip

on her leg, but without a sound, she picked up her knife and sawed through the plastic cuffs. Only after she had finished that task did she quietly begin to moan.

Her ripped tendon flopped like a living eel beneath her fingers until I was able to bind it as best I could with pieces torn from my shirt.

"It's all right now," she said. "Take care of yourself and Anne. I'll see to Bob."

After tying a makeshift tourniquet above my wounded thigh, I limped over to my daughter.

She tried to speak after I threw off the cowling and pulled the horrible plug from her mouth. But it was too soon for anything intelligible to come out.

"There, there," I stuttered inanely as I untied her.

I held her in my arms until she responded with a healthy round of sobs. Then I led her to Langston.

Josie had stanched the blood bubbling from his chest, but he couldn't speak. There was a little gleam in his eye, however. He held up his hand for a light high-five. I saluted him instead.

Our celebrations proved far too premature, however.

Blame it on the loss of the blood, the over-whelming relief of having escaped mutilation and death, or simply the dim lighting in that dungeon.

Whatever.

I didn't realize the consequences of not finishing the job until Anne nudged me and silently pointed to where Quist had been and now wasn't. He'd staggered away while we dressed our wounds and congratulated each other.

No doubt, he was heading to the elevator and would come back with his thugs to finish us. So much for turning the tables.

Crawling once again on my elbows, I retrieved the gun I should have secured the first time and desperately fired a burst of five or six semi-automatic rounds into the darkness of the tunnel before it ran empty.

As indicated by its name, the Glock 17 holds seventeen rounds. I didn't think Quist had used more than half a dozen on us.

Click. Click again.

The bullets must have been used on other poor souls.

From somewhere in the dark corridor, he shouted something at us. It wasn't the voice of a man in physical distress. I think he was laughing.

With our wounds, we were out of options.

Or so I thought.

Josie, Langston, and I may have had nothing left to give, but Anne Bevan did. Apparently, she wasn't a Royal Marine commando's granddaughter for nothing.

"I'll handle this, Dad," she said, jumping to her feet.

I don't know what astounded me the most: My daughter's sudden transformation from catatonic victim to determined warrior or the fact that she referred to me as "Dad." It was the first time in years she had called me that.

"No, babe. Save yourself. Go up the stairs that Josie came down. Maybe you can bring help…"

"Don't think so. Not enough time."

She put one hand on my shoulder and extracted the dart from between my ribs with the other. She then wrenched the crossbow from its base, drew back the cable, and inserted the dart in the grooved chamber.

"Go for it, girl," Josie whispered to herself as Anne rushed into the darkness.

Thrashing sounds ricocheted between the walls of the corridor, followed by Quist's maniacal laughter and the groaning motion of the elevator's wire cables.

"Sweet Jesus," I said, reaching for Josie's hand.

We listened helplessly to the tortured metallic sound, the prelude to the end of everything.

I clung to a forlorn hope. Instead of rising, the elevator might actually be descending. If the cage had returned to the kitchen earlier, we hadn't noticed it, but there had been plenty of other things to distract our senses.

The answer came moments later when bright lights flooded the chamber, followed by a dreadful yowling.

Anne, the crossbow cradled in her arms, stood with her back to us, facing the dark elevator shaft. Her head tilted downward, looking at something.

Wuummpppp.

The elevator cage landed like it didn't have brakes.

We heard a truncated howl.

The elevator door opened about a foot above the floor. Lieutenant Higgins and two burly men wearing star badges and Durango mustaches stepped from it. There was a lot of cursing.

Higgins got down on his knees and peered under the cage, looking for what had stopped it inches from the bottom. He got up after a few seconds and said something to Anne. She answered by pointing to where Josie, Langston, and I sat in our ever-growing pond of mingled blood. Higgins nodded, pulled out a cell phone, and began talking into it while following my daughter down the corridor.

As they approached, I noticed that Anne carried

the primitive weapon behind her neck and nestled across her shoulders. She looked like a hunter who had bagged her first deer.

"Quist?" Josie asked.

"Not to worry," Buford Higgins said, nodding in the direction of the elevator. "He's a pile of mashed potatoes, and there ain't enough for leftovers on Monday."

The hillbilly humor was lost on me because whatever adrenaline remained in my system packed its bags and seeped out.

The next thing I knew, white-coated EMTs were loading me onto a stretcher cart. When they rolled me past the body of Martin Quist, I saw that Higgins hadn't exaggerated. The flattened corpse lay on a rubber tarp, painted in the pulped colors of mutilation. An iron dart protruded from his right eye.

Chapter 29

Friday, July 5

Unlike many urban hospitals, St. Luke's in Kansas City hasn't swallowed the surrounding neighborhood. Its broad face of brick and glass stands regally on a hill overlooking Mill Creek Park and the J.C. Nichols Fountain. Norman Rockwell captured both in a painting produced for the July 1955 cover of the *Saturday Evening Post* and every family doctor in town has a framed picture of it in their waiting rooms.

Quist's bullet had missed my femoral artery by an inch and my privates by less than three. The exit wound left a two-inch hole of devitalized tissue on the back of my upper thigh. Dr. Fotopoulos scheduled surgery to clean the wound, suture torn muscle, and apply a plaster cast for the next day.

Unless infection or lead poisoning set in, I'd be eligible for tango lessons by Christmas. The dart had broken a rib and separated some cartilage, but I was used to such "owies" in rugby. No big thing.

Josie's Achilles tendon was treated in another area of the hospital. A few days after her surgery, she was wheeled up to my floor to see me, but I told the nurse I wasn't ready for visitors.

It was partially true. I hurt like hell and the painkillers had me babbling about Martians and marshmallows some of the time. The real reason, however, was during my more lucid moments, I had tried to come to terms with her appearance in that porn video and wasn't succeeding.

Long Bob Langston, having spent five hours on the operating table, was recovering in the intensive care unit two floors down. I wanted to thank him, but neither of us would be ready to relive our adventure with Mr. Quist for some time.

Nurse aides were rolling dinner carts in the halls when Anne entered my room. She looked strung out. Her eyes fluttered and blinked too much, and there was a pale line around her mouth.

She said hello and kissed me on the forehead.

"Hello, yourself. How do you feel?"

"Not great. I'm pretty itchy. Martin pumped me with something I've never experienced before. And, believe me, I've had plenty to experience."

She poked at a box of Kleenex and for a long minute made eye contact with the television set.

"Listen," I began.

"Don't," she said, fiddling with a plastic cup. "Don't say anything until I'm finished."

I nodded, pretending to study the electric gizmo that adjusts the hospital bed in all kinds of ways except the way you want it.

"I'm checking into the Allen Rehab Center in Lawrence this afternoon."

"That's very wise."

"Didn't I tell you not to say anything?" She looked toward the hallway as if ready to bolt.

"Sorry," I said, willing her eyes back to me. "I thought you were finished."

"Well, maybe I am. I'm not sure about it. ARC costs a lot of money, but I can probably handle this thing myself."

I just looked at her.

"Well, why don't you say something?"

"You told me not to."

She smiled for the first time since entering the room and sat on a corner of the bed.

"I'm sorry for how I've acted."

"I haven't set much of an example for you," I said.

I didn't mention how proud I was of her for going after Quist. According to the police report Higgins showed me, Quist had already pushed the descent button when Anne surprised him. She shot the dart when he lunged at her, striking him in the eye. He staggered backward, tripping into the shallow of the shaft, just in time for the descending elevator carrying its load of an overweight cop and three federal agents to finish the job.

Her fingers curled around my hand. They felt cold.

"Drug addiction is my problem, not yours," she said.

"Anything that causes you pain is my problem as well. Don't worry about the money. Think of what I'll save not having to pay for your next semester at CU."

Anne straightened her back and said without

anger: "I still can't disconnect you from Mother's death."

"I don't see how you can, honey. Every night before falling asleep, I ask the old 'what if', but second-guessing doesn't honor your mom's memory. Give it a nod when it enters, then let it pass just as swiftly. After a while, it might get tired of visiting."

"Josie Majansik told me it was all right not to forget if one can forgive as well."

I smiled at the old saw used by divorce lawyers to bring a semblance of reason to their emotionally fragile clients made irrational by jealousy and anger.

"That's nice of her to try to help."

"She's been very kind to me. I think she'd like for you to call her when you get out of here."

"Is that so?" I said in a way that meant "not a chance."

Anne arched an eyebrow. "I heard you wouldn't see her when she tried to visit."

"I wasn't feeling like flowers."

"I thought you two were…"

"Involved?"

"If the euphemism fits, yeah."

"We were for about ten minutes," I answered. "We've all got our issues, but Ms. Majansik, for all her good qualities, is too hard a case even for me."

"What on earth could she have done—aside from saving our lives, of course—to have put you off of her?"

"Let's just say she takes her work far too seriously."

I squirmed a bit, looking for the right adjectives to make the point without telling the truth about that porno tape. Discretion has always been a tricky business for me.

"Josie is nice," I said. "Very attractive and all the rest, but I'm just not comfortable around her."

"Oh, bollocks!" Anne snorted in a most British manner. "She's exactly what you need, whether you're comfortable with it or not."

"If you say so."

"Don't patronize me."

She pulled her hand from mine, and we both stared at the television. Maybe I should have turned it on. Instead, I asked how she was going to get to the clinic in Lawrence.

"Mark Winter offered to drive me."

I smiled with approval but wisely didn't comment on their similarity in age. "He's a great kid."

Anne shrugged. "I'd better go see how Bob is coming along in the ICU."

"You still care for him, huh?"

"Ridiculous as it may seem to you, I love him. Lots. He makes me feel worthwhile."

"Ouch," I said.

She laughed and her eyes softened.

"I put it badly. He's ready to make something of his career again. I want to be with him when he does."

I gave her the skeptical father look. Langston's past, combined with the glittering environment of Hollywood, didn't sound like a drug-free future to me.

"Give him some credit," she said, reading my thoughts. "He wasn't the one who hooked me on drugs. I was snorting coke by my junior year of high school. Bob's been clean as long as I've known him, but he couldn't get me to quit. When he became involved with Quist, I suddenly had a free supply of heroin. Bob was furious when he found out, but he had as much control over my addiction as you would have had."

I sighed. It's hard letting a child go, especially when you're just getting to know her.

"Tell him I'll get over to see him when we're both properly patched up."

She squeezed my hand. I grinned as best as I could.

"Honey," I said as she walked to the door.

She turned. "What?"

"Your mother and I were very much in love. You were our pride and joy. Do you recall the book we read to you when you were three or four? That story about the Chinese boy with the long name?"

"*Tikki Tikki Tembo*?"

"Yes," I said, closing my eyes as I recited its repetitive line: "'*Tikki tikki tembo-no sa rembo-chari bari ruchi-pip peri pembo* has fallen into the well.'"

"You remember that?"

"I was there, too, honey."

"Now that you mention it, I believe you were."

"I'm still here for you."

Anne returned to my side. Her hands trembled as she grasped my hands. I'd like to think it wasn't just a withdrawal symptom.

"Dad?"

"Yes, daughter?"

"How about a hug?"

———

A WEEK LATER, I had recovered enough to visit Bob Langston. He'd been released that morning from intensive care and was parked in room 467, around the corner from my room.

I wheeled in to find his chest swathed in bandages. He wore a linen cap with a flap covering the left side of his head and his tongue was decorated with a dozen or so black sutures.

He greeted me as if we were the best of friends. I suppose we would have been if he hadn't bedded my daughter without my permission.

"Thass a pwetty fowtin," he said, pointing his massive hand toward the window.

"Yeah," I said, pushing myself up from the wheelchair to see it, then settling back down.

"Fwanks fuh saving ma life."

"Hey, we saved each other. You might have been a little quicker on the rugby cue, however. I thought I was going to have to spell it out for you."

"Yu bastid," he grunted, flashing me the ugliest smile this side of Topeka. "Y'ud make a gud fadder'n law."

"Give that tongue a rest," I said, eager to avoid any talk relating to matrimony and Anne. "It's making me sick watching you try to make it work."

"Maaiik?"

"Yes, Bob?"

"Yur dotter's a wunner...wunferl guurll...'n so bwaave."

"I know. But I'm not a wonderful guy, so you'd better take good care of her."

His cobalt blues peeped at me from under the goofy hospital cap.

"Dun wuury, Pop."

"Don't call me that. Not ever."

He giggled. It wasn't a pretty sight.

"Ah'm goin' t'finis 'he Jethie Jame movie."

And ten months later, buoyed by a loan from Edward Worth and some slick editing work by Anne Bevan, he did just that.

Chapter 30

Wednesday, July 21

Ten days after my release from St. Luke's, I attended a memorial service on the UMKC campus for Julie Caxton, Rebecca Weitz, and Deirdre Eberly, the three girls found entombed in the walls of Quist's chamber of horrors.

I sat in the back of the theater listening to the tributes given by their teachers and coaches as photographs displaying their once-golden lives flashed on a large screen. The juxtaposition of those bright, cheerful images with my memory of the horrific pictures taken of their last moments soon became more than I could handle. When one of the girls' track coaches rose to speak, I gathered my crutches and snuck out.

In the parking lot, I encountered a man in his mid-twenties who had the well-scrubbed good looks of the young people I'd seen at Quist's bacchanal. His shaking hands fumbled for a cigarette as I passed him on my way to the Jeep.

"Excuse me, sir. Do you have a light?"

"Sorry," I said, turning to face him. "I don't smoke."

"Thanks, anyway."

His eyes were ringed with despair, but he wanted to talk.

"I'm Trey Eberly, Deirdre's brother," he said, shaking my hand. "She was a wonderful person but very modest. She would have been embarrassed by the speeches being spouted in there. Did you know her?"

Not having a delicate answer, I just said, "She meant a lot to everyone whose lives she touched. They all did."

He gave me a cold stare.

"Yes, of course. Have a nice day, sir."

As I drove away, a selfish thought emerged, one I could not resist and which I refused to let weigh on my conscience. The boy lost his sister, his parents, their child, but partly because of their terrible loss, I had regained the love of my daughter.

It's best to take what you can in this world. If you choose to believe in fate, I figure you might as well believe that it brings only good fortune.

━━━

A FEW HOURS LATER, I hobbled into The Peanut to meet Buford Higgins for lunch. His idea.

Pegeen Flynn poured two pints of Boulevard Pale Ale, said she was glad to see me alive, if not well, and reminded me that I owed her gas money for the use of her Saab. I tossed her two of those dollar coins found only in stamp machines these days, and she disappeared into the kitchen to prepare our order.

Being mid-afternoon, only three other customers were in the place. A lone drinker with the face of a flat tire sat at one end of the counter. He spent a lot of time shaking the ash off his cigar into empty longneck bottles placed neatly in a row like little brown soldiers. In a booth behind him, two women locked lips. When we tired of watching them, Higgins started talking.

"Weston Preston's out of the hospital and in a holding cell. He seems to be fine physically but complains of a 'melting mind.'"

"I don't envy you trying to get a sensible affidavit out of him."

"He's talking, and that's all that matters. Phyllida Law isn't saying a word, of course. She found enough money to hire David Scarpelli, so we'll be jumping through the usual hoops."

"What happens to all the photos and addresses? I'd just as soon see them burned before someone else gets hold of them."

"Not to worry," the big cop said. "No minors were involved, so the FBI authorized me to personally deliver all copies of sexually incriminating material to the affected parties. A lot of randy rich folks are resting easier at their country clubs this week."

"What about the district attorney?"

Higgins looked at me with those squirrel eyes.

"Some are more deserving than others," he said. "I've talked to him. If Crowell doesn't resign by the end of the month as promised, he'll regret it. At any rate, he won't be running for the Senate."

"Maybe not this year. Moral evil may carry its own curse, but I doubt this will destroy Denny."

"Yeah. He'll be back. There will always be a segment of the electorate too stupid to ignore the hypocrisy of politicians like him."

Pegeen brought out the triple-size B.L.T.s, and we ate in silence for a while. That's what you do at The Peanut after those monster sandwiches get plopped in front of you. It takes total concentration and jaws opened wider than a cattle gate to devour one.

When nothing remained on our plates but some orphaned pieces of lettuce and mayonnaise drippings, I asked Higgins if he'd heard from Josie Majansik.

"She's still in Columbus with no plans to return. Last I heard, she was filling out her expense reports for the General Accounting Office. What's it to you?"

"You know what."

"You weren't exactly Sir Galahad when she tried to visit you in the hospital."

"She makes me uncomfortable. What's her story, Buford? I know she had a role to play. Maybe there was no other way to gain Quist's trust, but Jesus..."

I hesitated because the drunk at the end of the bar took a swipe at Pegeen's beautiful bosom while she tried to clear away the empty beer bottles.

"Excuse me for a minute," Higgins said.

He walked to the end of the counter, grabbed the nape of the man's neck as if it were a rat's, and hustled him out the door. Upon Higgins's return, Pegeen tossed him the Sacagawea coins in gratitude.

"Majansik's not whoring for Uncle Sam or anyone else," he said after sitting down and collecting a free beer. "Staying undercover for eighteen months is a hell of a long time for that kind of work. With Crowell feeding Quist the names of our local vice squad operatives, we had to keep her on the job, even after she showed signs of burnout."

"And I know why," I said, staring into the bottom of my glass. "Marilyn Chambers wouldn't let happen to her what Josie did in that porn flick."

It's a good thing Higgins had eaten his sandwich or he would have choked on it.

"Hell's bells," he sputtered. "You saw that?"

I nodded solemnly, more solemnly, in fact, than I would have normally done if Higgins hadn't thought it so hilarious.

"Ah, you poor bastard," he said after catching his breath. "Is that what all this moping is about?"

I looked at Pegeen. She whistled something from *South Pacific*, then set about wiping the counter free of imaginary beer rings.

"Well, yeah," I finally answered. "Isn't that enough?"

"That wasn't Josie Majansik in the film. At least not all of her."

"Huh?"

"We weren't getting anywhere with Quist or his people. Initially, they didn't buy her act of a lonely nymphomaniac new to town. The regional FBI lab took a confiscated film featuring a woman with her body type, made some grainy shots of Majansik's face and a boob shot or two." He stopped momentarily for a swig of beer. "But mind you, no down-unders. They spliced those shots of her into the original."

I heaved a sigh, either in relief or partial disbelief. "Well, it sure fooled me."

"Hell, yes. The feds in Cleveland had recently collared a child pornographer in Lancaster, Ohio, and, given the choice of forty years or helping us, the charmer agreed to make the necessary introductions for Majansik by sending the doctored film to Quist. Within a week, Rolf Kramm paid a visit to her apartment, threatening to send the movie to her supposed boss at the *Gumbo*. To avoid exposure and to avoid actually prostituting herself, she tearfully agreed to lure the wealthy and oversexed Edward Worth into Quist's trap."

I smiled mirthlessly, picturing her sweet gamin face staring up at the Afrikaner, telling him she was just a poor girl from southeast Ohio who needed the money and "Please don't tell my mother."

"With Worth's cooperation, it worked beautifully," Higgins continued. "But got complicated when Langston and your daughter, not to mention you and that damned book, got into the mix."

"Josie walked into *my* life, not vice versa."

The detective glared at me with gunboat eyes before getting up slowly. He laid a twenty-dollar bill on the counter.

I started to say something else, but he squeezed my shoulder with that meat hook of a hand.

"Hold your gob," he snarled. "Majansik never had a chance to be 'sweet sixteen.' She was eleven when her father died from black lung disease working in the coal mines of southeast Ohio. Her mother sent her and a younger brother to live with an uncle who proceeded to have his way with both of them. Somehow, she survived and earned a scholarship to Ohio State. The boy wasn't as tough. He hung himself at fifteen."

Higgins released his grip. Pins and needles danced on my upper arm.

"How'd you learn all this?" I said, massaging my shoulder.

"She needed cover in her role as a reporter. I set her up in a room down the hall from my office, and I got to know her pretty well. She didn't share any personal stuff, however, until the night before she returned to Columbus."

Pegeen returned with Higgins's change. He pocketed it and started for the door but didn't get far with my hand grabbing his sleeve.

"You can't stop there, Buford. Did she say anything about me?"

The detective turned. "She asked me to tell you 'goodbye' for her."

"I understand."

He spread his big paws on the counter.

"No, you don't, Bevan. When she tried to see you at the hospital, it was to open herself up to you and explain certain things. I can guess what they were now. But there must have been something good on daytime television, because you had better things to do than give her that chance. She has pretty low self-esteem when it comes to men. Maybe that's why she's so good at enticing us. She's a pro when it's playacting, but when the emotions become real, she doesn't know what to do."

"Was she just playing me along as well?"

"In order to get close to Quist through your daughter and Langston?"

"Something like that."

"Maybe, maybe not. But I know Eddie Worth thinks she's pretty special."

Silence fell between us. The Peanut was beginning to fill with students pouring out of class from the nearby campus. Pegeen inserted a CD in the boom box above the bar and the place exploded into life. With its torn barstools, tattered booths, and cheap decorations hanging from every square inch of the walls stained by decades of cigarette smoke, only the music seemed to ever change in Kansas City's oldest bar. I like places that thrive on neglect. Maybe that's how I was with people, too.

"Tell her I'm sorry and maybe, maybe…oh, hell, I don't know."

"I'll think of something," Higgins said.

We walked into the sunshine.

"I hear you're being promoted to captain."

"The chief thought it might be a good idea after I showed him this." He grinned like the Cheshire Cat and pulled out a folded piece of yellowed paper containing a list of names under the logo of a new moon.

"Amazing how many folks are on this thing."

Chapter 31

Friday, August 5

I learned from Tim Winter that Josie was back in town giving statements to the federal prosecutor for Phyllida's and Weston's preliminary hearings. After Alice got on the phone to insist that I get in touch with Josie, I left a message for her from the bookshop. She returned the call that same afternoon.

"How's the leg?" she said.

"Fine. And yours?"

"It's still in a cast and it itches like hell."

"I'm sorry."

"It'll come off soon enough."

"I'm not talking about the cast."

"Oh."

"Can I buy you dinner tonight?"

I waited a couple of heartbeats for her to answer.

"I guess so. But nothing fancy."

"I know just the place."

SIOBHAN GREETED us at the door of Fitzpatrick's with a big smile and led us to a table in a secluded snug.

Aiden Delahunt was setting up his amplifier on the stage directly across from us. The usual after-work crowd of young lawyers, architects, and ad reps sat on barstools nursing their pints and yakking with Ronan Gill while he shucked mussels behind the counter. Upon seeing me, he waved a rubber-gloved hand and made a gesture of throwing his knife at me with the other.

While the Wolfe Tones wailed about the potato famine and that "bastard Lord John Russell" over the Bose speakers, we silently studied our menus as if they contained the *Book of Kells*. We hadn't said much in the Jeep on the way over either. There was too much to explain and no easy way to begin.

When the waitress came, we ordered Guinness and fish and chips. It was either that or the beef stew.

"I gotta know," I said to Josie after finding courage in my first pint of stout. "What led you to Quist's basement?"

She put down her glass, dabbed her mouth with the cloth napkin and leaned toward me.

"It was in my report."

"But I want to hear it from you."

"It doesn't make for pleasant dinner conversation."

"Irish bar cuisine doesn't qualify as pleasant dining."

"All right," she said tonelessly. "I got worried when we lost sight of Langston and Anne and was about to look for them when I recognized you. Believe me, your presence was an unwelcome surprise. I was sure you'd screw up our plans if you approached me, so I headed for the kitchen to stay out of sight. I was deciding what to do over a glass of milk when Martin's men hustled you right past me into the elevator. You stepped on my heel, you clumsy oaf."

"Sorry. I didn't know it was you, or I would have asked those thugs to stop and let me apologize."

"No matter."

She reached across the table to pat my hand. "I knew about the staircase from poking around the place the day before. God knows, there wasn't much else to do after Martin entertained us with a marathon showing of slasher-porn movies. Grabbing a knife and hammer from a drawer, I hustled down the stairs just in time to hear Quist's rants. I peeked through the curtains, desperately waiting for an opportunity to attack while you baited him and got Langston tuned in to your crazy rugby trick. I was ready when you jumped into action. You know the rest."

"Was I part of your plan to get Quist? Is that why you started coming to Riverrun?"

"No," she said. "The bookstore was an island of tranquility. I desperately needed it when the stress began to overwhelm me. But then came the Gareth Hughes business that got you involved with Quist. I knew you were in bigger trouble than you could have imagined. It was stupid getting emotionally involved with you and jeopardizing the case."

"And I thought I was a big help."

"We would have got him anyway. At least I think so. You just made it harder and a lot scarier."

"It's not like I asked for it," I said, trying not to make it sound like a complaint.

"Of course not, Mike. No more than Anne asked for it. I'm just glad it worked out."

After pretending to read the history of Ireland on the back of the menu, I said, "I'm glad you came back, even if only to provide evidence. It was wrong to avoid you at the hospital."

"I've been snubbed by worse," she said, smiling. She looked over my shoulder at the stage where Sandra Epstein had joined Delahunt and was testing the microphone by playing a few bars on her penny whistle.

When Josie looked back at me, her smile was gone.

"I chose this profession for reasons I don't want to go into. I've been an agent six years and worked vice the last four; time enough to put away a lot of scum. Martin Quist may not have been the worst, if you can believe that; in the top three, for sure, but there was a pair of grandparents in Dublin, Ohio, who still give me nightmares. I nailed them with life sentences, but they took a bit of my soul as well. Quist's getting so close to you and your daughter took more out of me. Most of what I had left. I don't think I'll be good at police work anymore. I'm taking a leave of absence."

I finished my Guinness and ordered another. Sandra and Aiden had finished setting up and would begin playing soon.

"Josie," I said in a voice that was an octave higher than I would have liked. "We've been on a crazy roller coaster ride. Now that we've climbed off, maybe we can start over under more normal circumstances."

"Any particular reason?"

"Well, for one, Alice Winter has been harping on my lack of female companionship again. She thinks it's unhealthy, and I'm beginning to think she has a point."

"Sounds to me that she wants you for herself."

"She's the one who insisted I call you. She's a dear friend, that's all. You'd enjoy her."

"Like I would have enjoyed knowing your wife?"

"I'm not comparing you to them. Will you consider moving in with me? I've got a nice house and a semi-nice cat."

She chewed her lip and didn't answer. Our food arrived and Aiden introduced the first number. It was my song, "The Wind that Shakes the Barley."

"I'm serious," I said at the end of the mournful tune. "I love you."

Josie silently turned her attention to the stage, but I persisted.

"If you prefer, I'll sleep in the bathtub."

"That would be uncomfortable."

"All right, the couch then."

She smiled sadly. "I don't think so."

I studied my plate, pushing coleslaw away from the crumbled fish flakes.

"Is there somebody else?" I asked. "One of your agent pals? Eddie Worth?"

"Maybe," she said, lifting my chin with her fingers. "Let's face it, Michael. You're still married to a ghost, and I don't know how to compete with that."

We finished eating and listened in silence as Sandra Epstein sang "Barbara Allen." Maybe the tragic tale of lost love had a palliative effect on me because by the time the check came, I wasn't feeling so much like a broken-hearted fool.

At the door to her hotel room later that night, I kissed Josie on the forehead and thanked her for all she had done.

She said, "Think nothing of it."

"Sure," I said in my best wise-ass voice. "So what if you saved my daughter's life and mine as well? I'll just forget it."

But we both knew I could never forget her. Before I got into the Jeep, I looked back to see her leaning against the doorway. The light from inside her room shone through the cotton dress outlining her perfect legs. She put a hand to her lips to blow a kiss like she had done an eternity ago in front of Riverrun, and I knew then that Edward Stuyvesant Worth IV had better be something more than just a handsome millionaire if he wanted to keep Josie Majansik.

Driving up Wornall Road, I played a Saw Doctors disc and sang at the top of my lungs to a song about happy wars and sad love affairs.

As Grandpa Bevan would say, "God bless the Irish for getting their priorities straight."

Chapter 32

Thursday, November 18

Indian summer had ended. Dead leaves covered the sidewalk like a brown blanket. I sat in the shop's bay window catching the last sun rays of an autumn afternoon, and studied the classifieds, searching for a new employee. It would soon be Thanksgiving, and the best retail season of the year would begin, but I was woefully unprepared for it.

Brian Canady, one of the Irregulars, had pitched in to run the coffee cart and found he still had enough energy after four hours of cappuccino-making to work on his newsletter. A couple of nice college kids helped with the afternoon shift as well, but my efforts to find someone to match Phyllida's expertise were going nowhere.

Riverrun had become dependent on the book-selling dot coms like AbeBooks and Alibris which presented my inventory to book buyers throughout the United States and the world. What a pity the person who had helped me establish the books on the internet had turned out to be a co-conspirator to murder.

I felt low for other reasons as well. The Colette, along with the other erotica, had been returned to Beatrice Land who, at my suggestion, placed it with Sotheby's for its winter rare books auction. She'd get an appropriate price, more than enough to keep her in whips and dog collars to the end of her days. I had dared to hope after numerous hints that she would give me one or two of the Japanese scrolls, if not in gratitude, then as a commission. But it was not to be. Riverrun would remain just a used bookstore.

Dr. Guffey's *in our time* was returned to Delaware's Special Collections Department, where it now rests in its half morocco slipcase three floors underground in the bowels of the Morris Library. I spent the two hundred fifty-dollar reward (approximately 1/1000th of its fair market value) on a first-edition biography of Captain James Cook by J.C. Beaglehole. It sits on my bookshelf at home next to *The Endeavour Journal* of Joseph Banks edited by the same Professor B.

Anne hadn't emailed or phoned from LA in a week. We'd gotten in the habit of communicating every other day, but I trusted her enough not to worry about the lapse. Like she had said not so long ago, I needed to get accustomed to having an adult child.

Even the Irregulars had stopped coming in regularly. It was as if the Phyllida and Weston Preston business had put a curse on the store. It got to the point that I seriously questioned whether Riverrun was worth operating anymore.

Although I knew the internet drill well enough to get by, I couldn't watch the shop, price books, go on buying trips and do everything else necessary to run the business by myself. In the five months since the encounter with Quist, it was more than I could continue to handle and still make a profit. My customers, having become accustomed to the place being open ten hours a day, began to dwindle after I cut back the hours.

Maybe Phyllida was right about my being a lousy bookman. Despite my love for books and the joy that comes with owning such a comfortable gathering place, I really had failed to make a real go of the business. Not ready to quit, however, I advertised for the kind of help I needed: a hardworking, sensible, devoted book lover with an eye for numbers and a good sense of humor.

A lot of people answered my ad. The first words out of their mouths were invariably, "I just love books and bookstores." When I told them what I could afford to pay, most said they didn't love books *that* much, and those who said they could live on minimum wage didn't know James Joyce from Joyce Brothers.

I interviewed several bright people who could make change, knew a good mystery writer from a bad one, and had spouses with good jobs, or had made their money in earlier careers and were bored with retirement. In the end, I passed on every one. It wasn't because of the nose rings worn by the grandmother in her sixties or the retired insurance salesman's ridiculous hairpiece.

The fellow with the toupee had been pleasant, even humorous, and he certainly knew his books. The grandmother claimed to have been on the magic bus with Ken Kesey and the Merry Pranksters and quoted whole poems by Gary Snyder in her interview. By all accounts, both seemed like honest, likable, and interesting people. But I didn't know them, and the two employees I *had* known and trusted for five years tried to set me up for a murder that they committed.

I got out of the chair by the window and went into the closet that serves as my office to place a call to one of the best used bookstores in Omaha. I knew its owner had long wanted to open a second shop in Kansas City.

"Pimpernel Books, Mingos speaking," answered the familiar gravelly voice.

"Hey, Carl. It's Mike Bevan."

"I heard you had some excitement this summer. Got any books for me?"

"You might say that. Riverrun's for sale if you want it."

There was a long silence, then an exhalation of breath.

"The whole thing? You sure about this?"

"I'll fax the details today. You'll be able to afford it, and there're three years left on a very favorable lease."

"Damn, I should be jumping out of my shorts about this, Mike, but you're a good bookman, and there aren't too many of us left."

"Thanks," I said, remembering that I'd thought something similar about Gareth Hughes after he was dead. "I'm tired of it, Carl."

"Horse-hockey! You can't be tired of books. That isn't natural."

"It's not the books or even the business. Maybe it's people I can't handle."

For a moment I thought the line had gone dead.

"All right," he said quietly. "Email me the numbers."

I hung up the phone, pulled a Diet Coke out of the

mini fridge and started to add some sales figures, not aware that someone had entered the shop while I was on the line.

"Are you hiring?" a voice said from outside the office door.

"No," I said as I tried to finish an entry in the accounting notebook. "I'm afraid that will be someone else's decision."

"Too bad. I so wanted to work with you."

I looked up to see Josie Majansik standing at the sales counter.

"Well, are you hiring?" she repeated.

"I just offered Riverrun to another book dealer."

"So I heard. Don't do it."

"Do you really want to work for me?"

"No. I want to work *with* you. I know books, but you should know that I prefer Chandler to Hemingway and Turgenev to Tolstoy."

"Can you operate a computer?"

"Second nature to my generation."

"It's not a very adventurous job."

"I've had enough adventure for a while."

"What about the FBI?"

"Like I said before, I wouldn't be good at it anymore. Besides, I broke rule number one."

"What's that?"

"I fell in love on the job."

"So you indicated to me that night at Fitzpatrick's. I suppose it's a fellow agent; if it was Eddie Worth, you wouldn't be looking for work. When's the wedding?"

"That's up to you."

"I don't get it."

She came behind the desk and laid a kiss on my lips.

"You're the one, you blockhead."

"But I thought…"

"You thought wrong. When you refused to see me in the hospital, I was terribly hurt. I thought you could never really care for me. After our dinner at Fitzpatrick's, I returned to Columbus to start life over again, thinking I could get you out of my mind. I couldn't. It just got worse with every passing week. I picked up the phone a dozen times to call you, but each time I put it down, afraid you'd reject me again. A week ago, Anne contacted me out of the blue. Her encouragement was all I needed."

"And you were the one who said you'd bring her back to me."

"She sounds happy."

"The editing work on the film is keeping her out of trouble," I said. That was as far as I'd go to give Langston credit for my daughter's continuing recovery.

A lady brought in a bag of paperbacks to trade. I told her to leave them on the desk and have a cup of coffee next door while I added them up. I looked back at Josie.

"That's the kind of excitement you can expect around here. Do you really think you can handle such pressure?"

"I love you, Mike. Do I get the job?"

"Just a moment," I said.

I dialed Omaha.

"Hello, Carl?"

"Yeah?"

"The deal's off."

"Riverrun lives?"

"Yup. I found all the help I'm going to need for a while."

A Look At Book Two:
LEFT TURN AT PARADISE

Our endearing hero is in deep water once again whilst on an unforgettable treasure hunt.

Michael Bevan is barely surviving with his used bookstore and rare book collection when he discovers a well-worn journal dating back to 1768. The dilapidated log appears to belong to legendary seafarer Captain James Cook and chronicles his first epic voyage—out of three—through the Pacific Islands. If it's as valuable as Michael thinks, the journal's sale might keep the bookstore afloat for another year.

Luck is on his side when he meets London dealers Adrian Hart and Penelope Wilkes, who claim to possess the journal of Cook's second voyage. Is it possible a third exists, which might detail another explosive voyage—and his death at the hands of the native Hawaiians? All three would be the holy grail of Pacific exploration. But before Michael has time to act, both journals are stolen.

Hunting them down will sweep Michael, Adrian, and Penelope across the globe—past a dead body or two—and into a sinister slice of paradise. High in the Southern Alps of New Zealand, in a remote Maori compound, a secret rests in the hands of a man daring enough to rewrite history and desperate enough to commit murder.

Can Michael retrieve the stolen journals and uncover a third one… before he ends up dead in the water?

AVAILABLE MAY 2023

About the Author

Thomas Shawver served four years as a judge advocate in the U.S. Marine Corps. His civilian career began as an investigator for the National Collegiate Athletic Association. He then practiced law with career breaks as publisher of *The San Jose Business Journal* and *Kansas City Magazine*. From 1995 to 2012, he owned Bloomsday Books, an antiquarian bookshop in Kansas City. He now writes full time.

A graduate of the University of Kansas, his interests are rugby, collecting rare books and international travel. He is married to a journalist.